BARROW WITCH

CRAIG COMER

CITY OWL
PRESS

BARROW WITCH
A Fey Matter, Book 3

CITY OWL PRESS
www.cityowlpress.com

Cover Design by Mibl Art. All stock photos licensed appropriately.

Edited by Heather McCorkle.

For information on subsidiary rights, please contact the publisher at info@cityowlpress.com.

Print Edition ISBN: 978-1-64898-028-2

Digital Edition ISBN: 978-1-64898-027-5

Printed in the United States of America

To Uncle Bill & Onkel Siegbert, whose devotion to family brought warmth and cheer to our lives, and us all together each and every year.

To grandma, who will live forever in our hearts, crazy chickens and all.

For Martina, who means more to me than she knows. Love you, always.

are tied to the same epic war, with different people from different walks of life, but, clearly in the same lands, at the same time, speaking the same language, right down to the swear words. It was graphic and captivating. I couldn't put it down."
– *GoodReads Reviewer*

"In The LAIRD OF DUNCAIRN, each character is unique and has a back story that allowed me to develop attachments to them. The story is very well developed and is told in a way that grabs you from the beginning. As the heroine, Effie, comes to know her race's past, she develops abilities that surprise herself, her companions, and her enemies...This book was a great read. I cannot wait for the sequel!"
– *Rita Cline, Reviewer*

"Excellent story-telling and well-rounded characters makes this a thoroughly enchanting tale of a strong yet compassionate female protagonist in a man's world. I was particularly enthralled by the geography and the period, incredibly well researched and invoked. Loved THE LAIRD OF DUNCAIRN, couldn't put it down."
– *Gillian Balharry, Reviewer*

"With few allies and the sniffers trying to catch her, Effie will have to race against time and the power of the Fey lords to establish an alliance between men and fey."
– *InD'tale, Sarah E Bradley*

SCOTLAND, 1885

E ffie hugged her arms tight about her chest. The coat she wore did little to stave off the biting wind, despite its thickness. She'd chosen it because its green reminded her of the deep heart of a forest. But the decision seemed foolish now. Frost collected on the heather and bracken around her. A thin blanket of white dusted the hills above. The afternoon light faded, stealing with it the little warmth the day had brought.

"Ruin," she breathed. She clenched her walking cane in frustration. Her nails dug into the wood. Even with the wind, the stench of death hung in the air. She and her companions had tracked it to its source.

Edgar Talmadge's slight frame knelt before her. The back of his woolen coat stretched as he examined the remains of Tam Lorrie. The poor farmer had not made it far from the village of Braemuir before something, or some things, had savaged his arms and chest. He lay in a tangle of bracken on the slope of a hillock overlooking a small glen.

Edgar had taken in the gruesome sight stoically. He'd seen more of violence in the past few months than his young years warranted—barely a hint of whiskers brushed his cheeks—but he prided himself in proving useful to Effie.

And lately that meant dealing with certain horrors.

"The same as the other," came a voice. The frozen ground crunched as Jaelyn stepped into view, emerging from behind some heather. The brownie of Clan Kae was tall for her kind, but that only brought her to barely above Effie's waistline. Her trousers and jacket had golden scrollwork on the cuffs, though the garments had seen rough use over the years. Her sharp eyes and angular cheeks were drawn into a fierce expression. She opened her mouth to add something more but chose to merely run her tongue over her snaggled teeth.

Effie didn't need the thought spoken aloud. They'd found Hamish Harrelson two days past in a similar state. Both villagers had been sturdy men, their arms and shoulders full of the muscles hard days of working fields provided. They'd known the land, too. They'd lived in the hills and glens around Braemuir all their lives.

"We don't know for certain," said Effie. "I won't turn back."

Jaelyn nodded. "Aye'ya, I ken ye well enough to know better."

"The girl might be hiding somewhere or hurt." Effie tried to convince herself the words could be true, but they felt desperate. Clara Bowman had been missing almost a full week. Effie had stumbled onto her disappearance from Braemuir while hunting for a pack of fell beasts. Wulvers, according to rumors in Dunfermline—wolf-like creatures with the snouts and curved fangs of a boar. Yet rumors in Stirling spoke of a rampaging giant, and in Dunblane they'd whispered of a host of goblins. The details had changed, but there were too many tales, and too much evidence, to deny something dark lurked in the hills.

Still, Effie refused to simply accept that Clara had met the same fate as Tam Lorrie and Hamish Harrelson. Not until she saw evidence of it. Hope, if ever so slight, was something she had learned to cling to over the past years.

Edgar rose and brushed clean his coat. "The good lieutenant best hear of this," he said. His voice held the thick brogue of a Glaswegian. He swung his gaze across the hills to the north. "Do you know? Er, can ye?" He trailed off. A blush rose to his cheeks, as it often did when he inquired after the abilities of her fey blood.

A Sithling, Effie appeared as normal as any other Scottish lass, a young woman with a rounded face, cheery hazel eyes, and thick crop of auburn tresses. But the blood of the ancient Daoine Sith coursed through her, granting her the gifts of Fey Craft.

She smiled kindly and pointed to the east. "The lieutenant and his men rove the hills toward Perth." With her fey senses, she could feel them, tiny auras in the distance that radiated the essence of each man. She bit her lip. They had split from the lieutenant in the village, each taking a different direction to search for the missing farmers and lass. But the days since had spread them farther apart, and they would lose the rest of the day waiting on the lieutenant to return, if he bade her call at all.

"They are too far to be of use to us here," she said. She adjusted her coat once more, wishing the dress beneath held a thicker weight, or better yet, that she wore woolen trousers like Edgar and Jaelyn. "We must carry on without them."

"Aye, as Caledon does without ye," quipped Jaelyn.

Effie glared at her companion but refused to take the bait. They had squabbled enough on the matter. The steward of the Seily Court negotiated with the crown near Balclune. She could almost feel him at the edge of her senses, if only because his strength was so vast. She had declined his invitation to join him there. Her place was not among lords. But more so, she knew the treaty they coveted would never be signed so long as the Barrow Witch roamed the countryside.

The Hag o' the Barrows. The Banshee. The Wailing Woman. The last of the Sidhe Bhreige who'd escaped the Downward Fields had many names. What people called her depended largely on which tales their mums told them as wee bairns. It was Edgar who'd taken to calling her the Barrow Witch, though they knew little of the creature beyond the impression of her gender, and that came from those twisted and wicked enough to revere her as their Mother.

"All our efforts must be spent aiding the crown's soldiers," said Effie, repeating herself for what felt like the hundredth time. They had spent months seeking the Barrow Witch's warren to no avail. Using Fey Craft, Effie had even called on the birds and critters of the Highlands to aid them. But her strength was not so considerable, even bolstered by the steward's blood, to scour every nook and cranny of the empire.

Jaelyn snorted, though her distain for the crown's soldiers held less bite in it than it had a year earlier. The Barrow Witch had seen to that, Effie knew. The ancient and devilish fey had spread her madness across the Highlands, into the cities, and as far south as Newcastle. The banshee's touch most called it. It warped the thoughts of men, turning gentle folk to thuggery and causing riotous mobs to form without rhyme or reason. Villages had been put to the torch, and crazed bands roamed the countryside, wreaking havoc on all they passed.

The Barrow Witch had found allies among the fey, as well. Rumors of fell beasts had sprung up on the heels of the banshee's touch, and Effie had little doubt those they now hunted were also part of this Unseily covenant. A chill rushed through her more frigid than the wind. She'd faced a cult of the Barrow Witch's disciples in the bowels of Edinburgh's Town Below. The memory of it still haunted her. Jaelyn might never admit she feared the Sidhe Bhreige, but Effie made no effort to hide her dread.

Edgar studied the remains of Tam Lorrie. When he spoke, it came barely above his breath. "We cannae just leave him here. We do that, and his soul may never find peace."

"Nor shall we," said Effie. She considered what to do, but her gut already told her what must be done. "You will go and fetch help from the village while we press onward. Gather a dozen men there and stay together."

Edgar shook his head. "Nay, that would leave you alone. I cannae do that. I've given my word to see you safe."

Jaelyn cackled. "Alone? Do ye think me a figment of yer imagination? Come, boy, it'd be a blessing not to have ye stomping around making so much noise, and with the stench of the cities on ye, scaring off everything a mile round."

"Oh, do stop," said Effie. She'd heard enough of her friend's displeasure regarding Edgar Talmadge. The man would likely never gain Jaelyn's approval on any account. "We are wasting precious time. Squabbling gets us nowhere."

Edgar ducked his head and blushed like a scolded school lad. Cursing something under her breath, Jaelyn folded her arms across her chest, one eyebrow raised. Effie glowered at her, but their gazes broke as a lone howl rose over the crest of the hillock.

"Gareth," said Effie. Her heart thumped. She could sense the hound's aura a short distance away and hear the anxious warning in his cry. He'd found something. Or something had found him.

She lofted the cane she bore so she could swing it freely. Long, straight, and lacquered dark, it had once belonged to Jack Canonbie, a fallen companion and giant of a man. She'd kept it to remember him by, and perhaps to remind herself of the closeness they'd shared for a brief time. Gnarled ruts and chips ran throughout the wood. Its length made it more of a walking staff for her own stature, and she'd had to wrap new leather about its grip to fit her smaller hands.

A shadow flitted across the hillock. Gwendoline screeched as she swooped overhead, the wee tawny owl adding her voice to Gareth's warning howl. The owl and hound had both chosen Effie rather than the other way around—a boon of her fey blood—but they'd proven themselves as loyal as any friend. She trusted them completely.

Her gaze darted to Jaelyn. She couldn't sense anything nearby, but that did not surprise her. Some fey were able to hide their auras from detection, and whatever it was they hunted had eluded them for many days.

"What it is?" asked Edgar. "What's out there?"

Jaelyn's lips widened into a snaggle-toothed grin. "This be not fer ye," she said in a hard tone as she stalked past him. She pulled a long dirk from a sheath at her belt.

"I can handle myself," he muttered under his breath. He drew a pistol from his coat pocket. Jaelyn clucked over her shoulder. Her footfalls barely made a sound as she climbed the hillock. Gareth fell silent, but Effie knew he was as yet unharmed. She scoured the area around him once more but could not feel another living creature besides Gwendoline circling high above.

As Jaelyn's form grew hazy in the dwindling light, Effie marched forward. She knew her friend was more dangerous alone, and a more capable fighter, but that didn't mean Effie hadn't a few tricks of her own.

Her breath puffed in thick clouds as she clambered through the bracken that clung higher on the hillside. Frost crunched underfoot. By the time she and Edgar reached the top of the rise, she could no longer spy the brownie. But that mattered little. She could follow her friend's aura without needing to keep her within sight.

The land dipped on the far side of the hillock before gently rising toward a ridge that disappeared into dark shadows and a thick grey cloud. The dim light reflected off the frost gathering atop a myriad of puddles. Effie heard the trickling of a small burn below. She felt exposed of a sudden—a cold and unsettling sensation—and hurried onward.

Scrambling toward the burn, the ground turned from frosted dirt to muck, and then to a soft and spongy bog of peat. The stench of winter moss and fetid water filled the air. An animal could wander into the slippery ground and get mired. Or a person. Either would be stuck until they froze to death.

Effie slowed and chose her footing carefully. It would not do to lose her balance in such a place. She could freeze from the damp just as easily on such a night as fall victim to the creature they stalked. When she sensed Jaelyn turn and begin edging toward her, she stopped and gestured for Edgar to do the same.

"It lies in wait and hides well," said Jaelyn. The brownie emerged from the murky dusk. "We'll need to rush it and take advantage."

Effie nodded. "We'd best see to it then, before we turn into blocks of ice," she said. "I'll draw it out." They had strength in numbers. It would have to be enough if the thing sprang at them, whatever it was.

She marched straight for Gareth, never-minding the racket she made as she tramped. Edgar followed at a more cautious pace. She heard his labored breathing coming in quick huffs. Of Jaelyn, she heard nothing, but she felt the brownie remained near, somewhere off to her side.

Gareth cowered in a thicket of heather sprawled over a patch of lower ground. Only a shadowy hint of his brown coat stuck out from the thicket. He shook and whined as Effie approached. The muck beneath Effie's feet made her slide and teeter along until her legs burned from the effort of keeping upright. She stopped a few paces clear of the hound and planted herself on the balls of her toes, ready to spring aside.

"Whisht, Gareth," she said. The wind picked up. She caught something in the air, something like mutton left to spoil under the sun.

Gripping the cane before her, she peered through the thicket.

A dry coughing sounded. The heather rustled, and the head and shoulders of the creature emerged. Tattered wisps of hair dangled, thin and oily, from an almost bald head. Pale grey flesh, dried and cracked, hung loosely about its frame. Heavy dugs and the hint of a once-kindly face gave the impression of a matronly woman. But the stench from the creature made Effie step back and clamp her mouth shut. She'd smelled the rot of corpses before, but never so strong.

"Grundbairn." It hissed the word, and the rasping noise came again. This time, Effie heard it for what it was—a mocking cackle.

The term proclaimed her affinity as a fey. A rarity, Grundbairns preserved the land and held a bond with all living things. It was why animals gave her such affection, and how she could sense the roots and veins of water trickling far below the earth.

Above, Gwendoline screeched, banking in tighter circles. Poor Gareth refused to budge. His tail slunk up to press against his belly. His bony legs trembled. Effie's heart swelled for him. Despite his terror, he'd done his job bravely. She sent him an impression of calm and strength through her fey senses, an image of him happily lapping up marrow as a crackling fire warmed his soft fur.

The hound relaxed, though her flesh still prickled with uncertainty. "What are you?" Effie asked. She delved as she spoke, reaching out to probe at the creature's aura.

But again she found none.

The creature locked its gaze on Edgar, who'd come to stand next to Effie. Its jaw slackened to reveal a row of teeth stained yellow. The man slunk back a step. He raised his pistol, only to drop it again and bring a hand to his head. He blinked and shook. An expression of confusion passed across his face.

"I will eat you, sweetling, before we are through," said the creature. Its voice came as a throaty rasp.

The hairs on Effie's neck rose in alarm. Such a change in countenance she had seen only in those afflicted by the banshee's touch. Hastily, she switched her probing to focus on Edgar. It did not take her long to find tendrils of Fey Craft ensnaring the man's aura. Decrepit things, they felt like befouled weeds. Effie grabbed at them with her senses. Wielding a light touch, she started to unweave their tangle.

"You have not the strength to save them all, Grundbairn," said the creature. It lurched forward, raising a lanky arm to swipe. Edgar dropped his pistol and crumbled to his knees. He clutched his head. Effie gasped. Swiping with her senses, she ripped the foul tendrils away from Edgar, freeing him from the banshee's touch.

Leaping back, her foot slid in the mud. She tumbled over, barely keeping a grip on her cane.

The creature's arm slashed through the night, nails long and sharp.

Effie sucked in a breath, bracing for the impact.

But Jaelyn sprang from the shadows and launched herself into the creature's exposed flank. The brownie's dirk bit into flesh and sent the creature flailing back, shrieking. It spun and swiped with both arms in a flurry. They were long and gangly, and Jaelyn stood only half the creature's height. Its arms crushed down on top of her.

Effie scrambled to her feet. She rushed in and cracked the creature's hip with a swing of the cane. Her teeth rattled from the impact.

Jaelyn danced away. A trickle of blood ran from a jagged cut along her cheek.

"The girl," Effie said. She brandished her cane. "Where is she?"

The creature eyed her. A sickly grey tongue licked at its teeth. "Dead," it said. "Eaten." Its lips pulled into a foul grin.

Effie's chest clenched at the pronouncement. Phantom tendrils born of Fey Craft flashed toward her as the thing leapt at Jaelyn. She batted at them, grasping and ripping as if she fought through a dense forest of thorny weeds.

Jaelyn darted. Her dirk flashed in the dim light.

Effie lurched forward once again, but the creature whirled, expecting the attack. A backhanded swipe caught the cane, ripping it from her hands and sending it spinning into the darkness.

The creature cackled as it sprang at her.

Edgar's pistol popped twice. The sound echoed through the night, carrying over the hills. The creature flinched and staggered.

"No!" Effie shouted as Jaelyn darted in and drove her dirk into the creature's back. But it was too late. The thing slumped. It struggled with its arms to reach the brownie before falling still.

"Clara," said Effie. A numbness overtook her. She couldn't shake the feeling she had failed yet another she had vowed to see safe. It mattered little that she had never met the lass. The creature had been right, she knew. She had not the strength to save them all.

"Most like, the lass was dead for some time afore ye ever heard of her." Jaelyn eyed Effie and spoke in a blunt tone. "Ye did all ye could."

Effie had no energy to argue with the brownie, so remained silent. The truth weighed heavily on her shoulders. Gareth found his legs and came to sit next to her. He leaned against her knee for support and burrowed in.

"What is that thing?" Edgar asked. He kept his pistol trained on the creature's body. His breath came in white puffs that dissipated into the frigid night air.

"A grindylow, I'd wager," said Jaelyn. Effie started in surprise, but the brownie merely shrugged. "It's as far as I can tell from the look of it, though none living would ken of the things. Not a sight nor whiff of them have been around the Highlands for centuries."

A grindylow, Effie considered. Another race of ancient creatures reborn unto the world, one that most considered naught but folktales. Had the Barrow Witch conjured them? And if so, what other dangerous creatures might lurk in the shadows, bound to her will?

Effie's body stiffened, as if her spine had seized. A foul taste came to the back of her throat. The array of potential answers troubled her. She hadn't thought it possible, but their position had worsened, going from bleak to desperate.

2

"Trows and wulvers hadn't been around for centuries either," said Effie. The impish creatures and lupine fiends had only reemerged since the arrival of the Sidhe Bhreige. She peered closer at the grindylow. "But they do not speak, nor have the Fey Craft to hide their auras. This thing felt...different."

The brownie shrugged again. She cleaned her dirk on some heather and sheathed it. "I can't say for certain, only that it fits with the tales told of the creatures. Their ilk is said to lurk in the fens and burns, snatching wee bairns who strayed too far from their mums' aprons. Abominations, the tales say."

Effie planted her hands on her hips. She worked through all the creature had said, and all it had done. "I felt the banshee's touch, just like in the cities. The grindylow used it to ensnare Edgar. It must be connected to the Barrow Witch somehow."

"Another disciple?" asked Edgar. Gareth whined and thumped his tail.

At the utterance of the word, a memory came to Effie of her confrontation with the cult, *Les Revinirs*, in the bowels of Edinburgh. "The phantom tendrils it used," she said. "I recognized them. Tallia, the Sithling woman who betrayed Cecily McCray, sought to bind me in such a manner. It is how I learned to recognize the Fey Craft used by the banshee's touch in the first place."

Jaelyn snorted. "Then we be in the same spot we've been in the past year. The Sidhe Bhreige does naught but hide and turn loose her minions to savage the land."

Effie chewed her lip. The statement wasn't completely true. The Barrow Witch had not always remained hidden. She had come to Effie near Inverness by means of Fey Craft. She had entered Effie's mind to taunt her. It was just after the arrest of Cyrus Reed, the madman who'd used alchemy to turn a trio of pixies into perversions of their former selves.

Into abominations. The thought clicked, and Effie froze in place. Gwendoline squawked, fluttering down to perch on her shoulder. The wee owl stared at her intently.

"Abominations," she said. "Tales speak of goblins in the same manner."

Edgar's brow scrunched. "You think there is a connection?"

"I'm not sure," she said. "The alchemy Cyrus Reed used to transmute the pixies into goblins changed their very auras." She had witnessed the change herself, though she found it hard to believe a creature like the grindylow had ever once been peaceful. And yet, hadn't the Barrow Witch's brethren, the Laird of Aonghus and Piper of Ceann Rois, used enthrallment to gain a host of trows, wulvers, and giants? Hadn't the Barrow Witch herself employed the banshee's touch on the humans of the empire, to the same effect?

"Perhaps Rose or Jane have uncovered more on the matter," said Edgar.

Effie nodded, though she found little encouragement in the remark. Their friends boarded in a cottage on the outskirts of Dunfermline, expending their efforts trying to reverse the fate of the poor pixies. They had, thus far, achieved not a speck of success.

Their attempts to stave off the banshee's touch had proved equally as futile. For every person cleansed, ten more sprang up somewhere else. Tensions in the cities and towns had reached a pitch not seen since the days of Cromwell. Any flick of tinder could ignite a blaze that would engulf the entire country.

Effie hugged herself against a blast of frigid wind. Her thoughts circled back to the Barrow Witch, as they always did. All of their problems stemmed from her. Until she was defeated, they might as well use handkerchiefs to hold back an ocean swell.

"It grows dark, and my belly grumbles," said Jaelyn. "Let us be gone from this place and find food and warmth."

"Aye," Edgar agreed. "We can see to this thing's remains in the morning. To Tam Lorrie as well. I'll fetch some lads from Braemuir for it, as you've asked."

And for Clara, Effie wanted to say. Her remains might be close by. But she held her tongue, despite how much it pained her. Kindness and civility would not bring them any closer to defeating the Barrow Witch. Wherever her resting place, she hoped the lass had found peace.

"I'll inform Lieutenant Walford as best I can," said Effie. She stared off to where she'd last sensed the man. All Fey Craft relied on the presence of fey blood. The more collected in a single place, the stronger the effects became. With Jaelyn standing near her, Effie could cast out her senses almost thrice as far as she could alone.

But she could not speak directly through Fey Craft. Instead, she shaped images and vague impressions of smells and sounds. As a Grundbairn, the effort came naturally to her, more so than other fey.

She found the lieutenant not far from where she'd last sensed him. The impression she crafted was simple: an image of Tam Lorrie's silent face and another of the grindylow. To these she added the image of an old plow horse plodding along a dull and lifeless road, its head bent, the flowers in the fields next to the road withered.

The lieutenant had no way of responding to her, nor she of knowing whether he was aware of or understood her sending.

Jaelyn took a final glance at the grindylow as she started back the way they'd come. Her footfalls fell without sound, picking a path through the muck and bracken toward the base of the hillock. Effie's bones ached from the cold as she followed, but she was glad to leave the rotting stench of the creature behind. She held the cane under an arm and rubbed at her hands as she strode. Gwendoline took to the night air. Gareth stayed at her heels.

Gentle, his name meant. Effie thought it suited him well. Jaelyn had wanted to call him Mutton, proclaiming he had more akin to a roasted haunch of sheep than anything else. Effie had laughed at that. She hadn't expected Gareth to stay with her long. He'd joined her in Glasgow at a time when a formal treaty between man and fey seemed all but lost. But they'd won a victory there and kept hope alive.

They'd won a victory at a high cost. Effie traced a finger along the grain of the cane that had belonged to Jack Canonbie. Memory of the churlish amusement that always seemed to sparkle in his eyes returned to her, and she lost herself in thought.

Ahead of her, Jaelyn's soft tread scraped the dirt. The brownie tensed, halting their march, and cocked her head to the wind. Effie blinked and cleared her mind. She felt a host of fey appear at the fringe of her senses, just as a ball of fire erupted into the night sky, coming from the same location.

Effie gasped, not knowing whether to be frightened or relieved. The fey host had been full of foul creatures—trows, wulvers, and some other races she did not recognize. The blast had engulfed them. The blast had slain the enemy.

3

The explosion's concussion boomed across the hills, echoing against the steep slopes. Gouts of smoke followed the distant flames. Grey wisps curled and danced on the wind. Some of the fey host winked from existence, yet Effie sensed a score remained. She had just the flicker of a moment to regard them before they too disappeared.

"I couldn't tell what they were, other than foul," she said.

"Aye," said Jaelyn. "Except for a pair. Did ye feel them as well?"

Effie shook her head. She hadn't. It had happened so fast. She caught Edgar glancing between them, but the man remained silent. He'd grown used to being left in the dark when it came to matters of Fey Craft.

She was about to inform him, but Jaelyn raised a hand and gestured for her to remain still. Just as she did, a sensation of dignity—like that of a proud stag atop a rise, gazing over the open land of his domain—washed over her. In her head, a horn blasted a long and tranquil note.

"Caledon," said Jaelyn. "He calls from afar."

Effie nodded. She recognized the steward of the Seily Court. The impression altered, and the stench of burning sulfur filled her nose. An image sprang to mind of two does racing not away from a fire but toward it. Effie almost laughed when she saw one had an owl perched on its back. As they raced, other deer appeared and joined them, until they formed a herd.

The impression ended abruptly, replaced by another. An oppressive weight pushed at her flesh. Her bones turned to lead. She could not move, not even wiggle her fingers. In front of her, a cloud of gas shimmered in prismatic colors.

Effie didn't grasp the meaning of the oppressive weight, but the gas she recognized. Thought of its destruction filled her with cold dread. The fey matter held the Sidhe Bhreige imprisoned in the Downward Fields.

"Aerfenium," she said. "It was Aerfenium that exploded." Her throat tightened, and she had to force herself to remain calm. She needed a level head. Three caches of the fey matter had been destroyed when Sir Walter Conrad rediscovered the substance a few years earlier. Each destruction had freed one of the Sidhe Bhreige. But each destruction had also sent a ripple of searing pain into those with fey blood.

No such pain had come this time. Hope of what that meant bubbled inside, forcing back her fear.

Jaelyn's expression turned pensive. "I don't know what the thing means," said the brownie, answering the unspoken question.

"Then we must find out," Effie replied. She turned to Edgar. "Our night's work is not yet done. The steward has need of us. He's bade us to hurry to where that explosion occurred and join him. A host of fey creatures have destroyed a cache of Aerfenium."

Edgar's eyes widened. He turned to the remnants of smoke billowing over the hills. He sucked in a deep breath. "Aye, all right then."

Effie expected Jaelyn to object, but the brownie trudged off without a word. Effie stamped her feet a few times to wake them from the cold, and followed. They cut a direct path. There was no need for stealth. Though the fey host hid their auras, they could undoubtedly sense Effie and Jaelyn's approach.

As they stomped through fields of wind-blown grass and clambered over jagged outcrops of stone, Effie wondered if the grindylow had been part of the host. She assumed its aura would've been as foul as those she'd felt. Perhaps the creature had stalked them all along, rather than they it. The thought brought little comfort.

They rose gradually to a ridge. As they did, smoke filled Effie's nose—charred wood and burnt grass blending with a hint of something acrid. A stand of pine trees ran along the ridgetop, with snow gathering in small drifts at their base. Jaelyn edged toward the trees and motioned for Effie and Edgar to hunker low and remain at her heels.

Gareth whined, nostrils twitching. His head rose to the wind. Effie reached out with her senses to soothe him. She wished he could tell her what else he sniffed, or better yet, from whence it came. Might as well wish for Gwendoline to pen her a letter. Fey Craft had its boundaries, despite its wonders.

She padded forward as softly as she could, peering through the trees. On the far side of the ridge, the land dropped steeply. Sharp crags were left bare where the higher ground had slipped into the ravine below. She pressed her palm against the rough bark of a pine. Her breath puffed in tiny clouds. Even in the twilight, it was not difficult to spy evidence of the explosion. Fresh churned earth formed a circle on the ravine floor. Shattered stone ringed the churned earth. Sprawled amid the stones were the bodies of a dozen fey creatures.

A few had large eyes and small, floppy ears, with ashen skin and heads overgrown for their wee bodies. Trows, Effie recognized. Those would stand no taller than Jaelyn. But some of the other creatures would cast shadows over Edgar. Thick around the waist and shoulders, they had flat noses and tusks protruding from the bottom rows of their teeth.

Effie's flesh curled as she took in the largest of the fallen fey. Tattered wisps of hair clung to its bald head. Pale flesh hung loose about its frame. Sight of the thing conjured up memory of the rotting stench.

"Grindylow," she said as quietly as she could.

"Fools." Jaelyn spat the word. Effie caught where the brownie's gaze fixed and sucked back a curse of her own. Coming through the ravine, almost in a straight line, were a dozen men. Each wore the bright red coat of a queen's soldier. Bandoliers crossed their chests, clinking with every step. Muck covered their high, black boots. They held their rifles at the ready, though it appeared they had not yet seen the fey bodies. At their head, Effie recognized the stiff gait and neatly trimmed whiskers of Lieutenant Walford.

"How?" she asked. She could not sense their auras and had not felt their approach.

"Masked, the same as the host," said Jaelyn. "By the host, I suspect. So we could nae sense them. So we could nae warn them." The brownie snarled, revealing her snaggled teeth. "The trap be well set."

Effie's eyes widened. She rose and cried out. "Lieutenant!"

"There!" shouted Edgar, at the same time. He thrust a finger at a shadow below.

The fey that emerged from behind a boulder along the ravine floor stood a head taller than the lieutenant. His arms and shoulders looked as if he'd spent the better part of his days tending to a forge. Ginger hair covered his body like a pelt. His face reminded Effie of carvings of the Green Man, though with a ridged brow bent more toward fury than peace.

With a bellow, he waved a thick, basket-hilted sword high over his head. The fey host stepped from their hiding places along the ravine, a troop of creatures full of tusks and snouts, hairy pelts and sickly grey scales. They clutched rusted hooks and broken plows for weapons. Some howled, while others hissed, hopping about under the rising pale moonlight.

Lieutenant Walford barked, and a dozen rifles cracked. The reports echoed down the ravine. A pair of the fey dropped, and Effie thought she saw the large one flinch. But the host turned its frenzy into a charge, swarming the soldiers from all flanks.

Effie lofted her cane and scampered down the brae. Blood rushed in her ears. It almost drowned out the cries of the men below and the howls of the fey host. Jaelyn and Edgar's footfalls thudded beside her.

Gwendoline screeched, swooping past Effie's vision. The movement drew her attention to a pair of tusked fey. They'd emerged from a deep shadow at the base of a large moss-covered outcropping of stone. One wore a coat of seashells, the other a gentleman's coat and trousers similar in style to Jaelyn's. Both brandished rusted tools, a hook and a shearing blade.

The shells of the coat clacked together as the pair stormed toward Effie and her companions. Jaelyn reached them first. Her dirk swept through the night and clattered against the shells. Its wearer squealed and leapt aside. The other launched itself at the brownie.

Effie's legs churned. She raised her cane, ready to lash out at the shell-encased fey, but a sharp hiss snapped her attention to the shadowy outcrop. A bolt of brilliant blue streaked from the darkness toward her. Its tail crackled as it met the cold night air, sparkling in a thousand tiny lights. Her boots skidded on the frigid ground as she struggled to dive from its path.

Edgar was less graceful. He slammed into her, knocking them both over and sending them tumbling down the brae. Effie's knees crunched into rock and root. She flung out her hands and jarred to a halt.

The bolt sizzled as it streaked overhead. Effie blinked to clear away the spots left by the blinding light. She tried to fathom what it had been. But only one thought, as confusing as it was absurd, sprang to mind. She sat up in a stupor, rejecting the notion. Her palms burned from scrapes and her knees throbbed. She'd lost the cane and could only make out a flurry of shadows where Jaelyn fought.

Help her! She sent the message as best she could to Gareth and Gwendoline. She sensed the hound slink forward and heard the screech of the owl high above.

Edgar groped the turf around them. His hand came up with a muddied pistol. He peered up the slope and levelled it, only to curse and let his arm drop.

"I cannae see," he said. Scrambling to his feet, he raced toward Jaelyn.

Effie pulled herself into a crouch. Below, chaos ruled. Grunts and cries rang out, but the rifles had fallen silent. The soldiers swung wildly at unseen foes, falling off balance and tripping over one another. A few ripped at their clothes, trying desperately to shed their coats, while others lay still.

The fey surrounded them, poking with their weapons but not engaging the soldiers directly. They were content to keep the men penned together. Trapped like hares, exhausting themselves until they collapsed, Effie realized with alarm. It had to be from glamours. The fey tricked the soldiers into seeing things that weren't there.

She could not sense the Fey Craft, but she had no doubt of its use. Above, Gareth yelped. Jaelyn barked something at Edgar, and a pistol cracked. Effie scanned the outcrop but saw no movement. Whatever the bolt's origin, it had not been a glamour. Something had fired the thing at her. Something in the shadows, no doubt with the power to do it again.

She bit her lip. Above or below. Her companions or the lieutenant's men. She had not the time to aid them both, not unless she conjured a glamour of her own. Reaching out with her senses, she pulled in as much power as she could, wracking her mind all the while for an idea of what to craft. She needed something to scare off the fey host, something to free the soldiers from their madness.

The gathered fey blood provided a wealth of power. It mattered not friend or foe. All was available to her, and she drank it in. Her body lightened. Her head swam. A tingling ran through her limbs like a soft kiss of butterflies on her flesh.

She began to shape the glamour, but as she did a tall and lithe fey with high cheeks and almond eyes stepped next to her. He appeared in a blink, as if popping into existence from the thin air. Effie startled and lost her concentration.

Another fey appeared next to the first. This one she recognized. A dear friend and mentor, his hooked nose and rugged handsomeness stood in contrast to the first fey's delicate features. Both held a regal bearing, and their fine dress possessed ornate scrollwork better suited for a city fete than a country brae.

"Caledon," said Effie. She felt the power of the steward press against her. It dwarfed all she had gathered from the host.

The steward nodded to her in greeting. His eyes twinkled with mischief as he worked his Fey Craft, and she felt a warmth return to the night air. It came in a sudden pulse. The fey below howled. The soldiers flinched, snapping free from their confusion. They scurried to find their rifles and close their ranks. Glamours no longer befuddled them.

Caledon's companion eyed Effie. His lip twitched, fighting not to curl into a sneer. "Remain here, Sithling," he said. His voice was calm but sharp. He drew a long and slender blade from a scabbard at his waist. It had a hilt of silver and quillions shaped to resemble a pair of falcon heads. As he marched down the brae, he flung up his free hand, fingers stiff, in a gesture reminding her not to follow.

When his arm dropped, Effie felt the power of the gathered fey blood ripped from her. She was left empty and with a slack jaw. Though they fought the same enemy, it was clear he did not trust her to do anything but stand back and watch.

4

Effie jerked in shock. She recognized the Fey Craft the steward's companion used. She could fight it and perhaps overcome it. She could reclaim the power of the fey blood to work her glamour. But the effort was not what the steward desired. Caledon trailed after his companion, marching into battle as if in a stately procession. He made no gesture toward her, nothing to signal she should do anything other than what she had been told.

He understood a simple truth as clearly as she—that despite the friends she had made and allies she had won, the fey of the Seily Court did not trust her. Not fully. In their eyes, she was still the daughter of an outcast and the granddaughter of a betrayer to their kind. She simply was not one of them and never would be.

A tremble started at her shoulders. It threatened to take control, but she forced herself to calm. She had no time to indulge in pity. Whirling, she scampered up the brae. If the steward and his companion did not want her to aid them directly, she would find another way. She wouldn't abandon the fight, no matter how they regarded her.

Her boots slipped as she climbed. The ground had dampened, yet she guessed all around her would freeze anew by morning. She hoped that would not include herself in the number. Already, her fingers and nose had numbed.

Rifles cracked below. Shouts followed from the soldiers. They had rallied as Caledon joined them in the fray, and it was now the cries of the fey host that carried a note of panic. She kept her gaze fixed ahead of her, though. Her friends needed her.

Above, she sensed Edgar huddled among the trees along with Gareth and Gwendoline. She could not see them, only feel their auras. Jaelyn snuck along the ridge. The brownie arced a path toward the outcrop of stone. Effie spied the movement of a dark shape there, but the aura was masked. A fey, and a tall one at that, she guessed.

Creeping closer, she tried to remain as silent as possible before she remembered the tall fey could sense her aura as surely as Gareth had a tail. Her arms prickled. She suddenly felt very exposed and very foolish. Stooping, she groped about for a rock, as if the weight of it might bring her some comfort.

"Come closer, Oak Seer." The harsh rasp held a mocking tone, but underneath it ran an edge of seething hatred. A blue glow lit up the features of the dark form, revealing a familiar and horrid face. The shield hiding the auras of the fey host disappeared.

Effie gasped. The fey woman's hair had thinned since the last time she'd seen her. Loose strands hung like an oily mop over a face of burnt and shriveled flesh. The angry scars and oozing wounds were Effie's doing. She had thrown a concoction of smoldering chemicals at Tallia as they fought in the warren of *Les Revinirs* beneath the streets of Edinburgh.

The ruined skin hung on gaunt cheeks. Effie recognized its grey hue and the hunched way Tallia stood, with her long arms dangling and brow lowered. In the warren, the fey woman had betrayed Cecily McCray and caused a violent rift in their cult. But now she had fully become a fiend, and she had done so in the name of the Barrow Witch.

Tallia held a slender stick in one hand. The brilliant blue glow burned from its tip. Its radiance made her fingers appear white as bone. Slowly, she made a slashing gesture. Flashes like embers flared from the tip and dripped to the ground.

Effie's chest tightened. The familiar blue glow confirmed what she had suspected earlier but refused to believe. The bolt had been made of stardust, a fey substance that burned brighter and hotter than perhaps anything save Aerfenium. Effie had grown up witnessing the substance being used to fuel wondrous devices, and she knew of fey who inhaled its vapors in rituals of Fey Craft. But she'd never heard any tales of it being used as a weapon.

Tallia's eyes lit with a sinister glee as she watched Effie. "Mother grants her most faithful children gifts more powerful than your pitiful mind can conceive." She waved the stick faster, and a comet's tail formed in its wake in a glittering display. "It is a kindness that your end will come so swiftly. You deserve so much worse."

"What have you done?" Effie demanded. "What have you become?" She knew the term of endearment referred to the Barrow Witch, and that the fey woman's aura had changed somehow, as if a rot had come to it. It reminded her of Cyrus Reed and the auras of the poor pixies he'd performed his alchemy upon.

"Something more. Something better." Tallia cackled. "Something unstoppable." She snapped her wrist. The tip flared, and a burst of blue light shot at Effie. The bolt hissed as it came. The stardust seared the air.

Effie dove aside, crashing into the turf once more. Pain flared along her arm. She bit her lips together to keep from crying out as the scent of singed cloth rose to her nose. She was bleeding, she could tell, but thought the bolt hadn't directly struck her. Only its radiance had kissed her flesh as it zipped past.

She hurled the rock she clutched at Tallia and scrambled to her feet. As she did, Gwendoline screeched overhead and swooped low over the brae. A pistol fired from the trees and pinged off the stone of the outcrop. Effie had come to aid her friends, but it was now they who rescued her.

The warmth of gratitude washed over Effie. She blocked out the pain in her arm and rushed forward. She had no place to hide within the bracken that would protect her from the bolts of stardust. Her only hope was to close the distance with Tallia and render the weapon useless.

The warmth increased. Her footsteps lightened. Behind her, a primal howl tore through the night, and one of the fey host winked from her awareness. She could feel them all now that the shield had dropped.

Their number had halved since the arrival of the steward. The onslaught of the rallied soldiers, now protected from Fey Craft, had turned the tide. What remained of the host began to tuck tail and flee.

Effie realized the warmth was not natural. Like the warmth of a hearth, it took the chill nip of night away and gave promise of something hearty and satiating. The impression came from Caledon, who sought to calm and encourage her.

The shadowed outcrop rose from the brae before her. Tallia stood, glaring at her, eyes narrowed to slits beneath a clenched brow. She raised the stardust device, but as she did Gwendoline swooped. Wee talons raked Tallia's head. The owl screeched, yanking free a tuft of hair. Tallia screamed and batted at Gwendoline, but the owl flitted away, too fast for the swipe.

Effie beamed in delight. She forced her arms to pump harder. Her scratched knees rubbed against the confining folds of her dress. Her boots slipped with every step, but she pounded a lumbering gait and willed her balance to steady.

The clack of seashells was all the warning she had before the tusked fey lunged from the bracken. Effie yelped. Her legs tumbled over the fey, and she flew to the ground once again. The tusked fey rose above her. Its body had the form of a fat sow. Thick arms raised the rusted hook above its head. The clacking shells fell quiet for a heartbeat as the weapon reached full height.

Effie brought her singed arm up to protect herself, though she knew it would do her little good.

But the blade didn't fall. The fey grunted and toppled to the side in a clatter of shells. Behind it, Jaelyn crouched. The brownie reached forward and ripped her dirk from the tusked fey's back.

"I didn't..." Effie said. She panted. She still reeled. "I didn't sense him."

"Aye, you'd forgotten about him," said Jaelyn. "'Tis good I hadn't, Grundbairn." The brownie wiped her blade on the damp heather. "Not all the host was revealed to us. A simple trick for those relying too much on their fey senses and not paying enough attention to that right afore their nose."

Effie felt her cheeks flush. "Thank you," she said, swallowing. Her gaze swung to the outcrop. Her body tensed. She expected another searing bolt to streak forth from Tallia's device. But the place she'd last spied Tallia stood empty. The woman's aura had receded into the darkness of the outcrop.

And in a blink, it disappeared once more.

Effie grunted. Anger fueled the feral part of her. She let it push back the fear and pain. Rising, she strode forward. Jaelyn marched with her, dirk at the ready. Vaguely, Effie registered that a quiet had fallen over the ravine below, and that Caledon and the lieutenant were among the auras milling about there. The knowledge bolstered her confidence, but she did not pause to consider them further.

Caledon had already made his position on her involvement clear, and she had no desire to hear it again. He could act as he saw fit. She needed neither his approval nor direction.

As she and Jaelyn approached the outcrop, a giant cleft revealed itself within the exposed stone. Effie guessed it had come from a slide in ages past, from the way the grass and bracken grew around and through the stone. The outcrop itself jutted from the brae like a giant wart. Its height loomed above her head.

She pressed against the edge of the cleft, peering within. But she could make out little beyond the few paces before her. Night had fully fallen, and only the light of the stars and moon illuminated her surroundings.

Frigid to the touch, the moss-covered stone gave off an earthen and damp scent. Effie breathed it in and considered. The dim light was devoid of the brilliant glow of stardust, but that did not necessarily mean the device's owner had fled. She had already fallen into more than one trap from Tallia, and she would not let her fury goad her blindly into another.

What she needed was a torch. She smiled. That, or a pair of eyes built for the dark.

Effie closed her eyes and used Fey Craft. Within the span of a dozen breaths, Gwendoline glided to her shoulder on silent wings. *Remain alert,* she sent the owl, using her fey senses. *Make sound only if you see danger. We hunt.*

She let her hand trail on the stone as she padded forward. She took each step slowly, testing with her foot before shifting her weight. A rustle came from within the cleft, and her heart froze. But she could not spy the sound's source. Her own breathing filled her ears, despite her efforts to remain quiet.

Jaelyn tapped her leg, urging her to keep moving. Gwendoline watched intently, perched on her shoulder as rigidly as a statue. Another step brought Effie onto a downward slope. The stone beneath her feet had worn smooth from years of constant battering by wind and rain. She risked looking down to help steady her balance. As she did the rustle came again.

Gwendoline screeched and took wing. Tiny prickles ran along Effie's flesh. Her gaze darted up, and she sucked in a sharp breath as a figure emerged before her, one that looked nothing like Tallia. One that appeared as a ghost, all the same.

The lass was perhaps fourteen. She trembled with a chill and rubbed at her arms. Her smock dress was torn. A week's worth of dirt covered her face and arms. Ginger hair sprouted in a nest atop her head. It hadn't been combed in some time. Taking in Effie and Jaelyn, her eyes went wide. She opened her mouth to speak, but fell into a shuddering sob that brought her to her knees.

Effie rushed to the lass. She took the girl's shoulders and hugged her tight for warmth. An odor she couldn't quiet place met her nose, but she shoved the worry of it aside. Jaelyn charged deeper into the cleft, disappearing except for the scrape of her footfalls.

"What's your name, lass?" asked Effie, though she already suspected the answer.

The girl gathered herself and wiped her cheeks. "Clara," she said. "It's Clara Bowman." She brushed aside a couple stray ginger locks. As her fingers pulled away, strands of the hair came with them. They floated slowly down to land in a clump near her feet.

$$\maltese \quad 5 \quad \maltese$$

E ffie's eyes pulled wide as she watched the ginger tresses fall. Instinctively, she reached out to feel the girl's aura, but the Fey Craft that hid it remained in place. Still, the balding could mean only one thing. The answer to the riddle of creatures long thought extinct suddenly appearing had revealed itself.

Tallia and the poor lass were mutating into grindylows.

"The creature fled," said Jaelyn, returning from the depths of the cleft. "Her lanky legs carried her out some hole faster than my own could take me." The brownie grunted and folded her arms across her chest. The admission touched on her pride.

Clara shuddered anew. Her head swung to where the brownie had emerged. Her hands returned to her face as her arms hugged tight to her body.

"We will find her," said Effie. Despite her shock, her fury toward Tallia had not fully abated. "Twice she has tried to kill me, and twice she has fled in defeat. I do not intend a third such assault to go unanswered."

"What of this one?" Jaelyn nodded toward Clara. "I do not need to spy her aura to ken what she is."

"A grindylow." Effie closed her eyes as she spoke the word. She thought again of the girl's tresses, what the balding signified. The first they'd encountered had seemed a creature from tales of old, but Tallia's aura had been known to Effie. And it had changed. It had rotted, as surely as the woman's appearance.

"Or at least becoming one," Effie continued, "through the same alchemy we have seen before. Tallia becomes the same, though I have no doubt the choice to do so was hers."

"Aye," Jaelyn answered. Her hand fell to the grip of her dirk. "Can the same be said of this one?"

"No!" Effie shouted. She read the brownie's intentions. Jerking forward, she planted herself in front of Clara. "The lass presents no danger. She has done no harm. Just because the aura befouls does not mean the creature is evil. Think of the poor goblins. They had no choice to become what they are, and even changed, their manner is more playful than wicked."

Jaelyn grunted. "Do not scold me, Grundbairn. The grindylow we slew held no mark of compulsion. Nor did Tallia. Whatever their auras once were, they hold none of it any longer." Her stare hardened. "And do not doubt for a moment them wee goblins would cast ye down and eat ye if you gave them the chance. Changed is changed, and they are no longer one of us. They are no longer of the Seily Court."

Effie stiffened, but the argument that found her tongue unraveled before she uttered a word. Still, she refused to remove herself from the brownie's path. They had not traipsed through frozen bracken and icy moor only to abandon the lass to a cruel fate. Nor would she stand to see any harm come to the lass when the girl had done nothing against them.

Not yet, anyway. The thought snaked into her head. It disgusted her, but she had to swallow it down.

"Miss Effie, your arm." Edgar broke the silence that had fallen. He strode toward Effie but stopped short of her, remembering his decorum. He held a torch in one hand that brought a flickering warmth to the cleft. A look of worry painted his face. Gareth trailed at his heels, tail tucked but wagging.

Effie had blocked out the sharp ache the stardust burn had left. It returned to her as she inspected her sleeve. The cloth had singed and blackened, yet thankfully it had not seared into her flesh.

"It must be bandaged." Edgar started to shrug from his coat. Gareth whined his agreement.

Effie held up a hand. "Thank you, but I will be fine. Let the lass have it before she turns to ice." She could tell he wanted to protest, so added, "Perhaps one of the lieutenant's men might have a suitable wrapping. See if they can spare any food as well, and let the lieutenant know we will join him shortly."

She tried a stoic face, but all of her aches—the bruising of her elbows and hands, and the scrapes along her knees—suddenly clamored for the same attention as her arm, and the weight of the evening sank in. Her body felt like lead, her mind like a jumble of beach stones pounded by vengeful waves.

But even as she fought to remain upright, a familiar warmth returned to her. She turned and found Caledon approaching, along with his companion. The steward's hooked nose gave character to a handsome face that appeared almost as young as Effie's own, despite his decades of maturity. His starched collar remained stiff and clean.

His companion's coat had not fared as well. Some of the scrollwork had torn free. Blood stained his chest and shoulder, though Effie guessed from the way he carried himself that it was not his own. The fey held his chin high, his sharp features pulled into a bemused expression bordering on mocking.

Edgar wrapped his coat around Clara's shoulders. She shied from the touch but accepted the offering, mumbling her gratitude.

"I will see to food and a bandage," he said, dipping his head to Effie. He shot a glance at Jaelyn before bowing to Caledon and the other fey. As he withdrew, the warm torchlight fled. Those remaining were painted silver under the star and moonlight. Their breath came in cold, white puffs.

Gareth's head found Effie's hand. He studied her as she stroked behind his ear. Caledon took in the sight and grinned broadly. With a wink, he bowed. She curtsied, feeling as if she'd better straighten her hair before the next waltz began. That they stood on a frigid brae in the aftermath of battle was lost on the charm the steward naturally exuded.

"It is good to see you both well," said Caledon after he bowed to

Jaelyn. He gestured. "This is Gaelyph, Warden of the Hunt. He has come from Elphame to act as the eyes and ears of the Seily Court."

Caledon's companion dipped his head in a shallow nod. The brownie nodded in response. Effie did the same, though a thousand questions overwhelmed her. Warden of the Hunt? Had Elphame finally sent someone to aid them in tracking the Barrow Witch? And if so, why hadn't they before?

Yet another matter pressed equally on her thoughts. "It is well you arrived and saved us from disaster," she blurted, "but how did you manage it so swiftly, and to the very spot where we need you most?"

Caledon laughed. "By a trick, and a good one."

Jaelyn snorted. "Only with friends in the right places," said the brownie. "Ye could've warned us of yer intent." Effie glanced between them. She felt left out of the joke, and it must've shown on her face.

"The way to Elphame is open to the steward," Jaelyn explained. "He has the strength with so many fey roaming about these days. And though his feet be nae so muckle, sometimes he can step farther than a giant."

Effie's brow knit. She pulled her coat tight. "You traveled to Elphame and back just to arrive here?"

The steward dipped his head in acknowledgement. "It seemed the swiftest route." He laughed again, the tenor light and full of amusement, but his companion's face grew sterner. Effie saw Gaelyph studied Clara with something more than idle interest.

"Perhaps such humor would best be shared while not in the presence of an Unseily," said the warden. His voice sounded as stodgy as his expression.

"Miss Bowman's aura is known to me and has not yet changed. She will provide us no harm," said Caledon. He took in the lass and addressed her directly. "You have the blood of our kind in your veins, though it has sadly treated you poorly."

"A curse, my mother always claimed." The girl hugged herself tight. She seemed close to tears. "What is to become of me?"

Effie heard defeat in the question. It tugged at her heart. That the lass didn't beg for the protection of the queen's soldiers, nor flinch at the mention of Unseily fey, meant she possessed awareness that a cruel fate awaited her.

"Grindylows are what Sithlings become when their auras are corrupted by this alchemy, as a pixie becomes a goblin," said Effie. She tried to piece together what she'd learned. She thought of the other creatures they witnessed in the ravine. "And these others, the tusked ones. They must be corrupted brownies and hogboons."

"She is as clever as you informed me," Gaelyph told the steward. His voice hung thick with something close to derision. "If not wholly correct."

Effie folded her arms across her chest but chose to ignore the warden. She'd borne such bluster and insult all her life. Her foot began to tap. She needed to uncover a means to help the poor lass. Her pain receded as her mind worked.

"I don't understand," she said. "We captured Cyrus Reed. How is this possible? How many can know the secret of this alchemy?"

"Only one is needed," answered Caledon.

The truth struck her hard. "The Sidhe Bhreige." Effie's heart sank. "The Barrow Witch spreads the knowledge of this alchemy as easily as she does the banshee's touch."

"Aye, it be so," Clara blurted. She swallowed and cast her gaze down as those gathered studied her. Tugging Edgar's coat tighter, she trembled.

"It's all right," said Effie. "I will not let harm come to you. Nor will the steward." She eyed Caledon and defied him to contradict her. "It will be difficult, but can you tell us what happened to you? Anything might be of help, no matter how small a detail."

Clara nodded. She took a deep breath. "I ken not the names and creatures of which you speak. But alchemy, aye. They forced me to suffer down an unholy concoction. The creature—Tallia you called her—came for me in the night a week past. She stole me away, binding my hands and covering my eyes. We marched until I'd lost count of the times I'd fallen, only to remain here on this frozen stone for days."

The girl shuddered at the memory. "Others of the host came and went, though I saw them not, blinded as I was. I only heard voices, squeals, and chittering. But it was Tallia who came in the night. Each night, to taunt me with horrid tales." Clara's voice caught. "She stalled, you see. I figured it after a while. We waited for something called the Aeger's Gat."

She shrugged. "I suppose it had to do with the alchemy."

Effie's eyes lit up. "Aegirsigath, could it be?" Aegirsigath was the ancient fey term for Aerfenium.

Clara's head cocked. "Aye, that could be it. The brew it made. It... It tasted of blood and something more. Something thick. Something that made my innards twist in knots until I thought they'd melt and flush away." She clutched herself around the middle.

"It is not an ordeal you should have had to suffer," said Effie. She placed a reassuring hand on the girl's arm. Yet in truth, her gut had curled as the lass spoke. Knowing the alchemy existed was far a different thing than hearing of it firsthand from one of its victims. Still, she focused on what Clara had told them. It shed light on many things, even as it begged more questions.

Though not Fey Craft, the alchemy contained Aerfenium and blood. Fey blood, Effie presumed, and perhaps more. Cyrus Reed had removed blood and brain tissue from a pair of fey before performing the alchemy on the pixies. The thought made her want to gag, and some of her warmth slipped away. But she kept her tongue on that account. The lass didn't need to know what she'd most likely ingested.

Effie bit her lip as a wave of guilt welled within her. Had the other grindylow once been a frightened lass just like Clara? Or perhaps a kindly village Spae Wife? What were they to do if the Barrow Witch raised an army of helpless victims? Surely they could not just cut them down, as Gaelyph had done in the ravine.

"If we had captured some of these Unseily instead of slaughtering them, maybe we could've helped them recover." She turned to Jaelyn. "There were two auras you sensed that were not corrupted. Clara's and another."

The brownie shrugged.

Effie glowered in frustration, but she could not hold honesty against her friend. Drawing herself up, she said, "We must find a way to return Clara and any other poor creatures to their rightful state. In the process, we might glean information on the Barrow Witch."

"No," said Gaelyph. He shook his head dismissively. "There is no returning. Once a fey is altered, their former aura is forever lost. It is best to put such creatures down. They are an abomination to our blood. Their kind have long plagued our court with their Unseily ways."

Effie planted her hands on her hips. "You would have us believe in absolutes? Do not frighten the poor lass." Her words carried a bite to them. The warden's arrogance had done naught but rile her since the moment of his arrival. "Though I am new to most fey lore, I have witnessed enough to recognize it holds millennia of half-truths and false certainties."

Gaelyph's face turned to stone. "I am Warden of the Hunt, outsider. Do you think that means I chase after rabbits? I know of what I speak when it comes to the blood of Unseily." He jabbed a finger toward Clara.

The girl shied away from the warden. Fear shone in her eyes. Effie stepped to keep herself between Clara and Gaelyph. She knew the warden would make quick work of her with that sword of his, but it mattered little. Scaring the girl with threats after all she had endured only drove Effie to resist his arrogance more.

Caledon raised a pacifying hand. A sense of peace and calm fluttered through Effie. She saw Clara relax as well, though Gaelyph remained as stone.

"Ye speak of Unseily beyond the nature of a cabal," said Jaelyn. The brownie seemed undisturbed by the tension between those around her. "Do ye mean these creatures be something more than pets of the Sidhe Bhreige?"

"They are Unseily in the original sense of the word," answered Caledon. "The present fey court of Scotland flows from the bloodline of a single Tuatha fey—Sidhe Righm. While the other Daoine Sith left for the stars and distant lands, Righm held his court in the Highlands and bred into life the pixies and selkies, the brownies and hogboons. His children formed a Seily Court and ruled the forests and hills, the lochs and the glens, for a millennia."

"Until the arrival of humans," said Jaelyn. Her lip curled.

"Until another Tuatha called Bhreige returned to the Highlands and became jealous of his brethren's happiness," answered Gaelyph. His countenance melted slightly. "Bhreige was close in bloodline to Righm, and he found a way to corrupt those of the Seily Court. He stole from them the pureness of their auras and tainted their very blood."

"They became Unseily," guessed Effie.

Gaelyph nodded curtly. "While Bhreige's direct offspring became what we now call the Sidhe Bhreige, these altered fey of Righm fell from the grace of the Seily Court. They became slaves to the Sidhe Bhreige and formed their Unseily Court."

Effie frowned. "But trows and wulvers are not evil. I have sensed in them only a base nature, one common in the wild. Can the Unseily not be persuaded to cast off this corruption?"

"Trows and wulvers are not Unseily in the eyes of the Sidhe Righm," answered Caledon. "They are born of other Tuatha fey and stand apart from our Scottish courts. The same holds true for all the other fey bloodlines on Earth."

"Like the gnomes of Germany and huldrefolk in Norway." Effie stamped her feet to warm them. What the steward said made sense, though her mind whirled in a circle.

"True Unseily have no love for those pure of blood," said Gaelyph. "Their corrupted minds are easily dominated by their creators. It does not take any Fey Craft or compulsion. It has already become their nature."

"But how?" asked Effie. She came back to a question that had long plagued her. "How does one alter a fey aura? What is the precise alchemy? Perhaps if we knew the answer to that, we could find some way to halt this corruption. To stall it before it takes hold."

Gaelyph glanced aside. "That we do not know," he admitted. "After the defeat and imprisonment of the Sidhe Bhreige, the great Star Readers foretold of a human betrayal. The Court of Righm had no reason to involve themselves with such petty concerns. They retreated to Elphame, carrying with them the knowledge of the Tuatha, and of Righm and Bhreige. This knowledge has been passed through the generations, but it is not complete, nor is all of it as precise as it once was. As Warden of the Hunt, it is my responsibility to learn the history of our enemies and to keep that knowledge safe. Until three years ago, the responsibility was a matter of function alone."

Effie balled her hands into fists. Her nails dug into the flesh of her palms. "You've confirmed the merits of my very argument. Nothing of fey lore is known with certainty. We cannot set about killing our own kind merely because they had the ill fortune to fall victim to the Sidhe Bhreige. There has to be some way to remove the bond they have to their new master and allow them to return to a life of peace."

The warden eyed Effie as if she smelled of rank cheese. "Only the sword will alieve Unseily of their corrupt nature. It is well you learn that, outsider, before it brings you harm." He drew his shoulders back. "Regardless, the matter is for those of the court alone. It does not concern you."

Effie's cheeks burned. But even as anger overtook her, a sadness crept in. Once again she'd been reminded that her place had never been beside the fey of the Scottish court.

6

Effie gulped in the frigid night air and slowly let out the breath to help ease her temper. Her blood still boiled from the warden's comments, though the hour had grown later. She stood now in the ravine apart from the soldiers who worked at lighting a bonfire. She'd left Clara with them and saw the lass sitting near Edgar, wrapped in a blanket and devouring a hunk of some coarse bread. Caledon had stayed Gaelyph's hand for the moment. The Warden of the Hunt had raised an eyebrow but given no other reaction to the command.

An outsider, he'd called her. The word stung, despite hearing it all her life. She had been an orphan as a child until Thomas Stevenson took her in. As his ward, she had found a home and believed herself fortunate that he cherished and honored her heritage. But she had never truly belonged with Stevenson. She'd had to hide from the public and all his engagements save those with Stuart Graham. His very association with her threatened to ruin his name.

She'd thought the Seily Court would be different. When she'd first found them on the shores of the Isle of Skye, a part of her had believed they'd welcome her as a long-lost daughter. But those hopes had quickly evaporated. Caledon had always treated her kindly, and she had earned

Jaelyn's respect, but most of the remaining court had viewed her as nothing more than the granddaughter of a murderer and the daughter of an outcast.

It was true she had changed the opinion of many in the years since that meeting. Some of her dearest friends and staunchest allies came from the court. Their love and protection provided a family she had never dreamed possible.

Yet an outsider she remained.

The bonfire nearby took to flame and sprang to life. Effie blinked against its light. Its heat called to her, but she wanted a few minutes more with her thoughts. Or perhaps she wanted merely to be free from the warden's infuriating gaze. She spied Gaelyph crouched over the body of the tall and hairy fey who'd led the Unseily host. He pulled something free from around the fey's neck and examined it. Effie was too far away to tell what it was.

"The creature is a bogill," said Caledon. The light of the bonfire played shadows on his face as he approached and offered her a hunk of the coarse bread. Her stomach gurgled, and she gladly took the offering. Her foul temper abated a little. The steward always had that effect on her. She wondered often whether his grace came from the mantle of stewardship or from his own natural charisma.

"It is what a male Sithling becomes, as a woman becomes a grindylow." Caledon smiled at something. "I have learned much from the warden since his joining our cause. I have seen much, as well, and know his support will aid us greatly. He is a wealth of knowledge."

Effie snorted. "It is support from Elphame we have greatly needed since the start of this mess. That he arrives now only begs to question his designs."

Caledon laughed. "Aye, you are too right. I can always trust in your clever mind to unravel a puzzle." He nodded toward the warden. "Gaelyph is not very different from the lords of London, in some regards. Those of Elphame believe the Scottish fey chose to abandon them by not leaving with the court. The Queen of Summer graciously allows us our choice but would rather we come to her and re-pledge our loyalty."

"The Queen of Summer?" Effie cocked her head in surprise. She had believed the Seily Court no longer held any fey of royal blood. She had never heard any fey speak of her existence, not even Caledon. The only tales she knew that even mentioned a fey queen were those of humans who chanced a meeting under a sacred tree or within a ring of standing stones. Yet none of those were likely to hold any merit.

"Righm's daughter," answered Caledon. "It is by her grace that I hold the position of steward, though she involves herself little in the affairs of Earth. Most often, even in Elphame, she does little beyond sleep and dream of distant stars. It has been thus since before the days of the Romans."

"But that must make her..."

"Aye." Caledon's eyes sparkled. "The royal fey do not age as we Sithlings do. Their Tuatha blood is closest to that of the Daoine Sith. The same holds for the Sidhe Bhriege. It is why they have survived these many ages in captivity within the Downward Fields."

Effie sighed. It felt sometimes the more she learned of the Seily Court, the more discouraged she became. "So if the warden did not come at the queen's behest, why did he come? And why now?"

Caledon gave her a small nod. He held a knowing look in his gaze but did not speak. Effie had seen the look before. Either the steward had no idea, or he possessed some information he did not wish to share. As a Star Reader, he knew well how his own judgements could shape future events, for both good and ill, and he often chose to give gentle encouragement rather than an opinion guised as truth.

Effie would need to remember to guard her tongue around the warden if she could not avoid him entirely. As for the Queen of Summer, she would waste no more breath. If the queen had not chosen to intercede by now, there was no hope of convincing her to do so. Effie had best focus on matters she could affect.

"Sir Walter Conrad has not yet found an efficient means to detect Aerfenium stores," she said. She mused aloud as she scanned the ravine floor where the circle of Unseily fey had sprawled after the explosion. Only a faint flicker remained visible, the frost catching on the starlight.

"He relies on his prospecting machines, which are slow moving and prone to breaking down," said Caledon.

Taking a pinch of bread, Effie chewed it slowly. The course flour tasted dry on her tongue. She would've added honey, had she any. "So how did this Unseily host manage to find it so easily? Can we imagine they stumbled on to it by chance? That does not seem likely, not when they needed a bit of the substance for their foul designs." The thought had churned in her mind as she watched the fire, one question among many others.

The steward clasped his hands behind his back and surveyed the ravine. "It does not," he agreed, "though it appears our luck held for the nonce. The stores we created at Balclune were enough to keep those Sidhe Bhreige still bound in the Downward Fields imprisoned."

"No more escaped?" asked Effie. "You are sure?"

Caledon nodded. "None of us felt the sickness such a release imparts. But if the Unseily have indeed managed to find a way to locate Aerfenium, it is only a matter of time before that balance tips against us and more are released."

The dry bread soured in Effie's mouth. "Then we are in even more peril than I imagined. Against a single Sidhe Bhreige, the empire might fall to ruin. Against a handful, supported by an Unseily host..."

"The world is in great peril," answered Caledon. "And on that matter, it is fortuitous in a small regard that we have come together this night—a silver twinkle in these dreary clouds. As you know, I have come from Balclune, where I discussed the fey matter with an emissary from Parliament."

The steward turned to address her directly. "London is in an uproar over threats from the continent, and rather than take an opportunity to forge new alliances, they are reverting to their auld ways of placing blame."

Effie felt a weight drop on her. "But Lord Granville will convince his lackeys to proceed with the treaty he promised, will he not?" She held her breath, though she could already guess at the answer.

"He will," said Caledon, "but only after this 'savage menace,' as the gathered lords call it, is defeated. They have no trust in the Seily Court as long as one of our own continues to wreak such havoc on their people."

Effie balled her fists. "The Sidhe Bhreige are not our own. We have debated this point with them ever since allying with London at Caldwell House!"

"They are of fey blood," said the steward. "That is enough doubt for the lords when faced against such a stern response from the continent. The Germans use the spread of this banshee's touch to demand access to Aerfenium. You know well they are justified in their concerns. They have heard the tales not only of the madness in the cities, but of the destruction the Sidhe Bhreige have brought on the Highlands. The French feel the same and have also demanded access to the substance."

Effie felt her weary bones sag. She hugged herself tighter for warmth. "They are justified in their fears, yes, and yet it is all a ruse to grab at power. The Germans and French, all the world, want access to Aerfenium now that they have heard of it. They will use any argument to gain its fortunes. It is always the same with humans. They see what they want and position themselves to justify bloodshed."

Caledon's tone softened. "What matters now is that the Germans and French are appeased. We have a need to treat with the fey courts on the continent and assure them that we Scottish fey stand for peace. Perhaps they can aid us in convincing the human governments to quell their tempers."

Effie snorted. "I'd like to see who could manage that."

The steward offered her a soft smile, but his gaze pierced through her weariness. Her snort turned into a choking cough.

"No," she said. She shook her head, trying to catch her breath.

"I believe your knowledge of human affairs and craft for negotiation would make our perfect emissary," said Caledon.

Effie blinked. "You desire me to negotiate after all the failures I've had?"

"Failures? Do not underestimate the progress of small victories, Effie of Glen Coe."

"But with Germany and France..." She paused to consider the complexity of the task the steward requested of her. "I've just proven I know little of the fey bloodlines within our own court. Outside of the Highlands, I know even less of politics and society." She shook her head. "Rose Brewer has lived among their courts, and Abigail Salisbury has treated with travelers from other countries for decades, working as she did at the university library. Surely, either of them would make for a better emissary."

Caledon's face remained expressionless. As she often felt in his presence, she thought he tested her. She clasped her hands before her waist to steady them. As always, she never knew whether she passed these tests or not.

"Abigail has not the aptitude for convincing others to join a near hopeless cause, and Rose grows weary with age for such travel. It is you who are the heart of this cause, the leader of our hopes. The foreign courts know of you and your efforts. You are the Green Lady."

Effie blushed. Her ears burned. The Green Lady was a moniker she had been dubbed after a royal procession with the Duke of Edinburgh. She'd worn an emerald dress, and while the newspapers of London had speculated she'd bewitched the duke, the Scottish fey had swelled with hope that one of their kind could treat with so mighty a person. They had praised her, and some had even pledged to her unfettered devotion.

Yet in her heart she knew her place remained unchanged. Green dresses were nothing but frivolity. She could fight to her last breath, inspire hope, and thrust herself into the public eye, but she could never take away how fey like Gaelyph saw her. She had learned that harsh lesson many times as an orphan when dealing with the threat of humans. For every cheery welcome she received, a dozen more would rather see her clamped in a dungeon.

"You do me a great honor, and a kindness," she said. "But it is precisely because those in Scotland see me as this Green Lady that I must remain." She found it difficult to meet the steward's gaze, so dropped her own to study the ground before her. Her words failed her. She had to find a way to make him understand.

"You ask me to speak for the Seily Court, but how can I when I don't even know how to reach Elphame? An hour ago, I had no idea the court even had a queen! The Warden of the Hunt is right. I am an outsider, no matter how well known I've become." The words stung as she said them, but they were also the truth. Beyond her lack of knowledge, she held no proper place within the court, and there were many who would reject her involvement in court business, no matter the steward's support.

Caledon nodded his head slowly. He seemed to study something deep behind her eyes, and she felt the weight of it drag against her shoulders. But he did not scold or let on to any disappointment. It was not his way.

"I will find another," he said, "until the time comes when you can see yourself as others do." He bowed and left her standing alone in the cold.

7

The sun crested the snow-dusted hills by the time preparations to march from the ravine completed. But the blinding rays did little to warm Effie. She stomped her feet and spread her hands over the smoldering ash of the bonfire, trying to stave off the morning chill that pressed against her cheeks. She'd padded her coat with thick wool and donned doeskin gloves, yet more than anything it was the waiting that allowed the cold to seep in.

Gareth lay with his head atop his paws, eyes glued to her, just as anxious to be moving again. Gwendoline had taken flight earlier, no doubt to hunt. Around Effie, the queen's soldiers hurried to form ranks. White bandages wrapped arms and brows, and more than one man moved with a slower, limping gait. That they had survived the fight without the loss of life seemed miraculous.

A horse whinnied behind Effie. She turned and found Lieutenant Walford astride a chestnut. The horse stretched its neck to nuzzle her, its breath tickling as it washed over her. It smelled of oats and the damp fields. She grinned and stroked its mane. She'd long grown used to the affections her fey blood drew from animals.

"Are you to Balclune?" she asked the lieutenant.

He nodded. "Aye, Sir Walter will want a report, as will His Royal

Highness, the duke." The lieutenant's dark hair had peppered with grey since they'd first met in Edinburgh a few years earlier, yet his cheeks remained stern and sunbaked. Days toiling in climates far south of Scotland had seen to that.

"And what of Mr. Billingsley, the Fey Finder General?" Effie asked.

The lieutenant didn't quite smirk, yet nor did he fully mask his disdain at the mention of the man's name. "Mr. Billingsley bothers himself with extravagant banquets and the company of his peers. If he desires any reports on this matter, I am sure he may obtain them from my superiors."

Effie's grin broadened. "You mean if Sir Walter encourages the man to act. He does nothing without Sir Walter's blessing. His or Lady Fife's." Her fingers twirled through the coarse hair of the chestnut's mane. "Still, the man is an improvement. I shudder to consider how worse our situation would be if Edmund Glover still held the position."

This time the lieutenant did not hold back a snort of derision. It had been he who'd ultimately rescued Effie from a violent assault by the former Fey Finder General, a man Effie had loathed above any other save the Sidhe Bhreige.

His horse shuffled sidestep, and he patted its flank. "Aye, though it is difficult to fathom our situation grimmer. This hag creature, the Barrow Witch you've called her, creates chaos at the whim of her thoughts, and now we learn she has the capacity to create devoted legions of tainted fey. That alone is dire enough, even without the peril of her releasing more of her brethren." The lieutenant's stiff posture somehow hardened further. "I fear soon the empire will have a need to defend itself from threats beyond its borders."

"It won't come to that, surely." A twinge of guilt shot through Effie as she recalled her refusal of Caledon.

"The French have risen to action already," said the lieutenant. "An airship of theirs was spotted over Aberdeen. Rumors in the city say there was an exchange of cannon fire, though the target remains unclear, as does the instigator."

A soldier approached the lieutenant and snapped to attention. With a young face and fair complexion, Effie guessed the lad had not yet seen a year in service. His eyes kept flickering toward her, and color rose to his cheeks. She wondered whether it was her fey blood or womanly shape that drew his eye. With young men, she couldn't always tell.

"All is ready, sir," he said.

Walford returned the man's salute and dismissed him with a nod. Turning to Effie, he dipped his head to her. "We must find this creature before the world burns around us. Fare thee well, Effie of Glen Coe."

* * *

Effie's legs begged her to stop, yet the promise of a warm hearth and hot tea kept her moving. Her muscles had long since grown weary. The cold made her bones ache. She'd reclaimed Jack's cane and leaned on it more heavily with each breath. Every step found a rock's sharp edge that dug into the pads of her feet. Each bend in the road revealed a slope to climb. But the cottage where Rose Brewer stayed was not far now.

She had left Rose there with the captured pixies that Cyrus Reed had transformed into Unseily goblins. For weeks, they and their friends had poured over ancient tomes full of crackling parchment, straining their eyes against fading smears of ink, scouring the text for some clue as to how to reverse the pixies' transformation. They had tried Fey Craft as well, all the mustered knowledge they possessed. They had barely slept. Their limbs had hung like sodden rags. Their cheeks had grown thick, and eyes puffy. Yet they had uncovered nothing to aid them, despite their efforts.

All the same, Effie hoped Rose would have good news for them once they reached her. Something to prove the warden wrong. Something to give the pixies, and now Clara, a chance. She sensed the corruption in the girl's aura, even not knowing what it'd once been. It felt wrong somehow, as if a pestilence of weevils and mites had taken root.

Clara kept pace beside Effie, with Caledon opposite. The steward's steady stride was carefree compared to the lass's wavering gait. They had left the rugged, untamed hills after a few hours. Gone were the long glens of trickling water and high ridges of frosted bracken. They crossed farmland now, and a hint of the pastures hung pungently in the air.

The abbey of Dunfermline rose in the distance, the crenellations of its tower barely visible in the failing daylight. To the south, across the dark waters of the Firth of Forth, the smoke and lights of Edinburgh painted the horizon in beacons of yellows and oranges.

Effie had known they wouldn't use the same trick to reach the cottage that Caledon and Gaelyph had used to reach the ravine. That trick involved traveling to Elphame, and neither she nor Clara Bowman were allowed its secrets. But she had assumed they would find horses or hire a carriage. The long day of marching felt like a leisure they did not have time to indulge.

Yet the warden disdained steam carriages and had made his dislike of riding animals likewise known. He had insisted they remain afoot, and to Effie's annoyance, Caledon had obliged the warden's request.

Marching behind, Gaelyph's crunching footfalls reminded Effie of a jailer prodding them along. She was grateful Jaelyn wasn't there to push them faster. The brownie's legs never tired. But she had departed with Edgar to see to the villagers of Braemuir and to let them know Clara had been found. Effie had sent Gareth with the pair, if only to guard them against each other and ensure the brownie did not leave the poor man lost in the hills.

Clara had chosen not to return home. Her present fate remained too much in doubt, and she'd broken down in sobs at the thought of facing her family. Effie's heart pained, but a part of her had felt relief at the choice, if only because she didn't believe Gaelyph would've let the lass go free. The decision had for the nonce avoided an argument, if not a shedding of blood.

Irritation welling, Effie's fists clinched around her cane. She forced them to relax again. She'd already done the same once for all the sheep in Scotland as they marched the day through.

"If only the tales be true, and fey could turn a turnip into a carriage," she said. Her tone wasn't quite as pleasant as she meant it to be, but Caledon laughed all the same.

"That would be something. And a toad for a footman, though I fear your Gareth would not make much of a steed," he said.

"Do...do they have carriages in the fey lands? In Elphame?" asked Clara. Her voice wavered, but she was able to meet Effie's gaze. "I've never ridden in a carriage before, only in Tattie Tom's cart."

Effie chuckled at the name. Not knowing the answer, she swung her head around to peer at Gaelyph. The warden stared at her blankly until she stopped and planted her hands on her hips. "Are all wardens as rude as you, or is it only women you dislike?"

Tilting his head, Gaelyph's brow narrowed. "Rudeness is not a topic commonly considered in Elphame," he said. "A harmony is reached when all fey know their place and abandon thoughts of self. Submitting to the honor of our court leaves little room for the willfulness of taking offense."

Effie's foot tapped furiously. "That sounds strikingly similar to the arguments of the Sidhe Bhreige. But I suppose your pure blood is closer to theirs than we lowly Scots."

Gaelyph's hand curled around the pommel of his sword. His eyes found Caledon. "You see, steward, it as I told you. It is the nature of your host to consider themselves first. That they would rather cling to life in these lands than join their ancestors in Elphame speaks loudly enough, but this contempt proves it."

He tilted his head down to glare at her. "Those who have chosen isolation should be left to their fate. They are not worthy of Elphame."

"Do not begin again," snapped Caledon. He raised a finger in warning. The steward's tone left little doubt an argument had passed between them earlier.

The warden stiffened. He tugged at the cuffs of his shirt. "It is time for the steward of our court to rejoin his duties in Elphame. The mantle has too long been distant. If you wish to remain here, the mantle can be relinquished. It belongs to our shared blood, not yours alone. Pass it to one worthy of our court in Elphame if you will not abandon your folly."

Effie's eyes bulged in shock. She had known the steward's mantle could be passed—her own grandfather had been close friends with the previous steward—but she'd always assumed the mantle, once taken, was kept for life. That Gaelyph dared ask for it openly made blatantly clear why he had come to Caledon. He had no desire to save Scotland from the Sidhe Bhreige, nor did he care about the fey of the empire.

A wash of rustling leaves on a warm autumn day passed over her. *Calm*, it said. Caledon treated her with a knowing look. He'd said earlier that the warden would aid them greatly. Effie calmed herself and bit her tongue. She would trust in the steward, as she always did. He could see things where all others, including herself, remained blind.

"We shall speak on this later," said Caledon.

The warden's face scrunched before relaxing. He brushed past Effie, marching down the road at a brisk pace. She saw no reason to hurry after and let him be. Now that she knew his true design, she determined not to let him goad her anymore. She turned her thoughts instead to Clara and asked whether the lass had ever been to Edinburgh. It always surprised her the number of Scots who lived within a day of the great city who'd never once visited it. When Clara shook her head, Effie began pointing out the different sections of the city across the firth, from the shores of Leith to the shadows formed by Castle Rock.

Caledon listened in silence, and Clara, while not an eager student, politely asked a handful of questions. It served well enough to lighten their step. By the time Effie finished, she recognized the trees and fields around them and soon spied the familiar cottage.

Warm light spilled from its windows. It begged her feet to hurry so she could find a soft chair and warm her toes by the hearth. The thatched roof stood a rigid sentinel over a small croft filled with wildflowers. Its pitch hung low but proud. In the summer, the soft buzz of midges had filled the garden. But winter had driven them away and left only a pleasant hush.

Until a horse whinnied. The sound made Effie smile. It meant visitors. She cast out her senses and found a pair of horses in the small stable on the cottage's far side. Letting herself roam within the cottage, her throat suddenly caught. She recognized the auras of those within. The visitors were the last she'd expected. Or, one of them, at least.

She felt Rose Brewer exit the cottage a moment before she spied the fey woman's ginger ringlets and slender frame. Rose wore a flowing dress in the Bohemian style, with a thick woolen blanket pulled over her shoulders. She raised a smug eyebrow as they embraced but kept her lips pressed together. Mischief twinkled in her gaze.

Caledon greeted her with a wry grin and kissed her hand softly. He introduced Clara, while Gaelyph greeted her with a formal familiarity. Rose relaxed at Caledon's touch, as if she had held her breath in his absence. Her eyes begged of him a hundred questions, but she held them in and instead slung her arm through Clara's.

"Whist, lass, come in afore you catch your death," she said. She prodded the girl toward the cottage door. "We'll get a hot tea in you and some soup."

Effie brightened at the motherly fussing. Though she'd barely known Rose a year, she'd welcomed such attention herself in the past months. It reminded her of the family she'd found, one she'd never imagined she'd have in the early years of her life.

Her thoughts returned to those in the cottage as she watched the women trudge away. Her head swam. That Rose had not yet mentioned the visitors was equally a mother's teasing.

"Will you nah... I..." Effie stammered, but her tongue couldn't quite form a witty riposte.

Rose stopped. She pulled herself and Clara around to stare at Effie. Her face finally broke into a broad grin. "Och, my manners," she said. "I'd nearly forgotten. You have a pair of callers, Effie of Glen Coe, and a penchant for picking up strays."

A flush rushed to Effie's cheeks, tickling up from her stomach. She wanted to feign indignation but grabbed her skirts instead and hurried inside.

$$\text{※} \quad 8 \quad \text{※}$$

E ffie all but leapt through the cottage door. A fire crackled in the
hearth. Its warmth buffeted her flesh. The scent of honeyed tea
and salted fish lingered in the air. A table held a stack of broadsheets and
musty, leather-bound books. One thin tome lay open atop the stack.
Inked drawings covered its aged parchment. Effie couldn't make sense of
them, but she knew they had something to do with alchemy and the
research Rose and Jane Porter had been doing.

On a sideboard nestled in the corner, sat a cage meant for carrying
songbirds. Within, three goblins scrambled about, brought to a frenzy by
her entrance. Their skin was a pale grey, their ears pointed and teeth
wickedly sharp. They stood only as high as a loaf of bread, with wisps of
hair that stood upright and tiny claws for hands that grasped the bars of
the cage, rattling it and making the whole thing teeter. That they had
once been pixies, a race of wee, colorful fey who zipped about open glens
on translucent wings, always brought a twinge to Effie's heart.

But it was the men in the chairs near the hearth that drew Effie's
attention.

Conall Murray rose and tugged awkwardly at his brown morning
coat. She watched his throat tighten as he swallowed hard. His hand

moved to brush back the black, curly locks that had sprung loose by his movement.

"Hello, Miss Effie," he said. He bowed, and her chest constricted as if all the air had sucked out of the cottage. The last time she'd seen Conall, they had parted on a sour note. Though they had drawn close for a time, she had been reminded of their different paths. Of their different desires. She did not know what it signaled that he had come to her, only that every part of her had wanted it.

Forgetting her manners, Effie only stared in return to his greeting. A damp piece of wood popped in the fire. The goblins chittered. Their clamor highlighted the awkward silence that hung in the air.

The man next to Conall saved Effie, as he had done for years. Stuart Graham rose, huffing as he swung his stockier and older frame about. He didn't stand on ceremony but crossed the cottage to embrace her as a favorite uncle might. Lines etched his rosy cheeks. Whisky coated his breath. Years earlier, he'd been one of the first to show her kindness after Thomas Stevenson had taken her as a ward. From that day onward, it felt as if they'd been kin.

"'Tis good to see you, lass," he said. "I've news, but I think perhaps a turn around the grounds might do our young friend here some good. We've been cooped up in the cottage for a spell after some hard riding, and the legs do need a stretch." The hint of a grin broke across his lips. He turned to Conall. "Not mine, of course, but your younger ones."

Conall started. He broke his gaze from Effie. "Oh, aye, um...yes." Graham clapped him on the back and winked at her.

The familiarity relaxed her. She took in a soft breath. "It is a pleasure to see you both, of course," she said. She reached to take Conall's arm as he extended it. The touch sent electricity crackling through her. She had just a moment to savor the closeness before the door banged open. A wash of cold came with it, dampening the heat that had arisen in her.

"We've tomes aplenty," Rose was saying as she led the others in. "But those old pages only go back so far, and the farther they go, the more they reek of fanciful tales rather than fact. None living, not even in Elphame, know what Fey Craft existed prior to Sidhe Righm."

She sighed as her gaze flitted to the birdcage. The warden's eyes lit up at the sight. His hand strayed to the pommel of his sword. The goblins screeched, rattling the cage and threatening to tip it over.

Caledon placed a gentle hand on the warden's arm. He smiled kindly at Graham and made introductions as if they all strolled in a sunny garden. The warden's expression turned into a blank mask. His fingers dropped from his sword, and he nodded as each man was introduced. Yet Effie could tell fury still burned behind his gaze.

"The books of man will tell you nothing of the Unseily," he said, clipping the words to show his contempt.

"That may be," Rose replied, "but it does not rule out other means of Fey Craft."

"I agree," said Effie. At their questioning looks, she explained to Graham and Conall what Gaelyph had told them earlier regarding the fate of the alchemy victims. She tried not to let each word feel like an admission of defeat, yet her shoulders sagged by the time she had finished.

"We had thought Cyrus Reed the only man with such vile knowledge," she said. "But others have gained the eldritch lore. We've run afoul of them, and their creations—grindylows and bogills."

"Aye, but certainly not too many as can't be defeated?" said Conall. He gave her a curt nod. The gesture made her straighten a little. They'd always had that effect on one another. When one shuffled toward melancholy or sorrow, the other lent whatever speck of hope they could muster.

Graham whistled. "Grindylows. Me ma used to tell me of them. Nasty hags who steal away with children who've misbehaved. Take the wee bairns right from their beds while they were sleeping and eat 'em."

"Not all of them," said Effie. She fixed her gaze on Clara. "Truth be told, we know little about their base nature. So we must trust all is not lost, and not all tales be true."

Graham caught the meaning behind her words from the way Clara shrank, drawing in on herself. "Och, lass, I didn't know," he said. "You have my apologies."

"It's all right," said Rose. She shuffled the girl into one of the chairs and produced a blanket to warm her. Setting the kettle over the fire, she readied a fresh pot for tea.

Gaelyph grunted. He'd come to stand near the hearth, planting his feet wide, with his hands clasped behind his back. "It matters not what tales are believed or told. Grindylows are Unseily and an enemy of our court. As are goblins."

"To what end?" asked Conall. The question came as inquisitive rather than challenging. He ran a hand through his hair as those in the cottage turned their attention on him. "Pardon me, Master Warden, but I wonder whether a pattern emerges that might give us some insight. Thus far the madness of the banshee's touch seems like random fits of violence, and now we see that she intends to raise an Unseily Court. Is that also to be random? Or is there some orchestration going on we do not yet see?"

Effie pursed her lips in thought. She had wondered the same but hadn't yet formed a theory. The only thing she was certain of was that the Barrow Witch was much craftier than her brethren had been. For all his bluster, the Laird of Aonghus had been blind to his own ego, and the Piper of Ceann Rois had seemed nothing more than a brutish warlord. The Barrow Witch, in contrast, had corrupted the minds of thousands and found a way to bind an Unseily Court to herself, all the while remaining unknown and hidden.

"Orchestration, aye, and no doubt one is meant to mask the other," said Graham. "As those in the cities become enraged, secretly these Unseily fey have spread throughout the countryside. They are searching for Aerfenium or to swell their numbers, or both. Whatever their design, it cannae be good. And it cannae be random. The alchemy itself needs be too methodical."

"There is also word from Aberdeen of unrest, and rumors of strange sounds coming from the hills in the lowlands," said Rose. She crossed her arms beneath her chest.

"Rumors cannot be helped," said Caledon.

"And of what can be helped?" Rose asked. She raised an eyebrow and tilted her head toward Effie.

"I made her the offer and she refused, as you said she would," said Caledon.

"Stubborn as a mule, I believe you told our steward," said Graham. He chuckled under his breath.

Effie drew herself up. Her eyes narrowed as blood flushed her cheeks, causing her head to swim. Had they all conspired to send her away?

Conall laughed. "Not for the first time she's heard that, I'd wager."

Her gaze swung to him, and his mirth dropped. He turned his head and found a piece of lint to pluck from one of the chair backs. A sheepish expression came across his face. Color rose to his cheeks to match her own.

"Er, what of this trinket?" asked Graham. He waggled a finger at Gaelyph, clearly trying to change the subject for Conall's benefit. "The one clutched in your hand behind your back. I saw you snatch it away from the steward as you entered. I'd bet a coin against three you wanted us common folk not to be the wiser of it."

Gaelyph glared at Graham, but the cheery man stood his ground.

"Well?" Graham asked. "Is it to be secrets among us?"

"It is an amulet worn by the leader of the Unseily host we encountered," said Caledon. "It bears a sunburst etched into the wood, the symbol of a cabal of fey known to us from France."

"France." Conall whispered the word, as if confused by the sound.

"Our warden did not wish you to know of it, as he believes all fey matters to be solely under the dominion of the Seily Court," said Rose. Her tone left no doubt as to what she thought of the position. Extending her hand, she waited as Gaelyph's eyes narrowed further. He regarded the steward in silence before finally relenting and handing over the amulet.

Rose let it dangle from her fingers. Effie saw the sunburst clearly; black lines scored the wooden disk in a crude arc, with rays shooting out to its edges. But the thickness of it caught her attention and gave her pause. It was not a delicate thing, not even attractive for a man to wear. Rather, it reminded her more of a child's device.

She frowned. "May I inspect it?" she asked. Rose handed it to her by its leather cord, and she took it over to the table. Her legs melted as she finally took her weight off them, but she barely noticed. She ran a thumb over the surface of the wood, feeling every imperfection in the grain and the scored ridges of the design.

Graham and Conall hovered over her. One of the goblins screeched and banged against the cage. The air had grown sharp with smoke from the hearth.

"It's a puzzle box," said Conall. He leaned closer until she could smell his breath. He'd had tea recently, perhaps while waiting for her, and he'd drunk it as she liked, thick with honey.

Effie grinned but did not take her eyes away from the amulet. She'd had the same thought. "Yes," she replied. "Like a locket, only for a child. It's meant for hiding something in plain sight."

Her grin broadened. She found the imperfection she sought. Taking the amulet in a firm grip, she moved her fingers into a precise place and twisted.

The sunburst split in half as the wood slid apart.

In the cavity nestled a thin stone covered in delicate runes. Effie gasped and almost dropped the amulet. The stone inside was nearly the size of her palm. The lines of the runes swirled in a dizzying pattern that made her vision swim.

"A thunderstone," she said. Her brow furrowed. "But why would there be a need, if the bogill was already Unseily?" The only thunderstones she'd ever seen had been embedded into victims' bodies and used to sway their thoughts. Somehow the connection of the runes and the victims' blood made the Fey Craft work.

"Not all thunderstones have a need to rend the flesh," Rose explained. "Nor are they limited to bewitching. They can do other wondrous things if the crafter's skill is great."

"Like what?" asked Conall. "What does this one do?"

The fey woman shrugged. "I dunno. You'd need a Rocksoother for such knowledge. But I've heard tales of thunderstones divining water in a desert, and of others pointing the way to buried hordes of gold."

Effie's eyes lit up at that. It was as if a fist slammed into her gut. "Aerfenium!" she exclaimed. "The stone is how the Unseily host found the cache. Their leader had it. He must have used it to guide them."

"Gods be good, you may be right," said Rose. She leaned over Effie, tracing her fingers across the stone. "A master must have carved this. A fey steeped in ancient lore." Her eyes met Effie's. "One with knowledge of Aerfenium." She did not need to state the obvious, that the criteria for its forging narrowed the list of fey to a mere handful.

And of those, the most likely one—the Barrow Witch.

"Assuming that's what it does," said Gaelyph. The warden had not left his stance near the hearth. "It could just as easily be a device used for communication, or one to dominate lesser creatures like trows."

"How do we find out?" asked Conall.

At the same time, Graham asked, "How does it work?"

Effie turned to Rose, who shrugged. "I dunno," she said again. "Maybe it's linked to its owner. Maybe it's not for our Seily kind to use."

"Gabus," said Effie. Her friend had helped her with the other thunderstones she'd uncovered in Duncairn. But she had no idea where the German Rocksoother had gone after they'd last spoke in Edinburgh years before.

Rose shook her head. "There is another Rocksoother closer. He may be able to tell us more."

"I know of whom you speak," said Gaelyph. "He is not of our court."

Caledon crossed to the hearth and stood before the warden. The fire painted him in warm shadows. His words came softly. "If we can learn how to find the Aerfenium stores, we can protect them and demonstrate to London that not all is lost."

The warden stood his ground, and the pair began a terse exchange. Rose joined them. Graham remained silent, except for the occasional grunt to let the warden know he'd said something foolish.

Effie tried to catch each word, but found her thoughts wandering. Exhaustion rolled over her in a steady wave. Besides, she had every faith that Caledon and Rose would win the argument. The steward held power over the warden. If it came to it, he would send Gaelpyh away.

She found Conall smiling at her. The attention made it difficult to concentrate on anything else, and she soon lost track of what the others said. The bench creaked as he sat next to her. He reached out a hand, only to let it drop short of her own. She found it difficult to meet his gaze now that she could feel his warmth and smell the horse and tea and musk on him.

"We did not part on good terms when last we spoke," he said. He spoke low enough for her to hear but not draw attention from the others.

"You stood by your beliefs," said Effie. "I had no right to assume you would do otherwise. I had no place." He'd made it plain he wanted a quiet life free from the entanglements of the fey cause and the ambitions that had become so desperately paramount to her being. She remembered the betrayal she'd felt at his declaration, the hurt, as if a part of her will had been stripped away. That pain felt selfish now.

"No, you did not," he agreed. "But I have come to realize one thing in these past months." He tucked his hands into his coat pockets and leaned toward her. "You will not leave my thoughts, and I cannot find peace without knowing you are safe."

Effie's heart froze. A flutter came to her stomach that had nothing to do with Fey Craft. She mustered what courage she had and shook her head.

"It is not enough," she said. "You are not my protector, to sacrifice yourself for my cause." She glanced at Jack Canonbie's old cane, where she'd rested it near the door. She'd had enough of blind sacrifices.

"Effie..." A twinge of pain coated his voice.

"No, it is the same argument as before. I cannot force you to share my dreams. You have a life apart, a life of obligations and a history."

Conall lowered his head. "I've broken with my father and left Her Majesty's service," he said. "I am a Fey Finder no longer." A crooked grin came to his lips. "I may not even be a Murray."

Effie sucked in a breath. "Oh, you foolish man!" She would've slapped him if she thought she could hold herself back from embracing him.

"So you see, I find myself adrift once more, with only a single mooring on which I wish to tether my life." His grin broadened.

She couldn't help but smile. "You amuse yourself quite well with that awful wit," she said. She took his arm. "Have you really broken with your father?"

"Aye, and he's as cross as he ever was. He'll be the ruin of me this time, I am certain." The last time he had gone against his father's wishes, Conall had found his business destroyed and the woman he loved embarked for America with his father's coin.

"So are you to follow me around like some obedient pup?" she asked. She leaned closer, breathing him in.

"Anything you desire," he said. He stroked the side of her face with his hand. Her body trembled, boiling with anticipation.

She didn't care that the other voices in the cottage had fallen silent.

9

Conall found Effie in the stables the next morning. He approached her dressed for riding. He wore thicker gloves to stand against the winter chill and a woolen scarf wrapped around his neck. Effie stroked the dark mane of his bay horse and fed it a last bit of apple. It nuzzled her as it chomped.

"Spoiling all you can, as ever," he said with a laugh.

She turned her head away from him and raised her chin. "I'm sure I don't know what you mean," she said. She tried to keep the grin from breaking across her face but couldn't.

"Effie..." he began, much like the night before. He took her hands into his. His eyes studied her, and the pressure of it confused her.

Outside, the wind gusted. The stable door shivered and groaned on its hinges. He glanced at it and swallowed down whatever he'd meant to say. Instead, he gestured toward Jack Canonbie's old cane. She'd brought it with her out of habit, half in case she needed its protection, and half because the weight of it helped remind her of the cost of even small victories.

"I am sorry for his death," said Conall. "He seemed a...capable fellow."

"He both betrayed and sacrificed himself for me," she replied. "Of what more he was capable, I hardly know. It feels sometimes like I barely knew him at all, and it is all I can do to convince myself that I had. That I had glimpsed beneath his boorish armor a time or two before the end."

Conall remained quiet for a moment. When he spoke at last, his tone had grown heavy and flat. "I know of what you speak," he said, and she knew he thought of Miss Catherine Thorton, the woman he'd meant to marry—the woman his father had paid to abandon him.

"But let us not slide toward melancholy," he continued. He sucked in a breath. His air lightened, and his smile returned. "Caledon has asked you to take the thunderstone to the Isle of Skye. I beg that you would let me join you." He stepped forward until his chest pressed lightly against hers. "I will be useful."

"You will," she agreed. She wrapped her arms around his waist and felt his eagerness. "But how?"

"I will fight," he said. "I will throw myself before you, come rake of nail, snarling bite, or fiery explosion." His body trembled as he chuckled. "You can feed me apples, too, if it makes you happy."

His horse whinnied its approval and stomped a hoof, scraping at the hay covering the ground of the stall.

Conall cupped her face in his gloved hands. The leather was supple and cold, but she barely felt it. Her mind clicked on something he'd said.

"The Aerfenium." She pulled her head back and watched him blink in confusion. "The Unseily host hadn't wanted it to explode. If they had, they wouldn't have been caught off guard and so many of them killed."

"They wanted to harvest some for their alchemy," said Conall. He sounded amused but did not let go of her.

"Yes," she said. "The alchemy requires it, which means Cyrus Reed had some too. He must have. And that means we've been wrong all this time. He didn't choose to ambush Balclune because he knew of a fey presence. He came there for the Aerfenium."

"I thought none was stolen during the attack?" asked Conall.

Effie grinned as she worked it out. "None was," she said. "But that's because he didn't steal any. He was *given* some by the very man who seeks to profit off its use."

"Sir Walter Conrad," said Conall.

"Yes, the very man," she said. "Lieutenant Walford spoke correctly.

Unravelling any clue as to the Barrow Witch's whereabouts must be our utmost priority. Rose can take the thunderstone to Skye. We must go to Edinburgh at once."

She knew Sir Walter could be found there. If he confirmed their assumptions, perhaps they could learn more about how and when Cyrus Reed approached him. That might lead them to where the Barrow Witch first contacted Reed, or how. It might even lead them to other madmen who'd done the same. The thought was chilling.

"Aye," said Conall. "We'll do just that." He jerked her back to him. His lips found hers as her mouth parted in sweet surprise. Warmth swelled in her chest, spilling along her arms and up her neck. Edinburgh could wait a heartbeat longer—perhaps two—she decided, as her head grew light and threatened to float away.

* * *

She smoothed her dress a hundred times on the way into the city. Ever since the stables, a part of her felt out of sorts, as if knocked akilter by the sudden emotions Conall produced. She had not expected to desire him so strongly ever again, not since she'd made peace with their breaking when last they'd parted. Not since Jack Canonbie had wooed her and stolen her affections.

But whatever her emotions, she had a need to stuff them down for now. She made the decision as the steam carriage rattled and squeaked, choking them with black coal smoke puffed from the boiler perched behind the hard wooden bench of the compartment. She had no time for self-examination.

A larger game was afoot.

Graham joined them in the carriage they had hired in Dunfermline. He had business in Edinburgh and wished to meet with Thomas Stevenson before finding Jane and Abigail, and relaying all the information they had learned. Effie wished she had time to go with him. She would love to see her friends and the man who'd all but been her father, once again. But that too would have to wait.

She would need to confront Sir Walter first. She knew the loose thread was delicate but also one she needed to worry at and see what unraveled. They had not so many options left to them as to let it sit untended. The Barrow Witch had to be found before her madness brought the world to the brink of war.

"May luck find ye well," said Graham. He patted her knee as the steam carriage squealed to a halt.

She took his aged and calloused hands, roughened from hard labor in his younger years, into her own. They reminded her of the peaceful home she had known not so long ago. "You as well," she replied.

Conall tipped his hat to Graham. He clambered down from the carriage and helped Effie alight. The city bustled around them, though it was quieter on the residential streets of New Town. The hawkers and urchins found in the older parts, coated in coal dust and weeks of muck, were replaced by sharply dressed gentlemen and women with bright scarves and well-mended dresses. Canes clacked along the cobbles. A polite murmur of greetings echoed between the buildings, which rose in bright stone, uniform and bold.

The steam carriage shuddered and groaned into motion. A breeze brought a hint of salt from the sea and pushed away the cloud of coal smoke left by Graham's departure. Effie let it wash over her. The stench of the tenements had no place in New Town, but that did not mean nothing rotten lay about.

"Sir Walter will not want a connection between himself and Cyrus Reed to be known," she said to Conall as they strode for one of the buildings. "It would undermine his position of trust with the duke."

Conall nodded. He used his cane to rap on a sturdy oaken door. It was opened by a footman who took their names and ushered them inside. The chamber within held sparse decoration but a refined taste. A plush couch with gilded scrollwork sat beneath an immense portrait of Arthur's Seat and the hills surrounding Edinburgh. Conall studied it while Effie chose to stare out the tall window that allowed sunlight to spill in from the street.

They did not wait long.

Sir Walter's study did not boast of wealth, but rather like the chamber outside served to remind its guests of a refined pedigree. The silver tea trays and candle holders were polished with a fervor, the snifters and other glassware finely etched with knot-work patterns. A pair of hearths warmed the room from either side, with a fire crackling in each.

Effie stepped within and instantly cursed herself a fool. She had been so caught up in considering how to best Sir Walter, she had blindly ignored her fey senses.

"Effie..." Conall hissed the warning.

Sir Walter leaned against a broad desk of teak that sat atop an ornamental rug from the East. His countenance was as impeccable as always. A finely tailored coat fit perfectly over a stiffly starched shirt. He kept his raven locks cropped short against his scalp. Dark eyes and gaunt cheeks made his lean frame appear even thinner, yet no one would mistake it for frailness.

"Welcome, Effie of Glen Coe. Mr. Murray," he said. He straightened and set down his whisky before offering a slight bow. He gestured at a sturdy, leather chair. "I believe you are both acquainted with my guest."

Effie's throat tightened. A nervous tremble passed through her. Sir Walter's guest stood. He'd had his back to her when she entered, but she would recognize him anywhere. Younger than Sir Walter, he had an athletic build and comely face. He smiled in a cheery way that made her skin crawl.

"I had no idea you kept such company, Sir Walter," she managed to say. She curtsied to the man. "I will leave and call on you when your matters have concluded."

Lord Granville laughed, a boorish sound from deep in his gut. "No, no, that is quite all right. I heard you announced and bade Sir Walter not to let you know of my presence. I knew you would likely seek to avoid me."

And why do you not seek to avoid me? The question blared in Effie's mind. It scared her, what the man might ask. She had not prepared for such a confrontation. He was one of the richer lords of the realm, and as much the schemer as any in London. In the past year, the man had bribed local gangs to lead riots against those harboring pro-fey sentiments, had concocted a plan to ship all with fey blood to a distant island, and had paid for the newspapers to print scandalous stories defaming the fey, all to undermine the good will she had fostered with the duke.

But Effie had faced him before and held her ground. She refused to buckle so easily from a simple attempt at intimidation. After all, she had made an ally out of Sir Walter, who'd tried to bully her in a similar manner when first they'd met.

"As you wish, my lord," she said. "Might I ask after your family's wellbeing?" The question held a hidden meaning. The man put more stake in his family's name than in its flesh and blood. His daughter, Catherine, had put herself in a precarious position the previous year, and it was a secret Effie held that rattled him to the core. She would never reveal it, of course. She could never bring herself to ruin a woman's reputation just to spite the father.

But Lord Granville, like Sir Walter, was a man who believed everyone to be as cruel as himself. The smile he wore in response to her query remained pleasant enough for outward appearances, yet he wore it like a carnival mask. His shoulders stiffened and eyes hardened.

"It is a pleasant day," he said. "Do not let us start with barbs. I believe you had business with Sir Walter?"

Effie painted a pleasant expression on her face to match the lord's and tried to tamp down the anger welling inside. The man was correct, she had to concede. She had business with Sir Walter. Provoking Lord Granville did her little good.

"The Aerfenium stores at Balclune. You have access to some of it, do you not?" She thought it best to be direct. Both men were shrewd enough to understand the importance of her questions, and she had no desire to linger in their presence.

Sir Walter perched himself on the edge of his desk. He reclaimed his snifter as he studied her. "It is in my right from the duke," he said. "I am charged with an allotment for scientific study."

Effie nodded, grateful the man was forthcoming with that much at least, its public knowledge aside. "We have learned Cyrus Reed had a small portion and used it in his alchemy. Yet none was stolen from Balclune."

Sir Walter's lips twitched. His eyes flared, but he quickly masked his surprise. He took a slow sip of whisky. "You believe I would have dealings with a madman?" he asked. "I never met the fellow."

She could see his mind working at something. "Then how did he obtain it?"

"I certainly do not know. Perhaps he stumbled onto it." Sir Walter waved an absent hand, as if the answer were in the winds. "There are several caches lost in the hills of Scotland. We both know this to be true."

"That would seem rather fortuitous for him," said Effie. "Yet he was found near Balclune and had knowledge of its use for storing Aerfenium. It is not a leap to assume the reason for this. So perhaps he did not meet with you directly. Perhaps he had an agent." She would allow Sir Walter that much. She did not believe he would jeopardize his position, and the wealth and notoriety he stood to gain, by knowingly conspiring with a madman.

"An agent?" he asked. "No, I rather doubt that. Though I suppose it is possible he stole it from someone given a portion."

Effie jumped on the opening. "Then we must know who you gave Aerfenium to, so we can account for any that might've been stolen."

"I rather feel that is my business," said Sir Walter. He glanced at Lord Granville. She couldn't tell whether he sought the man's approval or wished to keep his accomplices in secret. Either way, she wouldn't give up so easily.

"I will ask Cyrus Reed then. He may rave like a lunatic, but that does not mean he won't react when I mention your name." She blurted the thought out of frustration. Having Cyrus Reed react to Sir Walter's name would mean very little, they both knew.

But the man's face tilted askance. "You haven't heard the news?" he asked. "Cyrus Reed is dead. His jailors found him not a week ago with nary a mark on his body."

Effie jerked in shock. "H...how?"

"These things happen to those feeble of mind, I hear," said Lord Granville. He studied her with a smirk on his lips. "They just expire."

She sucked in a breath and shook the surprise from her thoughts. "Then we shall ask his jailors. They may have overheard something." The argument sounded weaker spoken aloud, and she cursed herself for uttering it.

Lord Granville chuckled. "Rather persistent, isn't she?"

"Yes, I am well versed in her manner," replied Sir Walter. The tension in his voice relaxed. He offered her a smug grin.

Conall planted himself before Sir Walter. "You jest as Germany and France gather at our borders, and Her Majesty's regiments hunt for cries in the wind. Our armies are ill equipped to handle the current crisis, and yet they are trying anything they can, as are we. We are not asking for your associates to gain currency over you. We ask because the connection may lead us to the enemy—the true enemy who brings madness and mayhem to the empire."

"So it is this demon again, is it?" asked Lord Granville. "The one no one can produce or find, yet all fey blame? The excuse grows rather tiresome." He let the statement hang in the air for a moment, challenging them to deny it, before continuing. "What assurances do we have to protect Sir Walter's honor?"

"My word," said Effie.

Lord Granville laughed again. "You hold your word in great esteem for one in your position. I am told you are not even a member of the Scottish fey's court. You are an outcast. And outcasts will always remain outcasts, no matter their aspirations. You may have tricked me into cowing to your wishes before, but I will not have my name shamed again by one devoid of authority."

"She is a more capable leader against this threat than all the lords of London," said Conall. He stiffened defiantly. "You have my word on that account."

"Do not make an enemy of me, Mr. Murray," said Lord Granville. He raised a hand and calmed his voice. "As it happens, I am in a position to offer assistance. I have formed a council that will oversee and approve all uses of Aerfenium, including Sir Walter's allotment." He nodded to Sir Walter. "And fortunately for you, you have found me in a charitable mood."

Sir Walter gave attention to his drink, swirling the amber liquid. The ice clinked softly against the glass. Making calculations, Effie guessed. She doubted Lord Granville was ever as charitable as he now proclaimed. He stood to gain something by Sir Walter's admission.

"I awarded small samples to men of notable reputation," said Sir Walter. "They were inventors and scientists who could aid me in demonstrating Aerfenium's worth to the empire." He threw back the remainder of his whisky. "All of these samples are accounted for, their successes and failures documented. Yet I also gave some to Mr. Edward Waite, for purposes unknown to me."

Effie choked down the urge to gasp. She saw it now, the vice that crushed down on Sir Walter. Lord Granville's council of lords and the coal barons were at odds. Each strove for the lion's share of profits from Aerfenium. Each wanted to put a stranglehold on controlling its usage. Lord Granville would win out, of course, because his profit would come under the guise of the empire's security. But that did not mean he had no need to fight.

"Mr. Edward Waite," Lord Granville said, as if mulling over the name. "He will not speak with you. He is a zealot who believes your kind are beneath him."

"Yet, I suppose with a kind word from you..." Effie saw right away where the lord headed. Her skin began to crawl.

Lord Granville's mouth parted as his lips pulled back. He laid bare his teeth. "Yes, I could use my influence in the matter."

"As you are in a charitable mood," she said. The words sounded as impotent as her earlier argument. They drifted about the room like a speck of dander.

Lord Granville brushed at his coat. "There is charity, and there is opportunity."

Effie's hands curled into fists. "I will not beg."

"No, I would think not," said Lord Granville. "Yet you witness the worth of a powerful name. How the empire thrives as its noble families thrive. How your crude behavior when last we met gained you only immediate satisfaction at the expense of ultimate victory."

Effie clamped down on her tongue and stilled her breath, which had become quick and shallow. The lord's gaze sharpened.

"I can see it in you again, here and now," he said. "That impulse to ruin all you desire merely to pretend at being my equal. A commoner, a fey, and an outcast at that. I don't believe you will ever treat me civilly, nor with the respect I deserve. With the respect the empire demands. It is rather against your nature."

"What is it you ask of me?" she all but spat.

"As you hold your word in such high regard, I will offer you a simple chance to prove its worth," he replied. "You will owe me a debt."

Effie dropped her gaze to the red pattern woven into the ornamental rug. The man's ego infuriated her, yet he had laid a perfect trap. There was no reason she should refuse his offer, other than knowing he would hold it against her forevermore. It would be something he'd use to remind her who held the real power.

She could not allow that, and not for selfish reasons. Who knew how the treaty might be impacted? Or some other dealing that would place the fey at a disadvantage with the crown? Her gaze rose, returning to Lord Granville.

"Our goals are much aligned at present. We both wish prosperity for the empire." She exaggerated her inflection to make it clear she meant the wealth he stood to gain from Aerfenium. "I will pledge you a debt but only until such time as the escaped Sidhe Bhreige is defeated. Then you will have the spectacle and proclamation of safety you've always demanded of the fey. The world will return to normal, and your council will have no fear over any demons other than yourselves. The debt at that point will be repaid."

She saw no reason not to pledge that much, at least. If they didn't stop the Barrow Witch soon, the debt would amount to nothing.

Still, Lord Granville hesitated. She could see him weighing his ego against his greed.

Conall saw it as well. He stepped forward, placing himself nearer to Sir Walter. "Aerfenium holds little worth until the empire is stable," he said. "Yet the delay in gaining this stability will amount to far more than missed opportunity if France and Germany obtain the leverage they seek. On many accounts, we must act urgently, my lord, before our enemies gain a crippling advantage."

Lord Granville's finger tapped against the chair's armrest. He regarded Conall in silence before nodding. "I will pen you a letter with instructions for Mr. Waite," he said. Effie tried to keep the flood of relief she felt from toppling her to the floor.

10

The train rocked gently as it trundled over ice-encrusted tracks on the way to Aberdeen. Effie and Conall had taken Lord Granville's letter to Edward Waite. The coal baron had not received it well. His veins had throbbed in fury. Spittle had flown as he barked at them. But in the end, his greed would not allow him to refuse Lord Granville's request. He capitulated and had given them a name.

They sat now on a worn wooden bench in a compartment near the rear of the train. The landscape out the window showed a blanket of white covering the gentle rolling hills. The peaks beyond shone through with brown and grey rock, the stone looking frigid next to the snow. The glass of the window had frosted at the corners, and a kiss of cold air rushed in as the train lumbered along.

They had the compartment to themselves. Hardly a soul had embarked for the service north. Effie leaned into Conall, pressing their shoulders together, trying to soak in the warmth he exuded. He smiled and shuffled his legs closer.

"Why, Miss Martins," he said, "I do believe this is not very proper." The name was one she had given when they first met. It was on a train to Aberdeen, in a compartment very similar to the one in which they now sat. Then, she had run from a wretched man who'd hounded her not for anything but to force himself on a young woman traveling alone. Conall had volunteered to protect her honor, though in the end only his presence had been necessary.

"No, Mr. Murray, I don't think this is proper at all." Effie cupped his hand in hers, entwining her fingers through his and holding it in her lap. The smell of horse and the road had left him, replaced by a hearty soap and the thin amount of oil run through his curly locks. The scents, so familiar and pleasing, confused her feelings.

"I am still cross with you," she said. She spoke softly. "I appreciate your willingness to sacrifice your career, and to bear the wrath of your father, for the sake of our happiness. But that does not mean I accept it."

"I understand," said Conall. "But it cannot be helped." He studied his boots. "I cannot pretend to live with your passions as my own, for it would be a lie. And yet our happiness, why can that not be achieved? You must see I find fulfillment dedicating myself to your endeavors, committing myself to your ambitions."

Effie bristled. She pulled away from him. "My ambitions!"

Conall's jaw worked. He sighed. "That is not how I meant it to sound. It's only...you have in these very months decided the world is a more important thing than yourself. It is a noble gesture, yet I cannot help but wonder who is looking out for you while you save us all."

She released his hand. "Would you be my savior? Do I need such protections from my own will?" She recalled it was he and Thomas Stevenson who'd inserted Jack Canonbie into that very same role not so many months ago.

"Effie, that is not fair. You know I share your beliefs for equality and peace." He tried to paint a smile on his lips, but it didn't quite take.

"Just not my willingness to abandon the security of passivity," she said, though she didn't truly believe he desired her to return to anonymity.

He turned his shoulders to face her directly. "You have a family and those who care for you dearly. You are part of a community. More so, you are one of its best leaders. Someone who is respected and admired. You have no need to feel apart, no need to risk everything alone. You are not an outcast but our very heart."

An outcast. She trembled. He did not pick the word at random. He had seen her reaction in Lord Granville's study, when the lord had called her thus, the same as Gaelyph, Warden of the Hunt.

Conall stood and shed his coat. He tried to wrap it about her shoulders, but she refused.

"No, sit here." She patted the bench next to her. Taking the coat, she spread it across both of them and leaned into his chest. She listened to his steady breathing for a while as the train rocked them gently along. The warmth of their touch melted away a part of her, a belief she'd held since she was young.

"So much like the first time," she said. They had argued then as well.

"It is our way," said Conall. He tilted his head so it pressed lightly on top of hers. His hand found her thigh, and she let it rest there, a firm anchor to keep her from floating away.

She dared not let it go.

* * *

The snowdrifts of the hills retreated as the tracks led them along the coast. By the time Effie spied the mouth of the River Dee, the acrid bite of seawater filled her nose. The bridge rattled as they crossed the water. She peered toward Aberdeen's large harbor, but it lay in shadows as the late afternoon sun fell to the west. Already the gas lamps of the city's broad avenues had been lit. Their flickering light caused the granite of the city's squat buildings to sparkle.

Alighting from the train with stiff legs and the weariness that comes from a long journey, she heard the lamps hissing. It took her a moment to realize why they sounded so loud. The train platform and station beyond held hardly a soul. Those she spied hurried on their way, as if they feared what might happen if they tarried.

"News of trouble in the city seems to be quite understated," she said. She'd brought Jack Canonbie's old cane and waggled it at a gentleman scurrying from the station. His shoe-clacks echoed off the stone.

Conall tapped his own cane on the platform. As he scanned about, his brow knotted. "Best we do the same as the locals," he said. "Until we know the cause."

A short lane brought them to Union Street, the main artery that divided the city. At its end, the Castlehill Barracks rose up like a prison and blocked the view of the sea. They made their way to a large square spread before the barracks. Normally bustling with activity—hawkers selling contraptions from the south, boys crying out with news from the latest broadsheets, and local tradesmen peddling their services—it stood now as quiet as the station.

Effie's foot tapped. She had hoped to beg the pardon of a passerby and ask for directions to the address they sought. She had hoped they might inquire an audience with the man before the evening grew too late. Neither now seemed likely.

She cast out her senses. She could feel the denizens of the city tucked within the buildings. It made her frown. Her foot stilled as an anxious twitter began in her gut, one that had nothing to do with Fey Craft. It came rather as a warning from the base part of her.

Conall's arm shot out. She jumped, nearly dropping her cane. "Do you see it there?" he asked. He pointed at a long shadow in the clouds. It took her a moment to distinguish the form of the airship hanging in the wind off the coast.

"Is it French?" she asked. The twinge in her gut intensified. She peered closer but could barely make out its rough outline.

"It is too difficult to spy," replied Conall. "But certainly if so, they cannot remain there forever." He turned around and gestured. "And why here, of all the places?"

A hoarse cry echoed toward them, followed by the clack of several boots striking the cobblestones. Effie whipped her head toward the sound. It came from a street running off the square. The hoarse voice barked again, but this time Effie caught a touch of fear in it. The footfalls stopped, and the eerie silence returned.

"Effie, wait!" Conall hissed the words after her as she strode across the square. She didn't turn back to him. Tightening the grip on her cane, she kept it from striking the ground. Conall caught up to her as the side street opened to them.

She startled and halted. Down the street, a pair of gothic spires rose at the front of a chapel. Before it, four soldiers surrounded a man and woman. The soldiers had their rifles leveled and bayonets fixed. Their red coats stood boldly against the granite stone of the buildings. Those they surrounded dressed in drab colors of a plain and modest style. The pair shrank toward the chapel, as if desperate to flee into its shadows.

One of the soldiers barked a question. Effie couldn't make out the words, but the man and woman shook their heads vigorously.

"Effie, this is not for us," said Conall. He snatched her arm with a gentle but firm hand. The touch jarred her. She hadn't realized she'd taken a step forward.

"We must aid them," she said. Heat rose in her chest. Her neck flushed.

"The soldiers or those they detain?" asked Conall. "We have no way of knowing their business, nor any reason to suspect it. The queen's men are our allies, remember."

She huffed as the truth of his words sank into her. She had no way to tell which side she should defend. Her assumption of the man and woman's innocence had come from her long history of mistrusting the crown's agents. Yet she refused to turn away. Something odd befell the city, and the scene before them stank of the same uncanniness.

"All the more reason we have no need to hide." She searched his face, wondering if it would've been better to come to the city alone. The thought made her twitch with guilt.

"Yes...but..." Conall exhaled a deep breath. Conceding, he nodded. "You are right. We need to learn more about what is going on. Shall we?"

Her eyes widened at his about-face. When she nodded back, he hollered down the street. "You there!" He strode toward the soldiers, clacking his cane against the cobblestones with each step. "I am a member of Her Majesty's Fey Finders. Tell me what transpires here."

The potency of his voice surprised her, as did the conviction of his lie. He marched with a stiff posture. It made him appear taller. Effie flushed the thoughts from her head. Striding behind Conall, she focused on the men with rifles.

The soldiers snapped their attention toward Conall. The one who had barked at those they detained stepped forward. As she approached, Effie could made out the blond hair that matted on his upper lip. His cheeks were lined and chapped. They held nothing of the youthfulness of his companions. The chevrons on his sleeve identified him as their sergeant.

The sergeant cleared his throat. He gestured. "Stand there, if you please, and kindly tell me your name."

"Mr. Conall Murray." Conall took a few strides closer before stopping.

"Well, Mr. Murray, if there were a Fey Finder in the city, I would know of it. So I will presume you just arrived." The sergeant's face remained passive. He knew better than to challenge Conall, but nor did he display any gratitude for the man's arrival. "The matter here is well in hand. You will find Major Barnes within the barracks."

It took a force of will for Effie to hold her tongue. Yet it would not be proper for her to speak over one proclaimed of higher rank. It would risk the gambit Conall played. Her gaze ran along the faces of the other soldiers. They were worried, and the way they held their rifles spoke of a preparedness to use them. They were not idle sentries on a routine patrol.

Her flesh prickled as understanding came to her. They hunted. Or something hunted them.

She swallowed. The gas lamps hissed at her. The dancing shadows their light cast over the chapel deepened as the last of the evening's glow vanished from the sky. She closed her eyes and cast out her senses once more. Before she had lightly grazed to gather an impression. This time she scoured every aura in the buildings along the street.

"You will not mind if I listen to your inquiry. I have a need to know what is being done about this matter," said Conall. The statement was truthful and sounded plausible enough. Yet he had barely uttered the words when Effie sensed something with fey blood materialize beneath her feet. She gasped and leapt to the side. But the aura was farther down, under the cobbles.

A low wail resounded through the city streets. It carried with it grief and pain, a lament for the dying.

The woman the soldiers questioned screamed. Toppling to her knees, she raked her face. Effie sensed the decrepit tendrils of the banshee's touch sprouting through the cobbles to ensnare the woman. Instinctively, she ripped at them.

The gas lamps nearest her exploded in a shower of embers. The shattering glass and whoosh of amber flame startled the soldiers. A rifle cracked.

"Hold!" bellowed the sergeant.

Conall stumbled into Effie, crying out. The bullet had struck him. He bled in her arms.

11

"Conall! Oh, Conall, please!" Effie helped him to the ground so he lay with his back pressed against her. She clutched him tightly, trying to push her warmth into him. The bullet had struck his arm. He clutched the wound, wincing as blood trickled between his fingers. It wasn't as much as she'd first thought, not nearly as dreadful as her initial panic had made her believe. Already it staunched and dried on his coat.

Relief flooded her, and with it came the realization she could see better now. The gas lamps had returned to their unbroken state. They hissed and flickered in a tranquil rhythm. The explosions had been a glamour, something to frighten the soldiers. She reached out with her senses, but as she suspected, the fey who'd been beneath the street had fled. The attack had been an ambush, though Effie wasn't quite certain of the target. Certainly the fey could not have foreseen the shooting.

The sergeant marched toward them until he hovered over Conall. He glanced at Conall's arm and grunted. "Apologies, Mr. Murray. The lad will be disciplined," he said. "Turing," he hollered at one of the younger soldiers. "Wilkes, fetch the surgeon!"

Effie couldn't tell if it was the same who'd fired his rifle. She watched the soldier run off. The pounding of his two boots dimmed as those of a thundering herd grew louder. More soldiers from the barracks hurried, across the square from their direction. They had heard the shot.

Several faces had appeared in the windows above them as well. None held any fey blood. They only stood and watched, some with candles or oil lamps in hand, others lit by the amber glow of the street's gas lights.

"I don't think the bone is broken," said Conall. He spoke through clenched teeth, grimacing.

"Lay still," said Effie. She squeezed the opposite shoulder from the wound. "The surgeon will see to it, though you will need a new coat." She smiled at him and was relieved when a glint of mischief came to his eye.

"On my current wages, I'd better learn to stitch cloth," he replied, so only she could hear.

"What of these lot, sergeant?" called one of the soldiers. He waved at the man and woman they had questioned. The woman had returned to her senses, though she swayed on her feet, in a daze. No evidence of the banshee's touch remained. Effie had managed that, at least.

"Let them go," said the sergeant. His tone gave no indication of an apology, but when he caught Effie's glare he spoke to her in a lower voice. "We were about to anyway."

He planted the butt of his rifle on the cobblestones. "You are fey," he said. "Where did the attack come from?"

The question surprised Effie, but it told her much about what transpired in the city. That the sergeant recognized a glamour meant he had seen them before. That he did not suspect her of the Fey Craft meant he searched for someone or something specific.

"From beneath us," she answered. "What is down there?"

The sergeant grunted. His lips pursed. "Aberdeen is a modern city. Its water flows underground—both the clean and the spoiled. It's carried from the river."

"It was only a single fey," she offered. "Have these attacks been more than flashing lights and false explosions? Certainly that is enough to drive folks from the streets, but we have heard reports of far greater engagements."

"That will be for Major Barnes to say," said the sergeant.

The soldiers from the barracks reached them before Effie could press any further. They ringed the street while the surgeon was brought forward. The surgeon helped Conall strip from his coat. The shirt sleeve he tore free to expose a wicked looking gash.

He inspected and prodded the wound. "The arm is not in jeopardy, but mending requires the needle," he finally said. The man had the same gruff temperament as the sergeant. "The light is better inside. Follow."

Effie helped Conall to his feet. The sergeant ordered a pair of soldiers to accompany them, and they marched as if under guard. The surgeon disappeared into the shadows of the large square, but she kept to a slower pace. There was no need to risk Conall fainting on her. His flesh had paled. His breathing came slow and ragged, yet his gait remained sturdy as they made their way to the barracks.

The barracks stood atop a gentle hill that once held a castle. They'd been built a century past to aid in the coastal defense against invasion. But they held none of the ramparts or battlements of a fortress. Were it not for the flurry of red coats marching through the grounds, and its dominant position within the city, the barracks might've been confused for one of the factories that lined the river. A factory, or a prison. Effie had thought of the latter when they first arrived. In her mind, the two could be much the same.

Granite walls stood stiff and unadorned. The sea air had washed away most of the scent of a hundred men living together, but Effie caught hints as they passed through the iron gates and crossed the courtyard beyond. Oil and grease lay under a wash of brewed coffee and potato soup. Musk and a tinge of gunpowder blended with the stench of the mold that clung to the damp, shadowed corners where the radiance of the gas lamps did not reach.

The surgeon waited for them at a small building that nestled near the barrack's main structure. He made quick work of the stitching with a practiced hand and wrapped Conall's arm in a clean, white dressing. Conall drank tea mixed with a tonic dripped from a small green bottle, and afterward some of his color returned.

Effie felt guilty not allowing him rest, but she was eager with questions for the major and warranted the matter could not wait. If Conall had not proclaimed himself a Fey Finder, she might have left him to a bed and gone alone. He waved her concerns away, however, and leaned on his cane as they were led into the main building and through a series of clerical offices.

Major Barnes sat behind a desk laden with paperwork. He glanced up from the report he read when the soldier that escorted them announced their arrival. A thick mustache covered his mouth. It fell like a walrus' on either side of his lips. He had sunken eyes that made his gaze appear disapproving.

"You are a Fey Finder?" he asked. He took in Conall's bandaged arm and returned to his report, as if the answer didn't interest him. The mustache twitched as he read.

"I am," said Conall. He slouched on his cane with his good arm.

The major did not look up. "I received no notice of your coming, yet I understood I was to be kept informed of your lot," he said. "Does that make a liar out of Mr. Billingsley or my superiors?"

The floorboard creaked as Conall shifted. "Ah, the Fey Finder General may not be aware of my movements. We had a need to travel in haste."

The major placed the report atop a stack of other papers. He studied Effie before returning his attention to Conall. "I see," he said. He waited for Conall to continue.

"We seek to find a certain man, a Mr. Jean-Nicolas Durand," said Conall.

"The Frenchman?" The major's eyes widened. "You will not find him in the city. He is under lock and key. He was found raving mad a week ago and thrown in the tollbooth with the rest of them."

Conall rose up excitedly. "Indeed? We must speak with him," he said.

At the same time, Effie blurted, "The rest of them?"

The major glanced between them again. "He is with the others who have been found wandering the streets witless, or even worse, inciting mayhem. It is a sickness that plagues the city due to the lack of work, the same that plagues the rest of this country. As for seeing the man, I fear it is not possible. The afflicted are under strict quarantine."

Effie barely kept herself from growling. "The banshee's touch is not contagious."

"So you say," said the major. "Yet these preposterous claims of it spread, and the so-called menace grows." He straightened in his chair.

"Do you know what wins wars, miss? Efficient lines of communication and supply. Sever those, and you sever the head of the snake." He waved an absent hand. "Or whatever this current madness is."

Effie's fingers curled into fists, but it was Conall who spoke first. His voice was hard. His face pulled tight with anger. "We must insist on seeing Mr. Durand," he said. "It concerns Fey Finder business and cannot be delayed."

"The days of Fey Finders bullying their way into catastrophe are over," replied the major. "Now, if you have been given orders, produce them. Otherwise, you may see yourselves off these premises." He curtly plucked another report from his desk and began to read.

A dozen arguments came to Effie at once, some lacking in civility, but she held them all back. She had dealt with men like Major Barnes before. Mentioning Sir Walter or Edward Waite, or even Lord Granville, would do them little good. Mentioning her theories on Aerfenium and the Barrow Witch would do them even less. The man read reports for a living. He would respond to little that did not come from a field manual or direct command. Their best hope was to send a telegram to Edinburgh in the morning and hope for a swift response.

Still, she would not be dismissed without further answers regarding the evening's events. "We require lodging in the city," she said. "Can we wander freely, or is the city under curfew?"

The major's brow furrowed. "I do not have that authority," he said. "But if you mean to inquire why the streets remain empty, it is due to the purported sightings of a beast. The thing is apparently nine foot tall and glows silver under the moon. Nonsense, of course. It is only tales of fear spawned by a bit of unrest and that damned French airship."

"Well, it is good to hear I was shot by one of your men merely due to tales of fear," said Conall.

The major snorted. "The attacks are real enough. It is their source that is fanciful. We have thus far been unable to track down the French insurgents, but we will. I assure you."

"Are the reports of cannon fire also a part of these tales?" asked Effie. She cursed inwardly. She saw straight away she had pressed with too firm a hand.

"Owens," the major called. "Please escort Mr. Murray and his companion from the barracks." He raised an eyebrow at her. "You will kindly leave military matters to the army while in this city. The tollbooth may have run out of space, but we would surely find other means for your detention, if necessary."

The soldier who had led them into the major's office reappeared. His boots slapped against the floor as he snapped to attention and saluted. Effie forced herself to curtsey to the major. Conall bowed stiffly before spinning on his heel.

"Well, at least we know Mr. Durand has not fled the city," he said once they were out of earshot of the major. "There is that in our favor."

Effie grimaced. They emerged into the crisp night air. A low bank of fog had closed over the barracks. It obscured the courtyard, yet she could hear the clink of tin and rustle of leather as men moved about them. She could feel them as well, along with those gathered within the buildings. Idly, she searched through their auras to determine whether any were familiar to her. It was not likely, but the process allowed her a small measure of hope. It was better than doing nothing.

She had almost given up when a slight tingling came to her gut. One of the auras in front of her held fey blood. Her flesh prickled in warning, but she didn't believe the aura to be tainted. It reminded her of wind blowing through the woods, and of an earthen forest floor thick with pollen in the springtime.

The fey had a human companion, too. They approached in a direct but steady manner. Effie placed a hand on Conall's chest to alert him as the pair of figures emerged from the fog. They stood on the far side of the barrack's iron gates. One was a soldier with a face barely of an age to bear whiskers. He didn't carry a rifle, she noted. The woman next to him wore a modest dress and coat, but the clothes held a week's worth of wrinkles and dirt caked at the hems. Her hair was pulled under a bonnet. Loose strands of it fell about the sides of her face. Her eyes had deep wells beneath them, as if she hadn't slept in days.

"Miss Effie of Glen Coe," said the soldier. His deep-set eyes sat over rounded cheeks and a thick chin. "I am Samuel Harper. This is Mrs. Graives. We would ask to speak with you about her son and daughter."

Effie studied his uniform and wondered how such a thing was

possible. It was he who held the fey blood, a member of Her Majesty's army.

Charging forward, the woman snatched Effie's hands. She clutched them against her chest. Her whole body trembled. Her eyes pleaded. "They are taken," she said. "But the major won't listen."

"They are taken by the Banshee of Aberdeen," said Harper. He glanced at Owens rather sheepishly. "Mrs. Graives and I have seen it and know where to find its lair."

12

S amuel Harper led them to an old coaching inn off Union Street. It had seen better years. The eaves sagged. The timbers had splintered and were in need of paint. They slumped against the granite stone of the inn's neighbors. But within, warm light brought a cheeriness to the place. A pleasant fragrance wafted from the hearth. Full of onion and carrot, it made Effie's stomach rumble.

They received a cheery welcome from the master of the house, despite the hour. The main room held a scattering of unmatched tables and chairs, each lacquered a different shade. A narrow stair rose to rooms above, and a long hall led to the service area at the rear of the building.

Effie chose a table that had a bench with a stiff wooden back, so Conall could rest against the corner it formed with the wall. She sat next to him. Her head grew drowsy the moment her back pressed against the wood, but she shook the weariness away.

"Tell me of this banshee," she said. Her heart had skipped when she'd heard the moniker earlier, yet she doubted instantly that the name referred to the Barrow Witch. The Sidhe Bhreige toiled at a greater game than terrifying the denizens of Aberdeen.

"The wailing started a fortnight ago, but even afore that there were

tales of strange beasts roaming the city at night," said Harper. He helped
Mrs. Graives into a chair and took one for himself.

"Beasts? More than one?" Effie asked.

"Och, aye." The young man glanced around the room, though it was
empty except for their table. "One's a hairy thing that skulks about in
the shadows. It don't do much but run away, but at least a dozen from
the barracks have seen it. Even Owens, not that he's likely to tell the
major. The other one's been seen less, for all the wailing it's doing."

"She took my Nettie," blurted Mrs. Graives. "First her, and then
Wallace."

Harper placed a gentle hand over hers. "Mrs. Graives and I are
distant cousins through my mother and the late Mr. Graives. I found her
wandering the city in an understandable state of distress."

"How long have your son and daughter been missing?" asked Effie.

Harper waited as the master of the house set down steaming bowls of
soup and poured cups of tea. "Nettie was taken first, from their cottage
on the outskirts of the city. She was at the washing and simply
disappeared. That was almost a week ago."

"I fetched my Wallace," said Mrs. Graives. "He's a bricklayer but has
a good head. He searched for Nettie for three days. Only on the fourth,
he never came back."

Harper read the question that came to Effie's mind, the connection
between the disappearances and the banshee. His cheeks flushed as he
spoke. "I get this kind of impression of Nettie sometimes, like I can
point to where she is even if I can't see her. I've had it since we were
both wee bairns. When I found Mrs. Graives, we went looking for
Nettie and Wallace both, and the impression came to me."

"Only it vanished," said Effie. She sipped at her tea, letting its heat
warm her bones. She saw now where the tale headed.

"Aye," replied Harper. He blinked in surprise. "That's when Mrs.
Graives spied the thing. It crept through the shadows dressed as a
woman. Only when the moonlight caught its face, we saw it had grey
flesh covered in scales. It led us to the pumping station at the far end of
Queen Street."

"The sewers beneath the city," said Effie. It all made sense. She
turned to Conall but found him with his eyes closed. His chest rose and

fell with a steady cadence. Some of the color had returned to his cheeks. He looked so peaceful, she had no wish to disturb him.

"Miss Effie," said Harper. He leaned in. "There are tales of others missing, too. The major sends out patrols, but they are searching for those causing unrest, or to guard against the French. They aren't looking for those who've been taken."

"Major Barnes does not believe in tales of beasts and banshees," said Effie. She thought of the cruel fate that awaited Clara Bowman and cringed. She had no doubt Nettie and Wallace would face the same, if they did not already. They shared the same fey blood as young Mr. Harper, through their father's connection to his mother.

A bogill and grindylow, his tale described. She was sure of it. The Barrow Witch's alchemy had spread to Aberdeen, along with her Unseily Court. What that meant beyond the immediate consequences, Effie could not fathom.

Glancing at Conall, her foot began to tap. The matter could not wait for dawn. It could not wait for the rest he required. She would never forgive herself if something happened to Nettie or Wallace while she idled about. Nor would she forgive herself if an opportunity to learn the location of the Barrow Witch slipped through her fingers while she sipped at tea. Conall would be cross with her, but that mattered little next to the fate of Mrs. Graives' family and the rest of the empire.

"Are you armed?" she asked Harper.

He nodded. "I have a service pistol."

She stood. "Mrs. Graives, may I beg of you to watch over Mr. Murray? He will need sleep and as much soup as he can manage to keep down." She reached into her reticule and produced some coins. "These will be enough until we return."

Mrs. Graives hands closed over hers. The woman's bony fingers felt like iron. Her eyes pleaded. Effie passed the coins over and gave the woman a reassuring smile. She kissed Conall lightly on the forehead before lofting her cane and striding for the door.

Harper held it open for her. They heard the wailing straight away as they emerged into the streets. It sounded far off, as if it came from the hills to the west. On any other night, Effie might have confused it for a lost hound howling for its master.

But she recognized the glamour the grindylow used from earlier in the evening.

"It drives everyone into their homes," she said. They made their way down a short street and turned onto a broader avenue. A clock tower rose in the distance, and Harper directed them toward it.

"Banshees are ill luck," he said. "To see one means death."

"Or madness," she said. She opened up her senses, but the only fey blood she felt nearby came from Harper.

"How is it you came to wear a soldier's uniform?" she asked.

"The crown tests for fey blood, but I was lucky. The Fey Finder who did the thing didn't know what he was about. I didn't either, truth be told, until a year ago. My company's captain assigned me a detail to deliver a missive to your steward. Caledon told me of it when I met him." Harper shrugged. "I had not thought such a thing possible—to not know, that is. My family hails from Carlisle. They aren't...but my mother, she's from the same village as the late Mr. Graives."

Effie smiled. "I've known all my life, but that did me little good when it came to what it meant. My mother taught me nothing of Fey Craft, or of the steward or the Seily Court, before she passed. She only sung a few rhymes and told vague tales of ancient days. Most of my knowledge of the fey has come to me lately."

Harper looked at her askance, and she laughed. "Not the stories you've heard of me?" she asked. "The Green Lady who communes with trees and fells giants?"

He swallowed. "You are more than those things, Miss Effie. So much more to so many. When I told Mrs. Graives of your arrival in the city, her face lit up with hope for the first time in days."

Effie had no response to that. She quickened their pace, as if to flee her embarrassment. Their footfalls, and the clack of her heavy cane, echoed against the granite walls of the buildings that lined the street. The gas lamps hissed. Their light beamed through the thin fog.

At the clock tower, Harper entered a narrow passage that emptied into a courtyard filled with young hazelnut trees. Beyond, a small square building sat. It had a crenelated roof, like that of a castle wall, yet it stood no larger than a cottage.

"The Queen Street pumping station," said Harper. "It raises the water from the River Dee high enough to flush the sewers beneath the streets into the sea."

The lock of the great iron-bound door was broken. The hinges creaked as Harper shoved the heavy door aside to reveal a long, steep stairway leading beneath the city. Effie took the steps carefully. Moonlight reflected off water that had collected on those at the top. On those at the bottom, green algae had formed.

She heard water running through the sluices as they reached the bottom. The air grew thicker with fumes of the city's waste. She tried not to consider them. A ledge ran alongside the central channel where the water flowed, and she motioned Harper to lead them down it.

He drew his pistol from a coat pocket. Though standing not nearly as tall, the action reminded her of Jack Canonbie. They had skulked beneath the streets of Edinburgh not so very long ago. Her chest grew tight at the memory, and a mixture of sadness, frustration, and regret set in.

"Miss Effie," said Harper, barely above a whisper. "We will need the torch you promised."

She shook herself alert and cursed herself a fool. Now was not the time for recollection. She fetched a pair of tiny paper packets from her reticule. Stooping, she emptied their contents onto the slick stone of the ledge and mixed the powders with the tip of her cane. The mixture sizzled and let off a soft silvery glow.

Harper handed her a strip of cloth, blinking as he stared in wonder.

"It's not Fey Craft, only a bit of chemistry," she said. She wrapped the cloth around the bottom tip of her cane and rolled the tied cloth in the mixture. "From a dear friend of mine, Mr. Stuart Graham."

Rising, she held the cane out before her. It was long enough that she had to brace it under one arm. A rat squeaked and scurried from the sudden light. The way beyond ran under an arched ceiling formed of bricks.

Harper set off at a cautious pace. Every fifty paces, a rib to support the ceiling would narrow the ledge to a hand's width. Scrambling past the ribs forced Effie to cling to the moss-covered bricks. At least that's what she wanted the slimy and somewhat furry texture to be.

Her heart thumped a steady rhythm. Her eyes had adjusted to the silvery light, but its glow only extended a few paces. In the darkness, critters skittered, water lapped, and the creak and groan of sluices and pipes echoed like the wounded cries of a metallic beast.

She searched with her senses as they stalked. She could feel the city above them, auras gathered together in small clumps, no doubt in bedrooms at this hour. But she didn't sense any fey blood nearby. It did not surprise her. The fey who'd attacked earlier in the evening had known how to obscure its aura, the way it appeared and vanished so suddenly.

They reached an intersection after a short while. Two channels ran together to form a larger. The fumes wafting from the water lessened as its flow increased, and a tang of salt came stronger.

"We near the sea," said Effie.

"Aye, I believe so," answered Harper. He peered up the second channel. "But which is the way we need?"

Effie thought for a moment before grinning. She should have thought of it earlier. The Banshee of Aberdeen might obscure its aura, but that did not obscure its intrusion on those who called the sewers home. Stooping down, she quickly found those she sought.

She sent them an impression of a nice chunk of moldy cheese. Two pairs of red eyes appeared with an eager swiftness. She added to the impression an impression of distance. The cheese lay in a field at the edge of sight, but they could smell its sharp tang still. It called to them. It was theirs, if only they could claim it.

One of the rats squeaked. It came forward into the silvery light and rose to its hind legs. It batted a forepaw in the air.

Effie brought crows to the impression of the field. They were dingy, mean things that circled and cawed, searching for the rats' cheese. Last, she brought herself into the impression in the guise of a tawny owl. She wanted to drive the crows off and let the rats run freely across the field. But she couldn't find the crows. She needed help.

Where are the crows that invade your field? She watched the rats. The one that had come forward edged closer. Its nose twitched. *Where are the foul intruders?* Effie asked the question again, within the impression.

The rat turned and scurried to the edge of the light. There, it waited, watching her. She strode toward it, and it set off again, only to wait for her once more.

"Thank you," she said. She brought the cheese closer in the impression.

"Marvelous," said Harper. He followed at Effie's heels. She heard the wonder in his voice and remembered when she had held the same when it came to Fey Craft. Despite all that had happened, it had not been very long ago.

Their guide led them down the larger channel. It joined with another after a short while and bent in a shallow arc. Effie tried to gauge the distance they had travelled. She wondered why they hadn't strode into the sea. But in the dark, with their slow and careful pace, she knew such things could be deceiving.

As the channel straightened, she spied a collapse in the wall. Piles of brick lay scattered across the ledge. They were covered in thick, black undersoil. She stepped carefully through the debris and peered into the fissure the collapse had left. It carried on for a dozen paces before it appeared to widen. An earthy scent wafted from the hole, smelling of damp clay and crushed seashells. It carried on a colder draft of fresh air.

Effie steeled herself. The fissure reminded her of the one she had found near the village of Duncairn. It left her with little doubt they had found the warren of the Unseily fey, and most likely the warren of the Banshee of Aberdeen.

The rat hopped onto one of the bricks. It pawed toward the opening but seemed reluctant to scurry any closer. She sent it an impression of warmth and the contentment of a full belly. It squeaked and looked at her, whiskers twitching. She knew it would rather have the cheese, but she would have to settle that debt later.

Harper checked the load of his pistol. They caught eyes, and she nodded. Leveling the weapon, he used his free hand to steady himself against the earthen wall and padded forward.

Effie stepped carefully behind him. She lofted the cane above their heads so it lit the way. There was no need to hide their coming. Whatever fey lay in wait would have already sensed their auras. The smarter thing would be to wait, to fetch the sergeant and a dozen soldiers. But for the sake of Nettie and Wallace, she would not turn back.

She could not abandon them.

The passage widened, and her silvery light spilled into the chamber beyond. Effie inhaled sharply. Several forms lay in a heap against the chamber's far wall. The captives were bound by thick ropes and gagged with rags. She could see the shallow rise and fall of their chests. They slept, though whether she had come too late to save them from the Unseily alchemy, she could not tell.

One of the figures, a younger man with light hair and freckles dotting his cheeks, opened his eyes. They widened in shock. He squirmed, straining against the ropes. He wailed a muffled cry.

Effie understood the warning and spun around. Her heart leapt into her throat. The chamber was barely larger than a train car, yet the Unseily fey had remained in the darkness at the edges of the silvery light. She swung the cane about and caught movement to either side of her as the light danced over the walls.

The bogill charged. Like the one she had encountered in the ravine, hair covered him in a pelt—a coarse black this time, in place of ginger. He had a ridged brow and shoulders the size of an ox. He held no weapon except for thick fingers that curled like claws.

He roared as he charged. The sound filled the chamber. Harper's pistol popped in rapid succession. Sparks of flames shot from the barrel. The bogill flinched but kept coming. It stalked to within a pace of them. Harper raised the barrel and fired once more.

The bogill jerked and slumped to the ground. In the sudden silence, Effie thought she heard the sound of waves pounding the shoreline. The morning tide must have come.

Dirt scraped to one side of her. A rasping cackle followed. She swung the cane so its light revealed the grindylow. Scaly grey flesh covered its head and arms. It regarded her with sunken eyes that had filmed over so they appeared as white orbs.

"You will not save them all, Grundbairn," the creature said.

A chill washed over Effie. Goose pimples rose on her flesh. The words were almost identical to those spoken by the first grindylow she'd come across.

Harper's pistol clicked empty. The man grunted and patted at his coat pocket.

"Get them out of here!" Effie shouted at him. She tightened the grip on her cane and waved it at those held captive.

The grindylow crept toward her. Its mouth gaped. Yellow teeth shone against the pale flesh of its lips.

Effie leveled the cane before her and braced herself to leap. The tip of the cane wavered as she struggled to keep her arms still. It caused the silvery light to cast dancing shadows at the corners of her vision.

She could hear Harper working at the bonds of those held captive. Grunts and muttered curses uttered from a pair of deep-timbered voices.

The grindylow cackled and lunged at her.

Effie raised the cane to swipe. She didn't see the rock sailing from the shadows until it struck her at the temple. The chamber spun and darkened. She stumbled and fell to her knees. A wetness dribbled down the side of her face.

A tittering laughter echoed above her.

13

Rotting vines entwined her. They sprouted from the chamber floor, from the walls, and from the arms of the grindylow. Their thorns bit into her flesh. Their weight shoved her down, yanking her through the hard-packed dirt and into darkness.

She fought them. She ripped and tore with her hands until her fingers grew slick with blood. Vines crept into her mouth, trying to suffocate her. She batted them away and snapped her teeth shut. She didn't panic. She had faced the assault before. She knew the Fey Craft for what it was —a trick. A deadly trick, but one all the same.

Light flared anew. Vines and stone and dirt dissolved in a swirling pattern of greens, browns, and greys.

Effie blinked and found herself in a broad glen. She stood beneath trees. Proud oaks ringed her in a circle, their gnarled bark twisted with age. A sweet scent of mistletoe and hazelnut hung in the air. Beneath it, a hint of wood smoke lingered.

An elderly fey watched her from one of the boughs. The woman had the almond eyes and sharp cheeks of a pixie, but she was much older than that race. She held a firm beauty, too, like that of a fierce storm.

Effie had met the woman once before. She forced her arms to remain still at her sides, refusing to give into the fear that crept through her bones.

"What have you done?" she demanded. "What is this place?"

"I have done nothing," said the Barrow Witch. "You sleep. You dream of the truth and deny your eyes."

Effie's mind whirled. "I must draw close, to provoke you thus." Her voice trembled. She heard the doubt in it. The Barrow Witch had taunted her with illusions of danger after the capture of Cyrus Reed. She had infected her dreams before that. But those had been faceless threats. The Sidhe Bhreige had only presented herself once before in this dreamlike state. In the underground chambers of *Les Revinirs*, while Effie lingered under the effects of opium, she had tried to convince Effie to join her cause.

Effie couldn't fathom what it meant that she came to her now in the bowels of Aberdeen, yet she doubted it random.

The Barrow Witch's pealing laughter held the power of thunder. The simple tunic she wore shimmered silver as she quivered with mirth. The oak trees rustled, as if an unseen force gusted against them.

"Draw close? You have not the power to hold back the wind, to deny the weight of stone, or to shatter a storm," she said. "You seek to punish those you deem corrupted. Why do you fear them so? They are only children of the forest, of the fields, and of the hills. The same as yourself. Can they not live as they please?"

"They...they..." Effie started to speak, but the argument that sprang to her lips dissolved. She blinked. The notion didn't sound nearly as absurd as it should. Her head swam, and she wondered why she feared the Unseily fey. It was true they only followed their nature. Wasn't theirs better than those who oppressed her kind?

She glanced at the oaks. A lingering thought confused her certainty. It tickled at the back of her mind, fighting to grab hold. She grasped at it and remembered. When last the Barrow Witch had revealed herself, a host of fey had frolicked beneath an intense moonlight. Drums had beaten, and the crackling flames of a great bonfire had warmed the night. But not all had been as it seemed.

The memory started to slip away. Effie chased it, clawing to keep it at the forefront of her mind. It was important, the part that came next.

Three men had come to the clearing and offered to sacrifice a young boy. They killed to please the Sidhe Bhreige. It was what the ancient fey considered man's true nature—that of subservient beasts.

Effie's eyes widened. She ripped at the fog that veiled her thoughts. Clarity returned, and with it, fury.

"You are a horror." She spat the words.

The Barrow Witch's lips curled into a hungry grin. Her eyes became shrewder. The angles of her cheeks sharpened. "I am many things, young Grundbairn. But I will return all to their natural order, to what was, and what was meant to be."

"Through slaughter and torment?"

"You steel yourself against your future. You fight it without cause. But you will see as I have seen. You will join my court, Grundbairn. You will know elation as the usurping queen is brought low and my rightful place is restored."

"Your rightful place is in the Downward Fields," said Effie. "Sealed away so you can no longer cause any harm. Yet you will never return there. The queen's armies will destroy you long before that becomes a possibility."

The Barrow Witch growled. Her flesh paled to the grey of stone. In the light of the bonfire, it appeared dead, like something left to rot. Her hair thinned and eyes sank until they were beady orbs that shone a fiery red.

"She will swing from her own usurper's tree. I will see to it." The ground rumbled as the Sidhe Bhreige spoke. The boughs of the oaks swayed and groaned. Their roots pulled up through the earth, snapping and splintering.

Something tickled along Effie's arms. She yanked back and felt the tug of invisible roots entwining her limbs. Ripping harder, some broke away. Yet others held firm. Without thought, she called on Fey Craft. She pulled water from the ground, causing it to spray upward in a dewy mist. The droplets kissed the invisible roots and allowed her to trace them as they sprouted from the trees.

There were thousands. She gasped at the snaking web. Even as she took them in, they grew barbs that scratched searing red cuts across her skin. She shrieked from the agony as she ripped and tore. She flailed madly with her arms and kicked with her legs. But the roots ensnared her, biting deep and constricting. They wrapped around her chest and legs.

She struggled to cling to what she had known before—that the roots were only a trick. But the knowledge did not matter. She could not convince herself of its truth. Fear had taken hold. Her breath shallowed. She grew lightheaded.

"Do not struggle, dear child," said the Barrow Witch. "Your breath will not be your last. My children have captured you and slain your companion. When you wake, you will be mine. You will be my most prized possession."

❧ 14 ❧

Sparkling dots flashed before Effie's eyes. Her throat burned from her dry, wheezing gasps. Her arms could no longer move, nor her legs. She tried to force the roots to whither. She tried to summon new-growth vines and grasses to aid her. But none of her Fey Craft worked.

The Barrow Witch strengthened her vines and held back the trees and undergrowth. She controlled the glen. She controlled everything.

No, not everything. A sharp scent reached Effie. It drifted from high above and smelled of the sea. Or rather, of salt mixed with the rot of seaweed and algae. The odor fought against the darkness that enclosed over her vision. It pulled her alert. She jerked and felt the thorns and barbs gouge her. The roots tightened.

If she could only come nearer the source of the odor, she might be saved. The thought drifted to her. She clung to it. She wished she could fly on wings like Gwendoline. But that would not free her. She wished her arms could stretch longer, so she could grasp whatever floated high above and draw it closer. But the roots would follow her hands and lash them down. She needed to loft her nose into the clouds.

She needed to grow as large as a giant. As quickly as the thought came, she forced her will to it. The Barrow Witch might control the landscape, but she did not control her. Not yet.

Her legs swelled and body lengthened. The roots, firm enough to hold her smaller self, snapped like the crackling of dry leaves. They squirmed in a flurry, trying to recapture her. But they became like strands of a spider's web. She swatted them away.

Thunder rumbled over the glen, shaking the ground. Thick clouds roiled overhead. The Barrow Witch shrieked. Her piercing wail brought on waves of nausea. But Effie rose to her feet and ignored it all. She'd grown larger than the oaks and could spy their tops far below.

As her head reached the clouds, she filled her massive lungs and recognized the sharp odor of Salt of Hartshorn. She started. Odd that the smelling salts would find her in the glen, she thought as she snapped awake.

She blinked against a bright morning sun. She lay on a hillside with her head cradled in a soft woolen blanket. Waves crashed before her sending sea mist jetting into the air. Conall came into focus. He held a small vial she recognized as one she kept in her own reticule. She sniffed its contents once more and jerked fully alert.

"She stirs." Harper's voice came from somewhere behind her. Relief flooded her at the sound. She had feared the Barrow Witch had spoken the truth about his fate. Boots clomped on grass dusted with sand. As she turned her head, she caught sight of more than a dozen soldiers roaming over the hillside.

"Effie." Worry painted Conall's brow. He stoppered the vial and leaned over her. He'd hung his injured arm in a sling of white cloth.

"I am fine. Do not tell me how foolish I was." Guilt overcame her instantly for her abruptness. Her cheeks burned. She hadn't meant to throw his concern back at him. It had come from her embarrassment.

Conall pulled her hand into his. "You did what you thought right. I cannot challenge your intentions, nor your courage." He grinned and cocked his head. "Though you might have had more allies if you'd considered it. Mrs. Graives was not the only person searching for a missing loved one, and Mr. Harper not the only soldier who would have followed you."

"Aye," said a gruff voice. The sergeant from the night before stalked next to her and knelt. "We pulled seven souls from that filthy den."

Harper knelt next to the sergeant. A jagged cut ran from his cheek to his chin, though it did not appear deep. "Nettie and Wallace were among them."

"Just like before," said Conall. "They captured those with fey blood from around the city and wished to practice their alchemy on them, to make them Unseily."

"They waited, as Tallia's host had? We were not too late?" Effie shot up and became dizzy. Her head pounded. Feeling at her temple, she realized someone had tied a bandage around it.

Conall helped her lay back against the blanket. He urged her to rest and offered her some water. It tasted metallic but soothed her throat.

"They waited," he said, with a note of sorrow. "But they had a young man with them they had perhaps recently corrupted."

"He's the one that struck you," said Harper. "I'm sorry, miss. I didn't see him at first, and once he rose up, I thought him another of the captives. He didn't look like the others. Just had some tattered clothes and a bit of dirt on him, is all."

"It is all right," said Effie. "You did no wrong. I did not see him either." She swung her gaze between Conall and the sergeant. "Do I have the pair of you to thank for our rescue?"

"Nay, miss," said the sergeant. "We came long after."

Harper shook his head. His gaze grew distant. "The roots sprang up as you fell. Eerie, they were, coming out of the chamber walls to lash at us, all thick with thorns. But Wallace stormed through them like they weren't there. He charged the banshee—or grindylow, as Mr. Murray called it—and there was a brilliant flash of light. By the time our vision cleared, the creature and the man who'd struck you were gone."

"The airship is gone too," said Conall. He released her hand and pointed along the horizon. "It left in the early hours."

Effie thought about that and frowned. "The Barrow Witch," she said, almost to herself. She leapt to the obvious connection, but it rang as false somehow. She didn't believe their enemy so reckless as to ferry about in an airship. Easily spotted and slow, the airship would draw too much attention. The Sidhe Bhreige was far more cunning.

"She revealed herself and threatened me," Effie continued at Conall's confused expression. "It was just as in Edinburgh, in a place of dreams." She shook her head. "But why does she taunt me? Why now?"

"She grows an army of Unseily, which you threaten," said Conall.

"That may be the heart of it," Effie conceded, though she had to believe there was more. "But why Unseily? Why not call on packs of fey beasts like her brethren—the trows and wulvers? What more does she stand to gain for this effort?"

Conall shrugged. "Her brethren's efforts ended in defeat."

"Who is this Barrow Witch?" asked Harper. He leaned in, his brow fixed and eyes intent on their every word.

"No doubt another beast from a bairn's tale." Major Barnes spat each word as if they befouled his mouth. He stalked across the hilltop, mustache twitching. Owens and another soldier scurried at his heels.

Harper and the sergeant scrambled to their feet. They snapped rigid salutes.

The major returned them, but his gaze never left Conall. "It comes to me from the Fey Finder General that you are no longer among their ranks," he said.

Conall's lips tugged in an embarrassed grin. "Ah, so I take it the paperwork has finally gone through," he said. He stared down at the major. "It took an age to file the needed documents. Government jobs, aye?"

The sergeant coughed. Harper shifted his weight. He gawked at Conall before remembering himself and snapping back to attention.

The major's gaze narrowed. "You wished to see Mr. Durand," he said. "I can arrange for you to take residence in the cell next to the man." He turned stiffly to Effie. "And you. I should have you in irons as well. It is not proper for a woman of any heritage to go skulking about in the sewers."

"Seven souls beg to differ," said Conall. His grin dropped. "More, perhaps, had the Unseily been allowed to fester any longer."

The major's gaze flicked to Conall. His expression grew pensive, and he craned his head toward the city to study something in the distance. "Mr. Billingsley also warned me against your involvement. He said unseemly business follows you wherever you go."

The sergeant frowned. His stance stiffened. "Permission to speak, sir."

"Denied," said the major. "I know full well these creatures arrived before Mr. Murray and Miss Effie. I have also spoken with those rescued and set men to scouring the city, above and below, for the Unseily fey that fled."

He knelt next to Effie and ran his gaze over her bandaged head. "But I will not have you running amok as you please. My soldiers are not for your personal indulgence, no matter the faith others place in you. You will give your word to leave Aberdeen once your interrogation is complete."

Effie perked up. She'd bit her tongue, not wanting to provoke the man further, but now she blurted, "You will allow us to speak with Mr. Durand?"

"Yes," said the major. "Afterwards, I will have Owens put you aboard a train."

❧ 15 ❧

The steel door of the cell groaned as Samuel Harper pulled it open. Painted to match the whitewash of the brick walls, it swung into a long and narrow corridor. Similar doors lined the dank corridor's length. The hay-strewn floors and stench of bodies reminded Effie of a stable. Muttering, weeping, and snoring echoed through the walls.

A single candle burned within the cell. It illuminated the small space. A straw mattress and blanket of coarse wool lay along the wall. A porcelain pot sat next to the bedding. The only other object was the stool on which a gaunt man perched. His suit had once been fine, but layers of soil and stain now marred it. His head had been shaved almost to the scalp. A thick nose dominated a face covered in whiskers.

"Mr. Jean-Nicolas Durand?" Effie asked. She stepped within the cell. Conall and Harper followed at her heels. Her head remained unsteady, and she leaned eagerly on her cane. They had come straightaway from the broad hill above the beach. Sand and grass still clung to her dress.

The man did not stir. He seemed transfixed on some distant object that none other could see. His lips were moist with spittle.

"We've come to discuss your dealings with Cyrus Reed," she said.

At the name, the man flinched. His head swiveled about. "Reed?" He spoke with a thick accent from the continent. His jaw worked and brow pulled tight. He seemed befuddled until his gaze fixed on her. Fury replaced confusion. Leaping to his feet, he shouted. "Where is it?"

Harper stepped in front of Effie. Conall raised his cane above his head, ready to strike. His wounded arm still hung in its sling. But Durand approached no farther.

"A trick! A bloody trick!" Durand seized his head in both hands and wailed. The effort doubled him over at the waist, and he sank to the ground. "Cyrus Reed, yes, but the deceiver... Yes, that's it. She chased. Hounded. Wolves at the ford! Howling!"

"The man is shattered," said Conall. He lowered his cane.

"Tell us, Mr. Durand." Effie begged, but felt her hope wilt. The ranting reminded her of Cyrus Reed—of a mind corrupted and left to rot. Conall was right. They had come too late to learn any direct information.

She pulled her shoulders back and stood straighter. She would not give up so easily. Even raving mad, the man might confess something vital. Reaching out, she felt through his aura. The withered branches and roots of the banshee's touch crumbled to dust as she pushed against them. Yet underneath, only a sense of emptiness remained, like a vast rent in the earth plummeting into an abyss.

Effie felt a coldness spew from it and gasped.

Durand tumbled onto his side and whimpered. He kept his head tucked into his knees, muttering something in French Effie couldn't understand.

"Mr. Durand," she asked, "where did Reed come to you?" From his aura, she couldn't help but think that even if the man had all of his faculties intact, he would no sooner tell her. There was nothing of warmth within the man.

He continued his muttering. She wasn't sure he had heard her at all, the way his body tucked and head remained bent.

"The dead hunt the hills," said Conall. "You cannot be saved. It will all crumble down." He turned to Effie. "That is the best my French can make of it. He repeats himself with slight variations."

"Variations?" she asked.

Conall nodded. He rolled his injured shoulder to stretch it, and grimaced. "You cannot be saved. I cannot be saved. We cannot be saved."

Effie couldn't help but snort. "The distinction seems rather important." She tried again to call to Durand, but the Frenchman didn't respond. She scoured his aura but could find no other trace of the banshee's touch, nor any other manipulation.

The effort of concentration caused the room to sway, and she hugged to her cane. "We must let him rest and try again," she said. She had witnessed before that the time of day, and whether a belly was full, could make a difference when conversing with an enfeebled mind.

She could use a hot cup of tea and some time with her feet up as well. They would just need to convince Owens not to report their delay to the major.

Another delay. Another lead that might fizzle into nothing, despite all they had done since their arrival in the city. Effie took a deep breath and let it out slowly. She left Durand's cell and eased her way down the corridor. Someone sobbed behind one of the doors. Another rattled as she passed it.

The sounds made her halt. Her eyes grew heavy with exhaustion. All that had kept her moving, that had kept her spirits eager, deflated. But she could not leave just yet. She could not abandon those she could still help.

Conall read her expression. "You mean to free them from the banshee's touch?" he asked.

She nodded. "Those I can, before the madness can't be reversed."

"Rest first," he said. "You have not slept, and they can wait another hour." He pretended to peer at the welt on her temple. "Perhaps three."

She didn't have the energy to smile. Her mood had soured to his wit. His own grin faltered. He stood there as wounded as she—more so—but with no better answers. They had nothing to show for their efforts.

"Perhaps you could show me how, Miss Effie," said Harper. "If I can, that is. If such a thing is possible." He stood rigidly with his chest puffed out. It hid his embarrassment, she thought. "I only did recently learn of Fey Craft, and of fey things. But I have sensed things before that I...well, I..."

"You will make a wonderful student, Mr. Harper," said Effie. "But I fear Mr. Murray is correct, as much as it discomforts me to admit it. I must rest first, or I will do all of us little good."

Harper's gaze dropped. From his expression, memories flooded her of not so very long ago. She had always known she held fey blood but had come to Fey Craft only recently herself. She remembered well the thirst for knowledge it instilled. She placed a reassuring hand on Harper's arm. She was too exhausted to worry over propriety.

He relaxed at the touch. "Aye, miss," he said. His tone sounded more eager than disappointed. He was not defined by his fey blood the way she had been, she realized.

She took in his uniform and wondered once again whether a childhood spent between worlds had altered her more than she would ever come to understand. What would've become of her if she'd grown up in a city unaware of her heritage? Would she have toiled in a factory all her years, blissfully ignorant, and yet somehow more content?

As well wonder if a horse could be a cow. It would not change who she was—the fey girl who did not belong in a city, nor within the Seily Court. Her neck and shoulders clenched in annoyance. They had no time for dwelling on such absurdities. Releasing Harper, she forced a smile to her lips.

The sun had reached its peak by the time they emerged onto Union Street, though the sky remained grey and bleak. Despite the hour, the streets remained quiet. A few shopfronts held open doors, and the pop and sputter of a steam carriage echoed down the broad street. But Effie spied fewer than a hundred denizens moving about, and those who walked did so with hurried strides.

Her gaze caught on a soldier marching toward her. She started, and it took her a moment to believe her eyes. She hadn't expected to see the man in Aberdeen.

"Lieutenant Walford," she said. She searched the expression behind his sunbaked cheeks, trying to divine the answer for his presence.

He stomped to a halt as she spoke his name. His gaze ran over her and Conall's wounds, yet his face remained stern. He greeted them both with crisp nods. "Miss Effie. Mr. Murray." Harper snapped into a rigid salute, which the lieutenant returned. "I am here to collect you and see to your safe passage."

"Passage?" She planted her cane before her. "No, not yet. We have much to do here. There is a grindylow on the loose, and Mr. Durand to interrogate, and those infected with the banshee's touch. I cannot abandon Aberdeen."

"Those concerns must wait," said the lieutenant.

Effie's brow pulled tight. "Surely Major Barnes did not summon you for such a purpose. What has happened?"

"It is invasion. The village of Duncairn has fallen. Montrose and Stonehaven are under assault," the lieutenant replied.

Effie gasped. Her eyes shot to the south as if she might make out something of the enemy through the gaps between the granite buildings. "But how? By whom?" she asked.

"It is unclear at the moment. There are reports of a fey horde, but also of the French being spotted. Some have the two fighting each other. The attacks began in the night and have scattered through the countryside." The lieutenant nodded at Harper. "Your major will want you to report. As the closest garrison, your regiment will deploy presently."

"Sir." Harper nodded and snapped a second salute. Turning to Effie, his gaze begged a question, though he remained quiet. He shifted his weight. Color rose to his cheeks.

"Mr. Harper." She gave him a polite bow. "Thank you for everything. I fear you must thank Mrs. Graives for us as well, when you have the chance. I will return to Aberdeen when I can and see to your instruction. You have my word." She smiled. "Besides, I owe a certain rat a bit of cheese, and I always pay my debts."

Harper laughed. "Until then, I shall count the days, Miss Effie." He bowed to her and shook Conall's hand. With a final nod to the lieutenant, he hurried off toward the barracks.

Effie closed her eyes and listened to his boots clap against the cobblestones. Taking a deep breath, she steadied herself and turned her attention back to the lieutenant. "Tell me more of this invasion," she said. "Has London responded?"

"There is a call to declare war," answered the lieutenant. "Parliament debates the matter as we speak. The duke has set up a defensive front stretched from Carlisle to Newcastle, and he himself has come to Edinburgh with an army."

"As the Romans once did," said Effie.

Conall snorted. "And the Danes, and the English."

Effie shook her head. Her grip tightened. The cane dug into her palms. "We have run out of time. Plans for war will matter little if our armies are turned to madness. We have not enough trust from the lords, and not enough fey allies, to turn back that tide."

"All is not yet lost," said the lieutenant. "I am here to take you to the Isle of Syke. Caches of Aerfenium have been found. All of them that exist in the Highlands, I am told."

"The thunderstone," said Conall. "They've cracked it!"

"Rose," said Effie. Sounding the name felt like throwing off a heavy weight. She pulled herself upright. At least one of them had succeeded. She glanced down the near-empty street and toward the barracks where red coats swarmed like ants. She would have to rely on others to achieve what she could not in Aberdeen.

"But how best to take advantage of the information," she mused aloud. "Do we move to protect all the caches or to lay a trap for the Barrow Witch?"

Lieutenant Walford nodded. "Aye, that is what must be decided."

"To the station then, and a train west," said Conall.

"No, Mr. Murray," said the lieutenant. "I have a more expedient means of travel available to us." He gestured with an open palm. "We are for the airfield."

❧ 16 ❧

E ffie's belly tickled in delight. Her arms prickled, and her lips pulled
so wide she thought they might kiss her ears. She'd never been in
an airship before. The wonder of it overwhelmed all other concerns for
the moment. Her neck craned as they approached the dirigible. Though
not as large as the one Lieutenant Walford employed during the battle at
Caldwell House, its wooden gondola would dwarf a fishing vessel. Above
and affixed to it, its canvas balloon stretched over a framework of wood
and steel ribbing.

The gondola had been painted as dull and lifeless as the balloon, the
better to conceal it within a bleak and overcast sky. Effie had seen many
odd and curious designs in the cities—those shaped and painted like
colorful dragonflies, and others made to look like sailing ships that
dangled in the wind from a harness. But the army favored function over
form, and the airship the lieutenant had procured for them was built for
hauling supplies to the outer islands, not for impressing great lords.

Effie didn't care about its appearance. She marveled at its network of
tethers and the way its rudder dipped below a pair of stabilizing fins.
She'd always had a passion for flight. Stuart Graham had fostered it. As a
young lass, she used to marvel at the airships drifting high overhead
while he pointed out how they remained aloft and cut through the wind.

Climbing aboard, she found the gondola held only a main cabin and a pilot house accessed through a small portal. Rows of benches were bolted to the floor of the cabin. An aft section could be loaded with barrels and sacks enough to outfit thrice the number of cabin occupants for a month, but it sat near empty now. She took a seat by one of the few portholes and breathed in a residue of coal smoke and spilt tea.

The lieutenant's men created a din of voices and jangling metal as they found places on the other benches. If any found her presence peculiar, none showed it. She had removed the bandage at her temple and attempted to improve her appearance as best she could. Conall sat next to her, his arm in its sling. His leg pressed against hers on the short bench. He leaned close, and she felt his breath dance along her neck.

She spared a quick glance at him and smiled before returning her attention to the airfield. "I suppose you ache to tell me of the tools used to frame the airship, or perhaps how your father owns a claim in the company that supplies the army its canvas balloons," she said. She meant the words in jest, though from his reaction they carried a stronger bite than she intended.

Outside, a few men scrambled about releasing the giant iron stakes that pinned the airship to the ground. Engines groaned, rattling the gondola. Coal smoke puffed. A man with a pair of flags signaled to the pilothouse in a series of sharp gestures, and with a lurch, the ground started to fall away.

She felt herself lighten, as if the airship's act of rising had somehow caused her to float in her seat. Her smile broadened. She had felt the sensation once before, with the stardust-fueled wings stolen from the trow warren in Duncairn. The memory of that flight brought on a flood of delight.

Conall laughed. "I confess, my knowledge lies with rail lines. I am as green to the experience of flight as you." His amusement grew as he eyed her awed expression. "More so, if I now recall."

"Then how do you avoid staring outside?" she asked. "Don't you want to see the ground fall away? I will never grow old of such a wonder." Below, the proud granite structures of Aberdeen retreated until they appeared only as quaint rows of grey blocks surrounded by clustered dots marking the outskirt villages. The airship banked, and she saw for a moment the open sea, with its white caps leaping to and fro.

He leaned closer and whispered so only she could hear. "I have a wonder of my own to take in," he said.

Heat rose to her cheeks, yet she could not keep her eyes from the porthole. Clouds began to roll across the glass. The frothy wisps obscured patchworks of rolling green fields and shadowed hills under a murky grey canvas.

She flicked her gaze about the cabin. The soldiers had made an effort to stretch out as they could and sleep. Snores and muttered breaths came from throughout the room. The lieutenant remained in the pilothouse.

"What was she like, your fiancée?" she asked.

He flinched in surprise. His brow narrowed. "Do you really want to know?"

"No." She shook her head. She didn't know why she had asked. Perhaps she meant only to remind herself that he had loved another. But whether that was to give her confidence that he could give himself to such an act, or to persuade her into thinking his love was easily given, she did not know.

He traced a finger along the back of her hand.

"You came for me," she said. "A dashing hero straight from an Austen novel." As she spoke the words, she wondered whether it meant their fates were intertwined.

"You need no dashing hero, Effie of Glen Coe. You never have. Your friends, the Croys, Thomas Stevenson, Stuart Graham, myself—all these years you have gained friends. But never have you needed another hero besides yourself."

Her head bowed. She recalled a harrowing escape from Edmund Glover, the crazed Fey Finder, and the starvation she faced, left alone in the hills with no direction, no home, and no sense of place. She thought of her mother and the loss that could never be repaired.

"You don't know what it is like to be orphaned," she said.

"Aye, I don't have any idea what it means, nor what it means to live between races, ostracized by almost all I meet. Yet I wonder if the same resilient skin that hardship fostered also acts against you now. You are no longer an outcast living on the fringe. You cannot run off alone to challenge the whims of fate."

She took in the words, but a part of her rankled, fighting against them. She managed to keep the snip from her tone, but asked, "What am I then?"

His face relaxed. His head shook slightly, as if in disbelief of her unknowing. "You are the center, the heart that beats hope into the lives of all who share our cause. Is it any wonder Caledon seeks your council? Or Lieutenant Walford? Or countless others, myself included?"

"Our cause?" Her heart warmed.

Conall's lips pulled apart. A glee came to his eyes. "It must be so, I have realized, if I am to call myself a just man. To live further with blinded eyes toward the plight of inequity is to enjoy a falsehood that stains the soul."

She forgot herself. Gripping his cheeks in both hands, her fingers twirled through his curled locks. She pulled him close, until their lips met. He tasted of salt and of the flowery whisky he nipped from his flask. He pressed in, and her breath grew quick.

A soldier's snore trumpeted through the cabin. The man's breathing changed rhythm as he rolled over. Effie pulled back from Conall. Her heart thumped as she remembered those pressed around them. Her eyes watered from the heat on her cheeks. Conall panted. He swallowed and blinked, as if to shake himself from a desperate hunger. His eyes darted about the crowded cabin before he slunk back against the hard wood of the bench.

Effie put a hand over his chest and felt its rapid beating slow. She smiled at him before turning once again to the porthole and the open sky beyond. Tucking herself into the bench, she drifted into slumber thinking of the rhythmic pulse of his heart.

* * *

The airship's engines whirled, puffing out clouds of coal smoke and shaking the gondola. The vibrations rattled Effie awake just as the giant pinnacles of the Storr came into view. Resting on the eastern slopes of the Isle of Skye, the jagged formation of broken rock plummeted toward the sea, leaving half its former might standing lone sentinel over trickling burns and shadowed ravines.

Gentle waves lapped against the shoreline of the isle as the airship began a circling descent. Of the Seily Court, Effie saw no evidence. The Scottish fey had long used the Storr as a gathering place, but their numbers were far fewer since the release of the Sidhe Bhreige. Many had left for Elphame, and those who remained had learned to hide themselves well.

As the airship touched down in a stony field, Lieutenant Walford emerged from the pilothouse. He ran a hand over a few days' whiskers as he greeted her and Conall. "Caledon invited us to bring you here," he said, "but it is a fey gathering not meant for the likes of lumbering soldiers. We'll encamp here and await your return."

Effie opened her mouth to protest but realized the lieutenant was right. Even in their current circumstances, most fey would rather run and hide than speak openly in the presence of the queen's riflemen. She and Conall took their leave as the lieutenant's men pounded giant iron stakes into the ground to tether the airship.

Tufts of wild grass sprouted along the coastline and continued as the ground rose toward the rocky crags of the Storr. There, deep shadows marked out a patchwork of clefts and hollows. The early snow from recent days had all but melted away, yet a cold wind bit at them from under an overcast sky.

They had not marched for long when a familiar aura popped into Effie's awareness. "Rose Brewer," she said to Conall, indicating the direction. She quickened their pace, and they soon found the fey woman awaiting them near a large thicket of bramble.

Several others stood with her. Though heads shorter than Rose and harder to distinguish from a distance, Effie could name them all. Surprise washed over her, but it was quickly replaced by joy and curiosity. The last she had seen of Freiherr Jörg and Ana, they had aided her in her efforts to rescue Catherine Granville from the cult of *Les Revinirs*. The gnome from the Order of Freiwald stood with his hands clasped before him. His white hair fell straight around plump cheeks and a bulbous nose. His great leather coat fell to his knees, with a high collar in the style of the continent. He nodded to her, yet his eyes darted warily toward Conall.

Ana stood almost as tall as Rose and had the same ginger tresses spilling from atop her head. The Sithling woman had worn a helmet shaped like a hawk's head when Effie had first met her beneath the streets of Edinburgh, and a thick brown coat that had hid her slender frame. She wore now a blue morning coat and grey trousers. The attire and unkempt hair made her appear like an overly large brownie.

Her gaze danced about Conall, and her lips pulled back into an open grin. "Where I am from, human companions wear masks and use—how do you say?—*monikers* so they are not easily known by proper society," she said in a slight French accent. "How should we call you?"

Jaelyn snorted. "Mr. Underfoot," she said. She folded her arms across her chest and raised an eyebrow at his wounded arm. The brownie was the last of Rose's companions.

Conall's cheeks colored. "I am fine with my own name and face," he said, "and as far as I'm concerned, I am among proper society." He bowed to Ana. She nodded with a look of approval.

"Welcome to our untidy moot," said Rose. She stepped forward and took Effie's hands into her own. Her eyes narrowed at Effie's temple.

"It is nothing," said Effie. "We have news of Aberdeen, but I am well."

"That is good," said Rose. "We have sore need for your counsel, Effie. Our host swirls about like mites caught in the wind, and goes nowhere."

"My counsel? But where is Caledon?" Effie studied her friends. Her gut twinged in discomfort at their heavy stares.

"None know," Rose replied. Worry broke across her face. "None have seen or heard from the steward, or from Gaelyph, Warden of the Hunt, in days."

17

The fey host camped in a grassy dell at the base of the Storr. A pair of bonfires warmed the clearing as the sun dipped toward the giant pinnacles that towered above them like trees of stone. Cooking pots swung on spits over the crackling flames, and Effie smelled a mix of onion, turnip, and tea wafting from them. Scanning the faces of the host as she approached, it surprised her how many she recognized.

A dozen Sithlings watched her with interest. She nodded to a couple she knew from her time in Glasgow. Their dress and appearance revealed nothing of their fey blood. Like her, only their auras gave any hint of their heritage.

Not so were the pixies that buzzed around the dell or the hogboons that sat on stumps around the fires. The former's colorful wings left a trail of flashing light as they zipped to and fro. The latter's plump forms were the size of children, yet the sharpness to their eyes and weathered lines on their faces declared their race.

A pair of brownies mended a canvas tent, one of several that dotted the grassy dell. The needles they wielded appeared as daggers in their hands. Like their brethren hogboons, they had sharp eyes and dressed in coats and trousers. Yet their cheeks held a gaunt line that made their faces more angular.

Effie spied more high-collared coats near a pair of tents and frowned. The gnomes of the Order of Freiwald appeared to be standing guard. Thick, round noses protruded above their collars, and almost all wore beards that fell to near their waists. Their bell-barreled blunderbusses hung on straps over their shoulders, but they stood in silence, peering off into the distance, away from the light of the fires.

"Jane Porter and that man that moons after her," said Jaelyn, catching her gaze. "The Order is not sae trusting of their human blood."

"They've been confined and watched since our arrival. As has young Clara," said Rose. She nodded at the second tent. "Effie, with the lass the Germans may have it right. She has changed in just these many days."

Effie's frown deepened into a scowl. "But they cannot be kept in pens like prisoners," she said. Caledon would not have allowed that to happen. Her gut twinged again at the thought of his absence, but she would not let dark tidings overtake her. The steward was most likely attending to some unknown affair, perhaps even in Elphame. Such an absence was not unheard of.

"They are not to be trusted," said Freiherr Jörg.

Before Effie could respond further, a Sithling man stepped in front of her. He had light eyes and a freckled complexion under a mop of brown hair. He stopped and bowed. "I beg your pardon, Green Lady, but you must allow me to welcome you."

Effie's jaw clenched tight, but she managed to relax the ire that had painted her face over the gnome's proclamation. "Call me Effie, please," she said as calmly as she could muster.

His eyes lit up. "I wish to thank you for what you have done, if you will allow me. In Glasgow, I joined your host marching against the lords, and I wish to offer myself again, if you have any need of my service."

Effie recalled the man dancing along her procession. He'd answered her call to make a public demonstration against Lord Granville. She nodded to him. "Thank you. Your offer is more than I could hope for, but it will be for the steward to decide our course of action, once he returns."

Jaelyn snorted. "Och, can ye go nowhere without gathering a flock of ducklings to squawk at yer heels? Come, let us break bread afore the sun flees too far over the hills."

Effie blushed, but the man laughed. She caught a whiff of the cooking pots, and her stomach reminded her she had not eaten in some time. Placing a hand over her grumbling belly, she said, "I will see Jane first and remove the poor lass from captivity."

Jaelyn folded her arms across her chest. "Ye'll be wanting ta' see the Rocksoother, and he won't speak in front of her."

"I will see to Jane and her moon boy," said Conall. "A prison it will be for three, if that's what it takes for friends to be become allies." He nodded to those gathered and strode for the tents. Effie watched him go and knew he wasn't far wrong. The host assembled within the dell stood little chance against the Barrow Witch if they did not learn to act as one.

"Do all know of the thunderstone and its properties?" she asked, turning to Rose.

"Word has spread on its own," the woman replied. "We waited for Caledon to debate the matter."

Effie's foot tapped. She planted her hands on her hips. Concern for the steward had allowed the Seily Court to waste precious time. Time they did not have. Her gaze flicked between Jaelyn and Freiherr Jörg. Their biases had blinded them as well, stealing from them desperately needed support.

"We cannot wait any longer," she said. "If I am to see the Rocksoother, let us all hear from him together."

"*Oui*," said Ana. She mimicked Effie's pose and gave a curt nod.

* * *

Effie leaned closer to the bonfire. Blinding rays of sunlight pierced her vision from the ridgeline above, but the night chill had already closed over the dell. It turned her flesh to ice. The stone she sat on seemed made of frost, and her coat did little to stave off the damp that seeped up from it. At least she had Gareth to warm her toes. The hound curled at her feet with his tail anxiously tucked beneath him. He'd charged out of Jane's tent as soon as Conall had opened the flap and greeted her with a chorus of whines and yowls.

She sipped from a bowl of piping-hot broth as quietly as she could. Jaelyn had shoved the broth under her nose while the host gathered closer. Its oniony scent had proved too tempting to wait on decorum. But no eyes were on her at the moment, anyway. The attention of the host was fixed on the Rocksoother. The gnome had a wrinkled face that scrunched in a permanent grimace, as if he'd been forced to devour a plate of rank cheese. Wisps of grey hair patterned his head. His beard tangled in knots and fell nearly to the ground.

"A great master carved this," said the gnome. "I have never seen or even heard tale of its like." He held aloft the thunderstone pinched between his finger and thumb.

"But you determined it does indeed find Aerfenium," said Effie. She set her bowl aside and stood. "And how to activate it?"

Dust puffed from the gnome's peat-smudged coat as he turned to her and absently patted his chest. From the lenses he wore, his eyes appeared as large orbs. He gave a wary nod.

"Gods of old," cursed one of the Sithlings. "It is a danger to have such a thing here. The Unseily will come for it!"

"We must protect it," said a hogboon. He rose and stepped onto the wooden stump he'd been sitting on. "We must secret it away and bury it."

"Fool," barked Jaelyn. The brownie glared. "Let the Unseily come. If we knew where they be, we could make an end of them."

"What if they don't need the stone?" squeaked a pixie. The wee thing flitted past Effie in a burst of pink wings. The pixie waved her arms. "What if they've already used it?"

"I don't believe it is that precise," said Effie. She had considered the question earlier. "The Unseily we claimed it from still seemed to blunder into the Aerfenium cache, even when they stood on top of it."

"Aye," said the Rocksoother. "The stone grants only impressions of direction, as if sensing an aura."

"Like a compass needle," said Rose. The fey woman had wrapped a green and blue tartan blanket about her shoulders. It made her appear older than Effie normally took her to be.

"So we may yet reach the caches first and protect them," said Ana. She thrust back her shoulders. "I will proudly undertake that task."

"As will we, the Order of Freiwald," proclaimed Freiherr Jörg.

A chorus of muttering echoed around the bonfire. Effie saw several heads nodding, but others glared and threw up their arms. One of the hogboons spat. His companion, who had spoken earlier, reclaimed his stump.

"The stone must never fall into the hands of one not appointed by the steward," he said. "Nor one not of our court."

Freiherr Jörg nodded kindly. "We are not asking permission, friend hogboon."

"The wards of Aerfenium are the only thing holding back an onslaught of Sidhe Bhreige," said Effie. "We must rally any we can to protect the caches, without question."

"What of the greater danger?" asked a Sithling. "The French have invaded. No doubt their German cousins will soon follow. What good is defending against the Sidhe Bhreige only to be enslaved by the continent?"

"That is not our concern," said the hogboon. "Let them fight. We need only worry about the Unseily."

"Hide," said another of the Sithlings. "Why not hide ourselves until the queen's regiments have destroyed this Barrow Witch and her minions?"

"Because they will not succeed without your help, and soon you would all face becoming Unseily yourselves." Conall's voice boomed across the dell. Several of the Sithlings startled and pulled aside to reveal him. He strode into the firelight with Jane Porter and Edgar Talmadge in tow. A buxom and comely lass, Jane wore a plain dress of white stitched with sprigs of mistletoe at the hem. A leather circlet kept her auburn tresses in place.

The guards from the Order of Freiwald had marched from the tents with their charges. They held their blunderbusses levelled at the humans but remained silent.

"Bah, we've destroyed the grindylows and bogills we've faced thus far and can do so again," said Jaelyn.

Effie ignored the brownie's bluster. She caught something in Jane's expression. The lass who had devoted herself to Effie and to the auld ways of the Oak Seers—the human term for Grundbairns—stood with pleading eyes. Her hands wrung before her stomach.

"What is it?" asked Effie. She found herself striding toward the lass. Gareth padded at her heels.

The hogboon who'd spat hollered. "It is not proper that she should speak at our moot!"

"Wheesht!" snapped Rose.

Jane swallowed. Her eyes darted over the gathering. She curtsied as Effie approached, a habit Effie hadn't been able to yet shake her of. "My lady, it's just...I've spoken with Miss Bowman." She curtsied again, as if to apologize for the fact. "She told me of her family and of the village of Braemuir. She remembered the blue ribbon her father purchased for her last Hogmanay, and the ring her mother gave her that had once been her nans'. She described both in detail."

Effie shot a look to Conall. He nodded encouragement. "I don't understand," she said.

"Don't you see?" Jane begged. "Her will dissolves, her aura changes, but she remembers everything."

Thoughts of Tallia snapped into Effie's mind. The woman had sought revenge even after sacrificing herself to the Barrow Witch's alchemy and becoming a grindylow. But she couldn't yet fathom what Jane hinted at.

Rose gasped. "Elphame," she whispered. "You mean that with enough strength of fey blood, the Unseily would be able to reach Elphame."

Jane nodded furiously. "With Fey Craft and the ability to scheme intelligently, their host is not confined to this empire like the Laird's trows and Piper's wulvers. Where better to bolster their number than a place inhabited by other fey?"

"They would only need someone to show them the way," said Conall. "Someone who travels between worlds with ease." He stared at Effie, and she felt the ground tilt beneath her.

"Someone with a steward's blood," she said, closing her eyes.

18

"We are nowhere safe!" squealed one of the pixies. The host erupted into a frenzy. The hogboons muttered among themselves, waving their pudgy arms. One of the Sithlings shuddered hard enough to force him to his knees. His companion stood in shock. He blinked, his head twitching like a chicken after corn.

Rose grabbed Effie's arm. "Conall has it wrong. It needn't be the steward. Aye, Caledon has the strength and kens the way better than any other, but any with the knowledge could lead them if their host had the strength."

The broth soured in Effie's gut. "But I thought such a thing wasn't possible," she said. "That the Sidhe Bhreige were too corrupt to reach Elphame."

"Unseily are not Sidhe Bhreige, Grundbairn," said Jaelyn. The brownie planted herself next to Rose. "Tainted they may be, but they remain kin of the queen."

"The Queen of Summer," whispered Jane. Her eyes grew as wide as moons.

Effie startled. A voice sounded in her head, mocking her. *The usurping queen. She will perish swinging from her own tree. I will see to it.* Her blood ran cold. They had been wrong all along. The Barrow Witch cared little for the fall of London. Humans posed no threat to her mind. They were a swarm of midges she could swat aside whenever it pleased her. She craved revenge. Revenge against the fey responsible for her imprisonment. Revenge against the Seily Court.

"It's a distraction," she said. "All of it. The banshee's touch, the attacks on the coast. She gathers an army for a single purpose—to slay the daughter of Righm and rule over Elphame."

Her hands balled into fists. She took in the gathered host as they squabbled and shook and fell into stupor. Their will had dissolved. But they were all that remained of the Seily Court in Scotland and could not fail to act. She would not let them wallow, nor let them cling to the auld ways when they faced extinction.

Climbing atop one of the wooden stumps, she used Fey Craft to bolster her voice. "Enough!" The word boomed over the clearing. It reminded her of when Caledon had done the same only a few years earlier. Then, she had not been able to recognize the Fey Craft for what it was. She'd barely been able to sense the auras of those around her, and her attempts at rallying the court against the Laird of Aonghus had fallen far short of successful.

But she had changed since then. She had learned of Fey Craft and gained hard lessons from the world. She could not fail this time. She needed to make them listen. Alone, none of them would survive.

The host fell quiet. They studied her, some with eager eyes desperate for good tidings, and others with suspicion. Yet they all waited on her to speak.

Calming her breath, she met each eye she could and nodded. The gesture made her stand taller, and the panic in her legs and stomach abated. "The Barrow Witch may have scored us wounds and ensnared us in her trap," she said, "but let us show her we are all the more dangerous for it. Let us show her we are the wolf and not the mouse."

"What would you have us do, Green Lady?" asked the freckled man from Glasgow.

"First, we must warn Elphame. Are we enough strength here for one to travel there?" she asked.

"Aye, we be," said Jaelyn, "and I ken the Fey Craft and the way, though I've never been."

"It is a time for firsts," Effie replied. "A time to speak openly and plain. We now know the reason the Barrow Witch has gone through the effort of raising an Unseily Court, but we must discern how she plans on getting her army to Elphame." She turned to Rose. "How does the Fey Craft of Leaving work?"

The hogboon who'd spoke before gasped. "That is not something for those outside our court to know."

Outside our court. The words stung instantly. Despair seized Effie to know all her efforts might crumble apart because of decisions made decades before her birth. It took her a moment to realize the hogboon's gaze fixed on the gnomes of the Order of Freiwald.

"*Merde!*" Ana threw up her hands and muttered something unpleasant under her breath.

Collecting herself, Effie spoke over her. "I do not ask for the way to Elphame, merely the Fey Craft involved. Will the Barrow Witch's army of Unseily need to be rallied in a single place?"

"No!" squealed a pixie. She spun in a circle of flashing purple wings around Conall. "Not in front of him! He used to be a Sniffer!"

"And the lass," said a Sithling woman who looked old enough to be Rose's grandmother. "She tries at being a witch. It is a dangerous path. We must speak no more until we are rid of them."

Jane sputtered in disbelief. "I...I do no such thing! A witch? Honestly!" She planted her hands on her hips only to wilt under the woman's glare.

The Sithling waggled a finger. "I heard you speak of performing a pagan rite. Don't ye deny it, or I'll find a good switch and bend you over my knee."

"Enough!" Effie barked the word once more and strained for patience. She eyed the gathered host, feeling anger wash through her. "We will not force our allies away, nor treat them without the respect they deserve."

"Are ye to speak for the steward then?" asked the hogboon.

The question took Effie by surprise, and she wondered whether the hogboon meant it as a cynical challenge. Surely, she thought, he could not have meant it in earnest. "I would never presume to speak for the..." she began but trailed off. She caught the way the freckled Sithling watched her with glazed eyes pulled wide, and shoulders that twitched as he leaned toward her. Edgar held a similar expression that begged for answers, as did Jane, and the Rocksoother, and most of the other hogboons and Sithlings. A pair of the pixies hovered near her head, waiting anxiously on her every word. Rose gripped her blanket tight, stretching it taut across her shoulders. The woman kept her lips pressed together. Even Ana shuffled uncomfortably.

They had wanted her to say yes, she realized. Not all, but most. Her anger and frustration melted away. A lightness came to her chest, and she felt like she might grow as tall as the pinnacles that ringed the dell.

"I am not of the Seily Court of Righm," she said. "I cannot speak for it, nor for Caledon. But I plan to fight. I plan to use all the strength and knowledge I have to throw at the enemy, whether the court accepts it or not."

Each word rolled easily from her tongue and served to bolster her confidence. "The choice is yours whether you believe in the daughter of an outcast and trust the granddaughter of a betrayer. The choice is yours whether you will heed my counsel. But the time for that choice is now."

She looked to the hogboon as gently as if she'd asked after a second cup of tea. Her breath came in a steady rhythm. She could hear the lapping waters of the sea in the distance, above the crackle and pop of the bonfires.

The hogboon's brow pulled tight. His hands came together before his worn coat, and his gaze shifted past her. She followed it and met Jaelyn's steady stare. The brownie raised an eyebrow and smirked.

"I stand with the Grundbairn," said Jaelyn. She nodded to Effie and turned to the hogboon. "Afore these past years, 'tis true I would not have, but she's proved her worth and honor, meddling as her nature may be." She folded her arms beneath her chest. "Let the auld ways be done, I say. Only fools worry over preening their feathers when they're about to be rightly plucked."

The hogboon's expression soured. He mimicked Jaelyn's posture, but he muttered to Effie all the same. "Aye, all right then."

Rose Brewer cleared her throat but paused a moment before speaking. A smile touched her lips, as if she had suddenly remembered something. Her eye caught Effie's, and she winked. "Caledon said this would come to pass, and in his word I will always trust."

Effie blinked, confused, but her friend did not elaborate.

Raising her voice, Rose continued for all to hear. "All Fey Craft is communal, and that of Leaving is no different. Besides strength of blood, the craft requires an anchor, the knowing of another within the place you wish to be. It is how the location of Elphame has long been kept secret, for it requires an intimacy with one already in Elphame."

"None other than Caledon has had the strength to journey there and back for centuries," said Effie, as understanding dawned. "Not alone, at least."

"Yes," Rose replied. "So the number who knew the way dwindled over time."

"The Barrow Witch may not count any among her host, then," said Edgar, sounding eager, "if they aren't old enough."

"No," said Effie. She watched the excitement drain from Edgar's face. "During his terror, the Laird of Aonghus frightened most of the remaining court into fleeing to Elphame. So we must assume those who stayed now have knowledge of an anchor, even if before the Third Leaving they did not." Her fingernails bit into her palms. Irritation flashed through her to admit the laird still thwarted them.

Jane's head cocked to the side. "If most of the Scottish fey left, how are there now so many created into Unseily?"

"The continent," answered Freiherr Jörg.

"*Oui*," said Ana. "They come as willing disciples. *Les Revinirs* was not the only such cult the Sidhe Bhreige infected." She spat into the dirt.

A murmur swept through the host, but this time silence fell when Effie raised her hand. "The news is troubling, but it aligns with what we have witnessed," she said. "The Barrow Witch began her Unseily Court in secret and has only recently escalated to enslaving the Scottish fey. We must assume from this that her plans have progressed toward a final step."

"It still doesn't answer the question of whether the Barrow Witch will gather her army in a single place or send them in smaller groups," said the hogboon.

Effie bit her lip. "Even with dozens who know the way to Elphame, each group would still require the strength of blood to do so."

"There is also a question of control," said Conall. "The major in Aberdeen had it right on that account. The Unseily will need communication and coordination if they are to mount such an attack. The Barrow Witch might play at chaos, but she is far too crafty to leave her plans to chance."

"You're right," said Rose. "The Fey Craft would take each group to precisely the location of the anchor."

"So the host would be scattered at random across Elphame unless they travelled as one." Effie finished the thought and considered it. "It is not proof, but it makes sense."

Jaelyn snorted. "Then we only have a need of finding the Barrow Witch and this Unseily rallying point. The same as we haven't been able to do over the past year."

"We have the thunderstone," offered Conall. He shrugged. "We might use that as bait to lay a trap for the Barrow Witch."

Effie shook her head. "She would not expose herself for such a ruse. We would only be laying a trap for one of her captains." She took in a deep breath. The frigid night air burned her lungs. They had to find another way.

"Why attack Stonehaven and Montrose?" asked Edgar. He stomped his feet against the cold. "What purpose does it serve? Perhaps that is a clue."

"Brilliant!" said Jane. Her face lit up. Her arms raised to throw around him, but she remembered herself and stopped short. Even in the dim firelight, her cheeks burned a cherry red. She returned her attention to the host with her hands clasped before her. "What I mean is, the better question is to ask why not anywhere else?"

Effie stifled her mirth at the girl's reaction. She had caught on. "You think the attacks are a diversion beyond fomenting random chaos."

Jane nodded. "If the Unseily rallied in the Highlands, they would have no need to make noise. The response by the army would work against them. Just look at the queen's regiments who are now on the march."

"Away from the Borders," said Conall. "The Barrow Witch moves her opponent's pieces like a chess master."

"The Borders stretch far south of Edinburgh," said Jaelyn. "'Tis nae small place."

"No," Effie agreed. But a thought came to her. "One of the Aerfenium caches is in Edinburgh, isn't it?" she asked the Rocksoother.

"Aye, near enough as I can tell." The gnome's lenses caught the dancing firelight as he nodded. "It is one among a half dozen others that remain."

Effie took in a deep breath. "We must make ready," she stated as a plan formed in her mind. "We few here may not be able to stand against the full might of the Unseily Court, and we have not the time to refuse the aid of those seeking our same ends. We must therefore call on the queen's army to stand ready to strike the moment we have uncovered the rallying point."

She waited for a storm of protests, but none came. The attention of the host remained fixed on her, eager for her next words. Even the pixies had stopped their flitting about. They hovered over her head like twinkling stars.

"So it must be," said one, wringing her wee hands together.

Swallowing down her surprise, Effie turned to Freiherr Jörg. "We must also find and protect the other caches. If the Barrow Witch knows their location already, it would not be beyond her to destroy them and release more of her brethren."

"Ja," said the wizened gnome. "The Order of Freiwald will do this task."

"We will aid them," said the hogboon. He grunted, and his companions nodded. "None ken the countryside better than we do."

Effie grinned. "Then you must call upon us all if you uncover the Unseily Court," she said. "Rose can teach you how."

"And ye?" asked Jaelyn. "What mischief will ye be working at?"

"Mr. Murray and I will travel to Edinburgh with Lieutenant Walford," she replied. "We will convince him to scour the Borders to the last blade of grass, and when they find the Barrow Witch and her Unseily Court, to destroy them. The treaty, peace with the continent, the safety of our kind, all of it rests on the Sidhe Bhreige's destruction."

Jaelyn's hand found the hilt of her dirk. "I suppose ye'll be wanting me to stay and fight? The gods know someone needs to save ye from yer own foolhardy self."

"No," answered Effie. "Elphame needs to be warned of the Barrow Witch's plan." Her grin broadened. Her head cocked to the side. "More so, as our best warrior, Elphame is the best place for you to be."

19

E ffie's bones ached from the bitter cold the moment she stepped away from the bonfires. The ground crunched beneath her like breaking ice. Her breath puffed clouds thick enough to obscure her vision. Gareth had been the smarter one. She'd left the hound curled near the warmth of the fire, sleeping soundly, while she trounced around the dell half frozen. Thinking of the hound made her wonder where Gwendoline had gone. Not that she had a need to keep track of the wee owl. Gwendoline had a knack for finding Effie when she wanted her to.

Rose strode next to her, bundled beneath her blanket. "Caledon's absence worries me," she said once they had left earshot of the others. The pinnacles of the Storr cast pitch black shadows above, while below the waters of the sea shimmered under silvery starlight. "He often wanders freely, but not now. Not when the court needs him."

Pressing her lips together, Effie kept her face blank. She would have to be blind to fail to notice the woman's discomfort, but she saw no reason for pretending roses bloomed on a rubbish heap. There could be only one cause for Caledon's disappearance.

"The Barrow Witch is craftier than we have given her credit," said Effie. "She's taught her Unseily to obscure their auras. It is a bit of Fey Craft only few of the Scottish fey know. As well, she has given over valuable items for their use—the Aerfenium thunderstone and Tallia's stardust device. Her brethren Sidhe Bhreige would not have done so."

Rose stopped. The crashing waves grew louder behind her as the moon pulled against the sea. "The Piper of Ceann Rois and Laird of Aonghus wanted to bask in glory. The Barrow Witch wants to win. It makes her far more dangerous."

Effie placed her hands on her friend's arms. "Jaelyn will let us know if the steward is in Elphame," she said. "You and Jane and Edgar will put your efforts to finding him, if he is here in Scotland. Enlist Stuart Graham and Abigail, as well." A lump grew in her throat as she spoke. She tried to swallow it down, but Rose's watery eyes fixed on her, and she couldn't hold back any longer. A shudder passed through her, and she released her grip.

"Och," said the elder woman. "Will you look at the state of me? Doom's upon us, and I'm as flitty-headed as a school lass."

"We are not yet lost," said Effie. "With the thunderstone and London's armies, we have hope." She would not allow herself to believe otherwise, but she saw her own doubts reflected in her friend's face. Even if they uncovered and defeated the Unseily Court, until they destroyed the Barrow Witch the threat of the banshee's touch would hang over London and the continent like a powder keg ringed by lit matches.

Effie felt her gaze harden. "We will find Caledon and see this thing through," she said. "We have no other choice."

A wry grin came to Rose's lips. Her eyes searched Effie, and the grin turned into a sputtering chuckle. She shook her head. "What would we do without you, Effie of Glen Coe?"

* * *

By the time she raised the flap to Clara Bowman's tent, Effie's toes had numbed. The girl's head rose from where she sat on a pile of woolen blankets. The tent held little else, only a lantern that burned low and a plate of food scraps. The gnomes of the Order of Freiwald had not trusted her with anything else.

Perhaps they were right to use such caution, Effie thought, as much as it pained her to admit. Clara's eyes had sunken deeper into her cheeks since the last time Effie had seen her. Her hair had thinned, too. The ginger strands barely covered her scalp and hung limp and lifeless.

Stooping, Effie found space on the blankets. She reached out and probed the girl's aura, searching for anything tainted or decrepit. But she found nothing amiss, nothing to match the change in the girl's outward appearance.

"It does not matter, what you sense," said Clara. Her voice came heavy and tired. "I can see the truth written on your face. I have become her creature. Do not try to tell me otherwise."

"Not yet." Effie tried to place force behind the words but faltered. She refused to concede that the lass couldn't be saved, yet she uttered barely a whisper.

"You did me a kindness to lend hope before, but I have no desire for it now. She calls to me, and soon I will succumb. I will let her have me."

Effie's head tilted. Her gaze slid from Clara to the blankets. *She calls to me.* The Barrow Witch had spread her influence across the countryside, yet those Unseily they'd encountered all acted with purpose. They acted as if they had orders as surely as if they were soldiers. She thought of Conall, and of Major Barnes. No military existed without a means of communicating.

The Barrow Witch called to her as well, Effie considered. But perhaps not in the same manner. The Piper of Ceann Rois had assembled a great host to assault Caldwell House, and yet even he could not compel all of his minions at once. It was a weakness Effie had exploited to defeat him. Those under the sway of the banshee's touch, and even Effie herself, had felt the touch of the Barrow Witch, but it never lingered long. Only those of the Unseily Court seemed to remain constantly under her thumb.

"Do you sense her when she calls," asked Effie. "Like an impression?"

Clara nodded. "It is like the chill from a fever, as if a hand reached up from some dark place to steal all my warmth."

Effie thought of her own experiences. "Do you see a stand of oak trees? Or a hill under a starlit night?"

Furrowing her brow, Clara shook her head. The response made Effie wonder. Had her encounters with the Barrow Witch merely been glamours all along? Powerful ones, to be sure, and worked from a great distance, but nothing more than tricks of Fey Craft? But if that were true, then it followed that the Sidhe Bhreige's connection to the Unseily Court might be similar to Caledon's connection to the Seily Court. A bond existed there. A tangible one, as if their auras had joined. The thought depressed her, as it weakened the notion that the Unseily taint could be removed.

"She has called to me, as well," Effie admitted, "and others I have known." She thought of the Sithling Jonas, and of Cecily McCray, the leader of *Les Revinirs*. "But her bond to you is different. It comes from within. I'd wager that is the necessity of the alchemy, this act of ingestion."

Effie delved into Clara's aura once more, scouring for a hint of the bond. Her head grew light from the effort. The blankets beneath her turned into a bed of stones, and no amount of shifting could bring her comfort.

Clara pulled back into the darkness of the tent, beyond the dim amber glow cast by the lantern. "Miss Effie, promise me you won't protect me. Promise me you will let me go once the transformation is complete, that you will let the others do what must be done."

The somber request buffeted Effie. She could see it, almost, as if the words hung in the air like an icy mist. She fell back and clutched at her throat. Her breathing came hard. She had no answers for the girl, no words of comfort. She was learning a painful truth.

She could not save everyone.

20

From the porthole of the airship, Effie watched the smoke billow from Leith. Smoke rose in plumes all over Edinburgh, but in the harbor-side burgh it came as a black cloud that obscured half the port. Someone had set fire to the dry docks, she thought, or perhaps some of the warehouses that lined the Firth of Forth. Mobs were the only answer for it, mobs born of the banshee's touch. Even at the airship's height, as they spiraled toward a landing field west of the city, she could see evidence of them everywhere.

Red-coated soldiers funneled through the streets in columns. Barricades had been set up at bridges. They ringed the aged and sagging tenement blocks of the Old Town. Near the gothic spires of St. Giles Cathedral, she spied a small crowd penned in like cattle under the guard of soldiers with fixed bayonets.

The scorched and blackened stone at the edge of North Bridge she recognized. She had first met Ana there. She and Jack Canonbie had rescued the French Sithling woman from a crashed airship before fleeing into the Town Below. It seemed a lifetime ago, a time when things could not possibly get worse.

How wrong they had been.

Conall leaned past her for a better view. She smelled the oil from his hair as it mixed with coal smoke and the salty tang of the sea air that buffeted the airship. His arm pressed against her, sling and all, but he showed no signs of discomfort. He squinted at the castle that lorded over the Old and New towns of Edinburgh.

"The duke's colors still fly from the ramparts," he said.

"From what Lieutenant Walford told us, I can't image it is any safer in the whole of Scotland," said Effie. Still, it was a good fortune the duke had not yet deployed his regiments to the north. She pulled her lips into a smug expression to show she jested, even if it were only a half truth. Conall used his free hand to take hers. The warmth of his palm felt familiar and right, but she fought the urge to pull away from it all the same. A sense their time had passed continued to weigh on her, despite all he sacrificed to be at her side.

The airship banked in a final plunge to hover over a grassy field at the edge of a village, one of the many that dotted the roads into the city. The early winter had eased and a light rain fell. Morning storms had flooded the landing field with pools that sloshed as a crew on the ground caught the dangling ropes affixed to the balloon. The gondola pitched as they heaved and anchored the airship in place.

Effie waited until it settled, and her stomach after that, before alighting. No sooner had her foot touched the slick grass than a sharp bark of command rang out. She startled and almost lost her footing. Conall caught her. He pulled her behind him as a dozen soldiers marched across the field in tight formation. Their boots pounded the field. Bayonets tipped their rifles. To a man, their faces were hard masks that studied nothing and everything at once.

Lieutenant Walford stepped forward a few paces and waited. His even keel steadied her, and she let go of the breath she held. Forcing herself to relax, she realized the folly of fearing these newcomers. She had arrived in the company of their comrades, after all, and within an army vessel. But something about the way the newcomers carried themselves, the menace in their manner, made her hackles stand on edge.

A rough-looking man with sergeant's chevrons barked for the newcomers to halt. The men grunted in unison, stomping their boots and snapping their rifles to attention. The sergeant saluted Lieutenant Walford.

"Sir," said the sergeant as rain dripped from his helmet. "Under the duke's orders, we are to inspect all those wishing to enter the city."

Even the queen's own soldiers. Effie thought to ask after how long the order had been in effect, and if a specific event had caused it, but the deadened stares of the men convinced her to keep her tongue. Lieutenant Walford merely gave a curt nod. If the order surprised him, he gave no indication.

At a wave from the sergeant, the newcomers broke ranks and hurried into the airship under a cacophony of squeaking leather and jangling metal. The sergeant's stare took in Effie and Conall. Only then did the lieutenant speak.

"They are known to the duke and here at my request," he said. His voice turned firm. "My orders are to escort them wherever they please. Safely."

The sergeant's brow pulled slightly. Effie could tell the man wondered after their names, but he snapped to salute once more. "Sir," he said.

The lieutenant returned the salute. Spinning on his heel, he left no opportunity for further delay. He ushered Effie and Conall across the airfield at a brisk pace to a waiting steam carriage. The driver, in his jet-black suit and chimney-pot hat, clapped the door shut once they had clambered inside the warm and dry compartment.

"They search for foreigners as much as those afflicted," said the lieutenant. Metal creaked, and a puff of coal smoke enveloped the windows as the driver put the carriage in motion.

"Have they caught any saboteurs?" asked Conall.

The lieutenant shrugged. "None that I have heard, but that does not rule it out."

Effie shifted her rump. The thin padding on the bench was an improvement over the bare wood of the airship. But she'd sat for far too long. She longed to walk and stretch her legs. Out the window, the streets looked eerily like those of Aberdeen. It brought a chill to her to see Edinburgh so quiet, as if in the wake of a plague.

Her lips pursed at the comparison. What else could the banshee's touch be called?

In the quiet streets, the wheels of the carriage thundered across the cobblestones. The boiler whooshed puffs of smoke that dusted everything with a thin black layer. Soon the smaller wood and plaster structures of the villages gave way to sandstone buildings that rose higher than castle walls. Edinburgh's own castle she could no longer spy atop its jutting rock as they made their way along the ordered, broad streets of New Town.

They were stopped twice at barricades. Each time the driver answered the challenge. Effie couldn't see clearly but heard wood scraping and clattering against the cobblestones as they waited patiently. Somewhere in the distance, whistles shrilled.

Conall blew out a deep breath. His brow pulled tight. "I see no coal porters with their wagons, and the shops are all but closed," he said. "The city will die a lingering death if its industry is not resumed."

"And with it, the whole of the country," said Lieutenant Walford. "You Scots are long removed from your agrarian past."

"Och, don't let the sheep hear that," Conall replied. He smirked, but if the lieutenant found any humor in the quip, he didn't let on.

"Heriot Row," said Effie in confusion. The carriage squealed and shuddered to a halt. As the driver climbed from its perch, it rocked gently.

Lieutenant Walford raised his hand before she could say anything further. "I will arrange for an audience with the duke and have a carriage call on you as soon as can be allowed," he said. Reading the expression that came to her face, he added, "There are too many obstacles for you to reach him directly, as things stand in the city. I have no doubt you would manage it, but the time would be costly, even with me by your side."

The argument rankled Effie, but she nodded all the same. She trusted the lieutenant. She always had. Not only did he favor reason over ego, but he strove for the same greater good as she, no matter the personal cost. It reminded her of the very men who dwelled within the house where the carriage had stopped. She could sense them now, their auras lingering in the drawing room, she judged by the distance.

She gave her parting from the lieutenant and along with Conall alighted from the carriage. She knew Thomas Stevenson's residence within the city well and greeted the maid who received them at the door with a cheery reception. By the time she had shrugged from her coat, a booming voice echoed through the house. The slap of footsteps on the floorboards followed.

"Effie!" Stuart Graham's round cheeks glowed red, and Effie guessed his nose would soon follow. She smelled the whisky on him as they embraced. When he pulled away, he looked at her askance. "We had no word of your coming. Is all all right?"

She snorted. "If you mean are there still barricades blocking the streets and parts of the city on fire, then aye."

Graham's gaze sobered. He patted her arms with a fatherly tenderness before greeting Conall. "Come now," he said. "He sits by the hearth to warm his legs."

Thomas Stevenson had aged since the last time Effie had seen him. The spots on his cheeks and pate had darkened, and his hair had thinned into silken strands, where it remained at all. But it was the way he slumped, as if weighted down by an endless exhaustion, that brought a lump to Effie's throat.

He sat in a chair by the fireplace, the wood as sturdy and proper as its inhabitant. A couch with a floral pattern brought color to the drawing room, and a tall window let in light from the street. Effie crossed to the man who had raised and protected her after the passing of her mother. She took his hand and felt an echo of memories flood through her.

"There ye are, lass," he said. "Miss Salisbury did tell us the moment your carriage arrived at the door."

"Hi'ya, Effie," said Abigail Salisbury. The ex-librarian of the university stood near the window. Her honey-colored dress had helped blend her into the curtains, which held a canary hue. Her once-black hair had greyed. Ink stained her fingertips, a result of years of ledgering among stacks of books.

Effie startled. "You hide your aura," she said. A device on her friend's dress caught her attention. She frowned at it. It reminded her of the badges of the Sanctity of Empire League. The anti-fey brutes had worn white armbands emblazoned with gold crowns. Abigail wore a patch on her breast that looked like sprigs of mistletoe shaped into a crude face.

"Aye'ya," said Abigail. She caught Effie's look. "We all do, those of us of the Green Lady's Auxiliary."

Conall barked out a laugh. "Is that supposed to be Effie?"

The ex-librarian touched the device absently. "Not precisely, but aye. There are a dozen of us Sithlings detailed by His Royal Highness to aid in removing the banshee's touch from the city." She nodded at Effie. "The same way ye showed us how in Glasgow."

Color rose to Effie's cheeks, both for her rudeness and for her embarrassment that such a noble effort would be named after her. But she could not bring herself to relax. Her neck pinched with tightness. It made sense that those who endeavored to remove the Barrow Witch's corruption would have a need to hide themselves from retribution. Even without that effort, it was a prudent action to hide from the Unseily Court. And yet... A pang thumped within her chest and rattled her nerves. *And yet.* She thought of Clara Bowman. Leaving the lass under armed guard had felt like abandonment. But it had also been prudent, despite the cruelty of it.

She searched her friend's hair once more, and her nails and teeth.

"Och, I haven't been tainted, lass." Abigail kept the hurt from her voice, but her posture stiffened.

The movement broke Effie. She rushed over and embraced her friend. "I am sorry, dear Abigail. You must accept my apology. I don't know what has come over me."

"It's her," answered Graham. He spat the words with venom. It left no doubt whom he implied. "The Barrow Witch has her grip on the city. It's all we can do to keep from drowning."

"It's true," said Abigail. "The mobs have grown, both in size and in their ferocity. We of the Auxiliary do what we can, but we are overwhelmed, and we cannot risk confronting their mass directly."

"I do wonder why the duke's men haven't been affected more than they have," said Stevenson. "The duke keeps an Auxiliary member near his person at all times to defend against intrusion, but surely his soldiers are at risk."

"No," said Conall. "Or aye, if the Barrow Witch truly cared to take over the city, she would no doubt focus on the duke's men. But we have learned that is not how the banshee's touch works, nor its intended purpose." He looked at Effie, and she nodded for him to continue. "The spread has always appeared random, like weeds infesting a garden, sprawling by the luck of the wind. The Unseily Court, on the other hand, is precise in its movements."

Stevenson tapped his hand absently as Conall explained what had been discussed at the Storr. Stuart Graham found his snifter. He put it to his lips only to pull it back, set it down, and grunt at the news. His face became pensive. Abigail clutched at her throat. News of the Barrow Witch's designs on Elphame caused her to gasp.

"What of Caledon," she asked. "You have made no mention of him."

The pain thumped in Effie's chest once more. "I had held onto hope someone had seen him in the city."

She started to shake her head but paused. Her head cocked to the side. Her eyes popped wide. Effie grabbed her arm to steady her as she stumbled.

"What is it?" Effie asked.

Conall crossed to a sideboard and fetched a glass of water. "Here, let her sit," he said, indicating the couch.

"The warden," replied Abigail. She took the glass and sat heavily on the couch. "He called to me." Her jaw worked as she sipped the water. "Uncanny strange, that is. I barely ken his aura."

Leaning in, Effie lowered herself next to the shaken woman. The hairs on the back of her neck began to rise. "What message does Gaelyph send?"

Abigail squeezed her eyes shut. "A tower house. Hermitage Castle, near Hawick, by the look of it. He is in danger, or in trouble of some sort. He seeks me to come."

"What? Alone?" Effie pulled back. "He makes no mention of Caledon?"

As Abigail shook her head, Effie's mind raced. Impressions sent via Fey Craft were often vague and subjective to the receiver, but she guessed her friend better skilled than most at deciphering such things. The woman had spent the better part of her life seeing to the comings and goings of fey within the city. Communicating via Fey Craft would be second nature to her. It made her wonder whether the warden had held back certain information, or whether her friend had not told her everything.

No. Effie shook her head. She would not continue down that line of thought. It reeked too much like the judgments she had just fought against at Skye. She had to trust in her friends. All of them. They were for whom she fought. They risked as much as she did and deserved better than her doubts. Gaelyph might stand opposed to her in certain regards, but he was an ally, and he needed help. She would take him at his word.

"I will go," she decided. She patted Abigail's knee, ignoring the choking sound Graham made and the sputtering of Conall. "From what I know of the warden, he would not ask for aid unless he had a desperate need. Besides, he and Caledon travelled together, the last we knew. So he may be the only means of finding the steward."

"But the duke..." started Conall.

"Och, lass," said Graham.

She stood and waved both men away. "The duke is more important, aye," she said to Conall, "which is why you must go with the lieutenant and convince him of our plans. He will listen to you as surely as he would me." She planted her hands on her hips. "You must make him."

Conall blinked. A wounded expression came to his face. "You wish to leave me behind, like in Aberdeen?"

She thrust a finger at his sling. "What good would it do to lose your arm from infection and lack of rest? You can fire a pistol, aye, but can you reload it? Or run, if the need arose? We need the duke's armies, but you do not need me to accomplish that feat."

As she spoke the words, she knew they hid something deeper. But neither of them had an appetite to press the matter further. Conall remained silent. He watched her like Gareth often did. She found her dress in need of smoothing and listened to raindrops striking the cobbles. Outside, the winds had swept in an ominous storm front.

"What of me?" asked Abigail.

"Your work in the city is too important," said Effie. "You also know the Town Below better than I. If there is an Aerfenium cache to be found in Edinburgh, you will find it. That is our other great need." She patted her friend's arm. "Gaelyph may have called you, but he will have to settle for receiving me."

Graham grumbled like a hungry bear. He swatted the air. "It is too dangerous. No matter what you have survived before, it is folly to risk yourself alone."

Choking down a growl that rose to her throat, Effie narrowed her eyes. Her foot tapped in irritation. "I do not intend to go alone. I will beg for some of Lieutenant Walford's soldiers. They have rifles, which will stand better against whatever confronts Gaelyph than any of us, myself included."

Concern painted Graham's face, but he gave no response except to fold his meaty arms across his chest and grunt.

She turned to Thomas Stevenson. "Do you object as well?" she asked. She regretted the bite in her voice, but it was Stevenson who'd hired Jack Canonbie to protect her person without her consent.

Stevenson's shoulders pulled back. His chin rose to meet her gaze. "Nay lass. I am proud of who you have become. Do what is right. You always have."

The words melted her. The last echoes of doubt fled. They would all do their part, and she would trust in them as they trusted in her. A fire roared from the center of her chest to the tips of her fingers and toes. Its warmth felt both familiar and comfortable. It felt like the love of family.

B lack smoke plumed from the stone walls of Hermitage Castle. The proud fortress stood alone in a field near the banks of a trickling water. Its owners had left it to ruin some centuries earlier, but its strength had held firm in neglect. The giant gatehouse rose like a mountain. The keep it protected huddled in its shadow. Yet signs of the castle's abandonment were also apparent. Green moss and creeping vines covered the crevices in the stone. The old curtain wall no longer ringed the bailey. Of the chapel at the edge of the grounds, only a low foundation remained. The arrow-loops high on the tower walls served only to house a murder of hooded crows.

The birds squawked and took wing as Effie slopped through the muddy field toward the castle's gate. She was thankful for the high boots she wore, and even more so for the wool trousers and morning coat she had borrowed from one of Thomas Stevenson's valets. The clothing splattered with muck with every step, despite using Jack Canonbie's cane for balance, but she enjoyed the freedom of movement they provided.

"We'll enter and clear the keep, if it please you, Miss Effie," said the sergeant tromping next to her. Of middling age, with a broad mustache and somewhat puckered countenance, Hugh McGrady seemed a capable fellow, if not a little hesitant around her. At least he hadn't asked her to wait by the carriageway with the horses. That detail had gone to a young lad from Huddersfield called Sweet Tom Reedling.

The rest of the soldiers who accompanied her marched in a column two abreast and three deep behind the sergeant. The sucking of their boots in the muck sounded a rhythmic cadence. Their rifles remained at their shoulders, but their cheery banter had ended at sight of the smoke puffing from the castle. They had not expected to find anything, Effie thought. Or perhaps that was just a soldier's way, this duality of disposition that could be flipped with a lever.

It had taken her most of the day to hunt down Lieutenant Walford in Edinburgh, and several hours of riding to reach the castle. The sun hung low over the hills. Dark clouds swirled overhead and threatened rain.

The lieutenant hadn't questioned her decision. He'd kept his face devoid of emotion and immediately barked for McGrady to attend him. He was used to taking orders from fools, she reminded herself. That brought on a snort of laughter she could not contain. Her foot slipped, and she barely caught herself from flopping into the mud.

McGrady eyed her. She waved him off, feeling color rise to her cheeks. Focusing on the castle, she scoured the ruins one last time for signs of Gaelyph. But she did not sense the warden's aura, nor any other's save the crows and the mice they had yet to find.

Smoke where there should be none, and a lack of life where there should be one. If not two. She bit her lip. She sensed an obvious trap, but for whom had it been laid? She had certainly not expected to come to Hermitage this day, nor had any of the men with her.

"Be wary," she told the sergeant. Her gaze lifted to the arrow-loops. She scanned each one but saw no movement.

She had only taken a few steps farther when the stench reached her. Under the scent of wet grass set alight and wood smoke came the hint of something foul. Effie recognized it. She had smelled it at Caldwell House, and again in the chambers of *Les Revinirs*. Her gut tightened. It smelled of death.

Sergeant McGrady caught the scent too. His mustache twitched as he sniffed. Stopping abruptly, he raised a hand and gestured for her to halt. Drawing his pistol from the holster at his hip, he barked over his shoulder. The men broke formation without pausing a step. They fanned out, their rifles swinging back and forth as they raced for positions against the castle wall.

A pair of the men motioned to the sergeant. He nodded, and they charged into the gatehouse. No gate or door remained to bar their way. Their footsteps slapped against stone and faded away as they disappeared from sight. The other men waited only a moment before following in pairs.

Effie sensed them all scurrying about like night birds pecking through the hedges. She found herself leaning onto her toes, as if pulled toward the castle by a hidden gravity. The seconds passed like ages. As each one ticked by, the cold of the afternoon bit deeper into her flesh. She yearned to dash inside, to see what transpired, to know what they saw, to not risk their lives when she could do anything to aid them.

Yet she waited. She held her breath. Next to her, Sergeant McGrady peered at the stone walls as if trying to see through them. He shuffled forward, seemingly without thought, as he craned his neck.

One of the men hollered. "Sergeant!" The tone gave no hint as to tidings good or ill, but Effie sensed the soldiers all gathered in the same area.

She forced herself to walk, albeit at a brisk pace. The sergeant matched her stride, and together they passed under the looming high arch of the gatehouse. Murder holes smiled down on them as they did. Moss coated the openings and clung to the dank corners of stone that were protected from the wind.

The ground turned from muck and grass to hard-packed earth and scattered pebbles. The gatehouse led to a small and narrow courtyard protected by the high walls of the keep. The wall on one side had dissolved into a shattered heap, exposing what was once the great hall. The soldiers gathered there. They encircled four bodies that lay broken and strewn among the rubble. Some stared at the bodies in silence, absently touching at their own faces and chests. Others studied the black smoke rising from a pile of charred wood and smoldering grass. It rested at the base of one of the corner towers atop a mound of stone.

Sergeant McGrady offered Effie a handkerchief, but she declined it. Despite the awful stench, she wanted both hands free to wield her cane if need arose. The fire had to be recently set. No later than midday, she judged, from the size of it and how well it still smoked.

The bodies had lain there for perhaps a couple of days. One appeared to be a shepherd, from his shirt and trousers. Another, a scullery maid. A tradesman in trews and coat, and a gentleman dressed in a fine dinner jacket rounded out the group. The oddness of the quartet made Effie wonder whether they had known each other at all. She squatted by the maid, using her cane to balance herself.

"Careful, miss," said one of the soldiers. "The dead left to rot carry disease."

"They ain't the dead," said another. "The way their faces are drained and hollow, they look like the barrow wights me nan used to say haunt the Lowland hills."

The first soldier's face scrunched in disbelief. "Blimey, Griggs, you see any barrows around here?" He threw a thumb toward the other man. "His nan, he says."

"They aren't right, though," said a third solider. Brandon, Effie thought he was called, though she didn't know if it was his family name or his Christian. "In my village they used to keep the winter dead wrapped in a cellar until the ground thawed enough to bury them proper. Us lads would dare each other to sneak in and uncover them." He circled a hand over the bodies. "Takes a while to look like this."

"A while, yes," said Effie. "But not long. Not if they were already starving." That's what the gaunt cheeks and pale flesh reminded her of—those who'd survived a famine. She frowned and slowly ran her gaze over the bodies.

"Look there," she said, pointing at a long cut running across the shepherd's thigh. "That wound looks like it's from a blade. It's too precise to be from stone." She found another such slash on the tradesman's arm. "And there."

Brandon knelt next to her and leaned on his rifle, squinting. He smelled heavily of sweat and horse. Both were welcome compared to the corpses. "Aye," he said, "by a broadsword perhaps. Something heavier than a knife."

A sharp crack rang out above them. Stones tumbled loose, clattering down like a hailstorm. One stone struck Griggs on the leg. He cried out and tumbled over, disappearing in a cloud of dust. The other soldiers scurried aside, raising their arms and rifles over their heads. Brandon shoved Effie back and threw himself on top of her.

She coughed from the dust. "I am all right," she said, pushing the man off. He scrambled to help her to her feet. His face drained of color. Stammering, he began several apologies, but she waved them away. "I am unharmed, both in person and in honor, and I thank you for it," she said, before raising her voice. "How is everyone else?"

"The castle is a dangerous place, Miss Effie," said Sergeant McGrady. He came to her side and inspected her. Blood trickled from one of his hands, and he wrapped the handkerchief he'd offered her earlier around it.

"It will become more dangerous if you suggest she wait outside," came a stern voice echoing from the heap of stone where the fire smoldered.

Effie leapt from her skin. The soldiers darted into firing positions and brought their rifles to bear. Sergeant McGrady stepped in front on her. But she caught her breath and moved around the man, crossing to the heap. She recognized the voice.

"Gaelyph?" she called. She could still not sense the warden's aura.

"Sergeant!" The shout came as a rifle cracked. Two more shots followed. The bullets pinged off the castle's stone high above. Clouds of chips and dust puffed where they struck.

Effie ducked low and followed the train of the rifles. They pointed at a shadowed recess in the corner tower opposite of where she squatted.

"I saw something move up there," said the soldier who'd shouted.

"Aye, a creature. Short and thick, with a long, thin nose," said the sergeant. The tinge of gunpowder wafted from his pistol.

"Talons like a hunting bird and eyes as red as the blood-soaked cap it wears," Gaelyph's voice came from beneath the heap of stone once more. "A redcap, and a fierce one. It was he who loosed the tumbling stone. Free me, and I will slay him for you."

"A friend of yours?" asked Brandon, indicating the smoldering heap with his rifle. Creeping closer, he kicked at some of the smaller stones and revealed the top of an archway built into the corner tower.

"He is Warden of the Hunt for the Seily Court," Effie replied. She would have laughed had her thoughts not been racing. The warden had gotten himself trapped in the castle dungeon. But her blood had run cold at mention of the redcap. Her mother had told her of such creatures, not in tales of fey lore but in the kind meant to scare wee bairns. The kind Griggs' nan would have told him to make him behave. Redcaps were linked to witchcraft, and they thrilled in murder.

She saw Sergeant McGrady looking to her. His face begged a hundred questions.

"Leave Brandon and Griggs with me," she said. "Hunt carefully for this redcap. There will most likely be more traps."

The sergeant nodded. Barking orders, he sent the men into the towers, the only part of the castle where stairs remained. Their footsteps and grunts echoed into the courtyard as they labored upward.

"That was folly," said Gaelyph. "You sent the men to their deaths."

Effie whipped her head around to glare at the stone heap. Goose pimples ran along her arms. Her throat and shoulders tightened. "Where is Caledon?" she demanded.

"There is no time, Effie of Glen Coe. Prove yourself loyal to the court and have your suitors do as I ask. It is the only way to save them."

Prove myself? Effie grimaced. She should ask the warden to do the same. But he was right. There was no time. She needed to either trust him or let him languish in the dungeon. She glanced at Griggs. The man lay clutching his knee. His trousers had torn, leaving bare a bloodstained and swollen leg. He'd be lucky if the bone wasn't broken, she guessed.

Brandon ran a sleeve along his brow. Beads of sweat returned as soon as his arm dropped. He clutched his rifle tight enough the blood drained from his fingers.

They needed Gaelyph. The warden spoke the truth about that. And she needed to find Caledon. Moving forward, she started picking away the smaller stones. Some were hot to the touch. She used her cane to knock those aside.

"Help me," she bade Brandon. The soldier did as she asked. Together they cleared an opening wide enough that she could spy the warden on the steps below. The stair to the dungeon dropped barely the height of a man beneath the tower. The air wafting through the opening stank of damp mold and the droppings of rodents.

Brandon kicked at the smoldering heap one last time and heaved aside a larger stone. The portal widened. Gaelyph reached his arms through, and with the soldier's help, clambered out. Dried blood caked his cheek. Soot and muck covered the rest of him. His coat had torn at the sleeve. He tugged at it, his lips pursed and brow scrunched in annoyance.

"Sir Warden," said Brandon, clenching his rifle. He glanced at Effie, uncertain what to do with the soot-covered fey.

Offering the barest of nods to the soldier, Gaelyph drew the slender blade at his hip. The silver falcon heads flashed in the darkening courtyard. Effie folded her arms across her chest, staring expectantly. Her jaw fell slack as the warden set off without a word.

"Caledon?" she asked, storming after the fey man.

"Taken," Gaelyph replied.

The word made her misstep, and she stumbled to a halt. "Taken? By whom? How? Where?" The questions flew from her lips in disbelief. The warden ignored them all. He disappeared into one of the towers and headed up its stair.

"Miss?" asked Brandon, behind her.

She glanced over her shoulder and gestured. "Th-thank you," she managed. "If you please, watch over Griggs." She reached for skirts that weren't there and cursed herself a fool. In a trot, she chased after the warden.

The narrow stair spiraled up above the old kitchens. The stone was cold and lifeless. Whatever tapestries and sconces had been used to adorn the walls had long since been removed. The steps had worn down, and she became dizzy watching them flit past as she circled round and round.

At a landing, Effie paused. Boots scraped the stone farther up the stair, but the sound came too heavy for the warden's graceful stride. She caught a glimpse of movement down a narrow corridor and crept after it. Her heart thumped. It reminded her to keep her wits. She could not let her frustration with Gaelyph walk her blindly into a trap.

The corridor narrowed and bent before one wall dropped away at the entrance to an old chamber. But nothing remained of its timber flooring. The opening plunged to the kitchens below. She peered down and saw the light tumbling in from the courtyard. Voices echoed back at her, but she could not make them out.

Above, a shadow moved past another, higher opening, the floor of the chamber overhead also gone. She caught a hint of red. Her breath caught in her throat. But she could not tell if the cloth came from coat or cap.

Rain began to spit against the castle, the few drops becoming a sheet that pounded the stone. She gripped her cane tighter. The chill stillness that came with the downpour unsettled her. It felt as if the storm gathered a momentum she would never withstand, one that would drown her and sweep her away.

The feeble sunlight streaming through the arrow-loops faded. The corridor darkened behind her. In the dimness, the warden appeared. He kept his sword pointed forward as he marched toward her. He wore a scowl that deepened as he approached.

"He is fled," Gaelyph snarled.

Effie's heart thumped hard at her breast, but irritation won out. She planted herself in the warden's path. Gripping her cane in both hands, she asked, "Where is Caledon?"

The warden did not slow his pace, yet his face lost some of its glower. "Look with your eyes, Grundbairn," he said. He stopped a mere breath away. The tip of his sword slipped past her ear, with a casual flick of his wrist. It clanged off the stone just behind her.

She flinched but held her ground. Was the move a trick, she wondered? No, she doubted the warden would employ any tricks if he desired to harm her. He'd have no need. Pulling her gaze away from Gaelyph, she eyed where he indicated.

Streaks of black crisscrossed the wall, radiating from a large splotch almost oval in shape. Crisscrossed, and yet perfectly aligned across several blocks of stone. It meant the coloring was not natural. She squinted and felt the rough texture. No soot or dirt or residue came away on her fingers. *Scorch marks then, and not from a natural fire.*

Her body stiffened. The marks had to be from stardust. "Tallia," she breathed.

"Aye," said Gaelyph, "working in league with the redcap and the wights, as the human called them."

Effie stood dumbstruck. "You allowed the Unseily to take him," she said without thinking. Of course, he hadn't, not willingly. A picture painted in her mind of the warden and Caledon ambushed. Gaelyph was trapped below and the steward made captive. The redcap had stayed to try and burn the warden out, until she arrived.

The warden pulled back. His eyes dropped for the flicker of a moment before growing stern once more. She reached a hand up to take the words back when a cry of pain rang out. Shouting followed, and a thunder of boots. The warden hurried for the spiraling stairs. She stayed at his heels.

Sergeant McGrady spun to meet them as they emerged into the courtyard. Rain dribbled from his hair and dripped from his coat. "A deadfall was set inside the gatehouse," he said. "The trigger set loose a tumble of stones that split Mayhew's skull."

Behind him, several of the soldiers tended to a slumped form. They all spoke at once. Blood soaked the rags they held. The rain had lessened to a mist, but it was enough to make them slip and slide as they scurried about.

"Oi, stay back! Stay back! Sergeant!" The hollering came from outside the castle. The last word was thick with fear. Rifle shots cracked in quick succession.

Those in the courtyard froze and glanced at one another before all save the wounded charged for the gatehouse. Effie's legs churned. She danced through the muck. Gaelyph stole a step on her, but they tore through the gatehouse before any of the others.

The soldier who'd hollered struggled to reload his rifle. Scratches etched his cheek in puffy red lines. Three bodies sprawled near his feet. A dozen paces beyond, a woman in a simple woolen shift stumbled toward them. She looked pale and tired, as if she hadn't eaten in days.

Effie gasped. Her hand found her mouth. Across the open field, a mass of bodies shambled like a mob from Edinburgh toward the castle. She had not sensed any of them approach.

"They are masked," she said.

"The redcap," Gaelyph replied. "He has sprung his final trap."

E ffie cast out her senses. The decay she felt within the woman in the woolen shift made her hiss and flinch back. She had never felt the banshee's touch corrupt its host so severely. It was as if dark masses of fetid weeds had sprouted within the woman's aura, their roots slithering everywhere, leeching and draining life.

She used Fey Craft to yank at the weeds. The masses came free in oozing, moldering clumps. A few of the roots snaked toward her. She batted at them. Envisioning a wall of force, like a crushing wave, she smashed away the remaining corruption.

The woman shrieked. She clutched her head and dropped to her knees, wailing in torment. Gibbering, she clawed at herself.

"The banshee's touch is stronger in them!" The words struck Effie as she yelled them aloud. An understanding came to her. She had witnessed this madness before—with Cyrus Reed and again with Jean-Nicolas Durand. Of humans, they had served the Barrow Witch more devoutly than any other. She had assumed this came from an existing corruption of morals, but now she realized it came rather from a more focused enslavement.

Like the Piper of Ceann Rois, the Barrow Witch could not control all of her minions directly. Not all at once. It required too much focus whispering in ears and nudging with Fey Craft. But she could control a small amount of them forcefully.

Those with a purpose she desperately needed, such as Reed and Durand.

Those tainted fey of the Unseily Court.

Effie's lips parted in a broad grin.

And those nearby she needed for protection. It meant the Barrow Witch was near, in the Borders, at least, as they'd suspected.

Effie scanned the gibbering woman and the dozens beyond who shambled toward her at a meandering pace. Not even in Edinburgh did the banshee's touch corrupt so strongly. They had not eaten in days, had not bathed, nor tended to torn clothes. The Barrow Witch kept them firmly under her iron will. The human part of them had wilted away.

Sergeant McGrady clomped through the muddy grass and came to stand beside Effie. His breath wheezed in huffs from the dash from the courtyard. He eyed her grinning face and took in the approaching mob. Blanching, he swallowed hard.

"Halt!" he cried. But his voice held no conviction. He recognized the deadened gazes facing them. He knew those of the mob wouldn't heed to reason. They would attack in a fury as they had in the cities.

The rest of the soldiers fell into a line. They levelled their rifles, peering into the dim light that painted the grassy field a pale amber. None spoke a word. Their eyes remained fixed on those approaching.

The sergeant raised his arm.

"No!" shouted Effie. She spun to Gaelyph. "We must do something. We cannot just kill them. They are innocent."

The warden's jaw was locked. He held his sword before him, the blade angled toward the ground. "The redcap seeks to trick your suitors with glamours," he said. His eyes twitched. "I thwart him. Those approaching are already dead."

A lump came to Effie's throat. She stared at the gibbering woman and thought of Jean-Nicolas Durand. The truth of the warden's words crushed her, but she refused to let it take hold. She grabbed the sergeant's sleeve.

"Please, you cannot do this," she begged.

"Hold fire!" the sergeant boomed. Dropping his arm, he studied

Effie's face with regained composure. His soldier's training had taken over. The protection of his men overrode any other concern. "Until ten paces!"

Effie released him. Whirling, she stepped forward and planted her cane before her, clutching it in both hands. She cast out her senses, not at the mob this time, but at the fields and hills surrounding them. She felt for the critters who rooted in the hedges and those that took to the sky, for those that tunneled underground and those larger who grazed at pasture.

Hidden around her, she found allies.

Forming a simple plan, she molded Fey Craft into a plea for help. She sent an image of a skulk of foxes stalking across the field. *They come to steal your eggs and harm your younglings*, it said. *Come. Help. Hurry.*

Cawing sounded within a copse of trees at the edge of the field. The call echoed from the high tower roofs above. Effie closed her eyes. Raising her arms, she made her inner self sprout feathers and lift into the image. Soaring into the murky night, she cawed and felt the vibrations rattle her throat.

That's it. Join me. A flutter of wings swooped into the sky. Circling from tree and tower, the murder of hooded crows flocked into a whirling storm of wing, beak, and claw. Effie banked the crow version of herself. She dipped and shot like a bolt for the foxes. Shrieking, she pecked and flapped and ripped with her claws.

The ground spun beneath her. She became disoriented. Yanking herself from the image, her body became heavy and cumbersome. She used her cane to brace herself, to keep from tumbling over. As she blinked away the remnants of her Fey Craft, waves of nausea made her sway.

But the murder followed her lead. They did as she wished. Only it wasn't foxes they assailed. The crows swarmed the mob. Flashes of black and white and brown feathering swirled in the failing light. The racket of their cawing rang in Effie's ears.

At first, those of the mob ignored the crows. They continued their steady march, tramping through the grass with deadpan stares. Effie steadied herself and threw up another glamour. Each crow became four, and then ten. The swirling, darting shapes blotted out the mob as if a dark cloud had swallowed it whole. Their cawing drowned out all other sound. It came, blaring and riotous, fueled by a predator's wrath.

The soldiers lowered their rifles. Mouths fell slack. They shuffled anxiously. Some pointed in disbelief. Effie caught out of the corner of her eye their jaws working, but she couldn't hear any of their exclamations. The din of the crows was too loud. She glanced at Gaelyph and saw the warden nodding to her, urging her on. The gesture startled her, but she kept her concentration on the glamour.

A man from the mob, one who wore a brown frock coat that had seen a month of soiling, jerked as a crow battered his ear. Another in a dark suit flailed his arms. Neither halted their advance. But they slowed, and soon others of the mob did as well. Their pace crawled.

The small victory thrilled Effie. She sought out another group of auras she had sensed earlier, those already familiar to her. Sweet Tom Reedling had mounted his horse. Perhaps the lad had spied the mob from afar, or perhaps he had heard the crows. Effie didn't care either way. She didn't call to him. She called to those he tended.

The horses knew her from their journey from Edinburgh. She had no need to persuade them as she had the crows. Her Grundbairn nature had created a bond of friendship with each of them as they'd trotted down the carriageways from the city. They recognized her call. The gentle touch of Fey Craft begged them to hurry.

The one she'd ridden, Barnaby, charged first. He broke at a gallop. She couldn't hear the pounding of their hooves over the cawing of the crows, but she could feel their rumbling progress trembling the ground. Barnaby crested the gentle rise and came into sight. His companions trailed a few lengths behind. Sweet Tom Reedling clung to his saddle. The lad fought the reins until he saw where the horses headed.

"Sergeant McGrady, prepare the wounded." Effie shouted through the din. She indicated the horses with her cane. "We must distance ourselves from the mob."

The sergeant swung his gaze between the charging horses and shambling mob. He eyed the high stone towers behind them. "We can make a defense here. The gate is open, but the walls are strong."

Effie shook her head. She had to force her hand from grabbing the man once more. "They will trap us inside and force our hand to kill them," she said. "That is no defense at all."

"Halt! Stay back!" Brandon cried. His rifle popped in his hands, blasting smoke and fire. The warning shot blew up chunks of dirt at the feet of a young man whose hair had been pulled and yanked by the crows.

A trickle of red ran down the young man's nose. His steps quickened. His hands curled into fists, and a snarl came to his lips. Behind him, a score of others did the same. The mob was upon them.

Brandon leveled his rifle.

Without thinking, Effie reached out with Fey Craft and ripped free the fetid weeds of the banshee's touch. The young man wailed. He covered his eyes, as if from a blinding flash, and sank to his knees. The sound panged her. She might as well have pulled the trigger of Brandon's rifle for all the good her efforts had done.

The others didn't slow. They charged like a pack of starving wolves.

Effie tore her gaze from them. The horses thundered across the field. They overtook the bulk of the mob but would not reach them in time. Not before the first wave crashed into them.

She reached again with Fey Craft, girding herself to tear free the banshee's touch. But she froze. Her gaze swept to the young man and to the woman who still huddled in the grass, gibbering. Her heart thunked to her knees. She cursed herself a fool. The warden had been right, and she knew it. These afflicted were already dead. Freeing them of the banshee's touch only to leave them to starve, befuddled in a field, was no better fate than a bullet.

Brandon stepped forward. He bashed the butt of his rifle into the young man's temple. The young man flopped over and lay still. Brandon hovered over him, head bent. His shoulders trembled.

"The Sidhe Bhreige did them harm," said Gaelyph. He came to Effie's side and flicked his sword toward Brandon. "It was not his doing. Nor yours."

She shook her head. "I...I cannot abandon them in such a state. We must take them with us or remain here." The words tumbled from her lips, but she knew them for folly. She could do nothing to save the infected. The Barrow Witch had already stolen their minds.

"No," said Gaelyph. "The steward needs us, Grundbairn. We cannot tarry here, nor laden ourselves with a needless burden. It serves no purpose for the greater good."

The warden slapped her cane with his blade. The jolt of it startled her. *The greater good.* They were words meant to justify a heinous action. They were words Sir Walter Conrad would utter, and Lord Granville. They had even passed the lips of Stuart Graham.

It infuriated her that the warden would use them. But it infuriated her even more that she agreed. She had to accept defeat. She saw no means to heal the afflicted mob, and no means to rescue them from their terrible fate. She and the warden could not seal themselves in the castle and hope for a better tomorrow. They had to abandon the afflicted for the steward's sake. His rescue mattered more.

Rifles cracked. Muck and bits of grass sprayed into the air. The soldiers shouted. They waved their rifles, warning the charging mob to stand back. Another volley rippled from their line. The tinge of gunpowder came sharp.

"Go!" hollered Sergeant McGrady. He clicked back the hammer of his pistol. "Our wounded would only slow you down. Take Brandon and Tom and go. We will make our stand in the castle."

"Trust in them, Grundbairn, or in me," said Gaelyph. "Or in none at all. But choose quickly." He swiped with the flat of his blade and caught one of the mob at the temple. The thwack felled the charging man, and the warden danced aside.

Effie nodded. The decision came to her without thought. *Trust.* The sergeant and his men had already shown her much. She refused to fail them by not honoring it. Nor the warden, who'd remained at her side when he could have fled.

Nor to Caledon, to whom she owed her life.

"We will fetch help," she said. She turned to the sergeant. "You have my word." Hands caked in mud and filth reached for her. She smacked them away with her cane. The thump of wood against bone rattled her arms.

"Can you hold until morning?" she asked. Her breath came fast. She swung the cane and dodged a groping hand. Her feet started to slip in the slickening muck. Gaelyph's blade flashed before her, and a wet thwack sounded as he felled the afflicted man who'd come at her.

"Aye," said the sergeant. "And I promise you, we'll save those we can." He smashed the butt of his pistol into the face of a pudgy man who wore a farrier's apron. The farrier dropped, clutching a broken nose that streamed blood.

Around the sergeant, the soldiers swung their rifles like clubs. Dull thumps chorused with grunts and shouts beneath the squawking crows. Those of the mob swung wild fists and clawed as they charged, but the soldiers strained and heaved, and held their line.

Barnaby barged through the mob, sending those around Effie reeling. She grabbed his reins. Vaulting into the saddle in trousers did not come naturally to her, but she managed to clamber up as best she could. Sweet Tom Reedling reached out a hand and helped her keep her balance. The boy sat astride a roan mare, a wild expression painting his comely face. He'd kept his rifle slung over a shoulder and struggled to reach for it while whipping his head all around, wide-eyed.

The remaining horses stamped anxiously, rearing and whinnying, eyes as wide as Tom's. Effie reached out with her senses to calm them. As she did, a new presence came to her. She cocked her head to it and wiped away her glamour.

The murder of crows shrank to its true size. Their squawking dampened, allowing Effie to hear the rumble of horses in the distance just before a hunting horn blared. A cry followed, a dozen voices at the least.

Cresting the last rise, the riders bellowed and whooped. They waved sabers and makeshift spears, some glinting and polished, others dull and rusted. Their leader bore a flag affixed to a slender lance—royal blue crossed with gold, styled in the shape of a shield.

Their cry came again. Effie understood a part of it this time. Her shoulders relaxed as a chill washed over her.

"*Teribus ye teri odin!*" *Land of Death!*

❧ 23 ❧

Effie recognized the cry. The charging riders hailed from the town of Hawick. Their ancestors of old had guarded their lands for centuries against English reivers. They came now in a gallop, kicking up clods of grass and muck in their wake. A few had donned battered helms of steel, with broad brims. The armor clashed against their bearers' riding coats and tweed trousers. Their leader wore a quilted doublet studded with iron. It was he who blew the hunting horn.

Their whooping quelled at sight of the mob, but their pace didn't slacken. Sabers and spears snapped forward. The riders fanned into a broadening line, their movements practiced, if not executed with a military precision.

Effie pulled at Barnaby's reins. Snapping her attention away from the charge, she swung her cane with one hand. The wood thwacked against the forearm of an older man with sallow cheeks and a stooped back. The man grunted in pain but kept reaching for her, fingers curled like claws. The snarl at his lips looked inhuman, the glaze in his eyes vacant.

Gaelyph swung into a saddle with the grace of a swan. Spinning the horse around, he ducked low and urged it into a gallop. That he mounted without complaint startled Effie. The warden had to believe their situation dire to do such a thing. A feeling of dread swept through her. She whirled Barnaby to give chase, calling after him. "Wait!"

Along the line, the soldiers had tightened together. They clutched their rifles in both hands, arms extended, pushing back the mob. Grunting, their boots slid in the muck as the press began to encircle them.

"Hold!" Sergeant McGrady called. Effie heard the command as Barnaby broke into a sprint, churning up the grassy field. She had a moment to wonder why the sergeant hadn't yet retreated to the castle, before the riders of Hawick crashed into the rear of the mob.

Spears and sabers hacked through flesh. Those of the mob barely cried out as the riders tore through them, striking them down from behind. For a moment, only the wet slap and thud of steel, flesh, and bone rang out above the pounding of horse hooves.

A sickening pang twisted Effie's gut. Even knowing those of the mob were too far gone to recover did little to quell the belief that she had somehow failed them. But she had learned these past years to stifle such emotions. Wallowing did nothing to serve her purpose.

Her vision narrowed to the back of the warden. Barnaby raced beneath her, powerful legs driving her through the frigid night air. They chased over the grassy field, crested a rise, and charged down a game trail that ran along a trickling burn.

In the shadows of twilight, Effie saw a small figure move ahead. It wore a blood-red cap and carried a staff as long as her cane. She thought she heard a mocking cackle and slowed Barnaby. Thoughts of the deadfall traps within Hermitage Castle sprang to mind.

Gaelyph had also slowed. The warden trotted along the trail with his gaze locked on the redcap. Edging closer, Effie could spy the fey creature better. He stood a head shorter than her, thickset, with long gangly arms and coarse black hair that streamed to his waist. His eyes beamed as blood red as his cap. His stave ended in a sharp iron hook.

The warden and redcap glared at one another. Effie felt the hatred throbbing between them. "Face me," growled Gaelyph. He dismounted and stalked toward the creature.

The redcap grinned, revealing a row of long, sharp teeth. He tipped his cap in a macabre greeting. Brandishing his pikestaff, he scurried up the small bank rising away from the burn. Gaelyph sprang after. His longer strides closed the ground between them.

Effie saw the folly of pursuing while astride Barnaby. The bank held too many dark shadows among the bramble and grass. One false step could lame them both. She slid from the saddle and hurried after the warden.

Scrambling up the bank, she heard a grunt and the clang of steel and iron. Atop the bank, the warden rose from his knees. He batted away the cruel iron hook of the pikestaff with his sword, and lunged forward. The redcap darted aside.

The hook flashed, and the warden grunted once more. Effie could see the wet splotched on his thigh and shoulder. Her heart thumped in alarm. It had not occurred to her the redcap would pose such a dire threat to the warden. For all his arrogance, Gaelyph had always defeated his foes with seeming ease.

She crept closer, searching for a means to aid him. He sensed her arrival and stepped in a circle, trying to force the redcap between them. She took her cane in both hands like a sword. Glancing down, she tried to find firm footing.

With a sudden rush, the redcap snapped his pikestaff toward her. She jerked and felt a kiss of cold iron brush her cheek. The shock of it sent her reeling back on her heels. Her foot caught, and her balance failed. Landing hard, she rolled away. Bramble raked her arms. Her lungs burned from her sharp inhale.

A sensation passed through her, as if a bucket of icy water had been dumped on her head. She startled and let out a soft whimper. But she recognized the Fey Craft. She had felt the sensation before—with Jaelyn at Caldwell House, and again with Rose Brewer.

Gaelyph, Warden of the Hunt, had linked with her. The joining of their auras allowed her to sense more fully his predator's nature—that of a lion slinking through a savanna rich with prey. It also allowed them to meld their Fey Craft, as if one's thoughts could guide the other's hand. Rose Brewer had done such a thing as Jack Canonbie had lain dying in Effie's arms on the streets of Glasgow.

The warden never glanced her direction. He kept his gaze locked on the redcap. But within their link, Effie sensed an urging for her to rise. She did so and saw the redcap leap at Gaelyph. The warden flicked his wrist. His blade clattered against the pikestaff. The pair swiped at one another in a furious exchange.

Come now, charge! The sensation tugged at Effie through the link. Her feet rumbled forward before she could think. Before she could panic. She rushed with her cane before her, clasped tight in her hands. She watched the spinning, whirling pikestaff this time.

Drop! The command barked at her through the link. She flung herself to the ground. The pikestaff cut through the night. The iron hook whooshed past where her neck had just been. It smacked against her cane, yanking the wood from her hands.

She skidded to a jarring stop. The redcap loomed over her, his pikestaff held high. His mouth opened in a snarl. His eyes burned blood red. Drool dripped from his teeth. He tittered, and the iron hook screamed down at her.

Gaelyph caught the shaft and ripped the weapon free. Effie blinked, gasping and confused, until she saw the warden's sword. It had impaled the redcap through the back of the shoulder and out the gut.

The redcap tumbled to the ground. The tittering sound came one last time from its lips before it lay still.

The link between her and the warden dissipated like a fading mist. Its absence left Effie feeling cold and hollow. She shivered, realizing how damp she'd become sitting on the ground. The warden reached out a hand and helped her to her feet.

"You bore such hatred, was this creature known to you?" she asked. She brushed at her trousers, as if she could remove the chill with a bit of dirt.

Gaelyph shook his head. "Not until we reached the castle. But their breed is malicious and cruel, hunting and maiming for sport. Theirs must be put down."

Reclaiming his sword, he flung the pikestaff away. His eyes met hers. They remained stern, and yet somehow she no longer saw the arrogance in them. "Against the tainted humans, that was no easy choice," he said. "I see your struggle with it."

She swallowed. "Th-thank you," she said. "I appreciate your understanding, and your mercy."

He frowned at the words.

"You used the flat of your blade," she explained. "Before, I mean. With those of the mob." The events of the day returned to her, and she found herself mimicking his expression. "But why did you wait so long to let us know of your presence? Or that the redcap stalked us?"

The warden pulled back. "I needed to see that you didn't work in concert with the creature." He spoke as if the notion should be obvious.

Effie flinched as if struck. "You couldn't believe that!"

"Four humans came at first, as a mere distraction," he said. "Caledon argued as you had, that they should be saved, that there might yet be hope for them. It allowed the redcap and his Unseily cohorts to ambush us as we quarreled."

"But you knew it was me." She tried to keep the hurt from her voice.

"I expected Abigail," he said. "Not you, nor the queen's soldiers." The warden made no move to apologize.

Anger swirled with an onrush of sadness in her chest. *Trust.* He had commanded her to do so even after his own lacking had placed them all in jeopardy. And yet, he had linked with her in the end. He had placed both their lives in the faith she would do as he bade. She no longer knew what to make of that.

She broke her gaze away. Her head began to ache. The nicks and bruises she had suffered inflamed as the excitement of the fighting waned.

"Why had Caledon come to Hermitage?" she asked.

At the question, the warden ducked his head. "I failed him. Word reached me that the Erbgraf wished to join our cause along with his Wild Hunt. We were to meet an emissary at the castle and agree to an accord. But no emissary ever arrived."

Effie's throat tightened. She reached for it unconsciously. The steward had asked her to treat with the Germans, and she had refused. She had not felt it her place. How could it be, with her an outsider of the Seily Court? But now that harm had befallen the steward, her reasons seemed so foolish and childish.

"That they have taken Caledon and not slain him directly must give us hope," she said. Her voice rasped. Clenching her fists, she swallowed down her guilt. "But we must hurry."

Gaelyph nodded. He bent and picked up her cane, handing it to her. As he did, the clop of horses sounded. Three riders trotted down the game trail. Effie squinted to make them out. But it was too dark. Night had fallen.

❧ 24 ❧

Torchlight painted Gaelyph's face. The warden strode through the night, picking a path through gently rolling hills. Water trickled over stones nearby, a splinter from the burn that ran past the castle. Starlight had etched the hills in silver for a time, but a bank of clouds moved in, and with it came a dank wind and the soft patter of rain.

The woolen cloak Effie wore kept out the droplets, and though it hadn't removed the damp of her trousers and morning coat, it at least stopped her shivering. She rode Barnaby behind the warden alongside three men from Hawick, Sergeant McGrady, Brandon, and Sweet Tom Reedling. One of the lads from Hawick had offered her the cloak. He'd taken it from some luckless soul to give to his sister. Effie tried not to dwell on its previous owner. The riders from Hawick spoke of scores of mobs roaming the countryside, each as large, or larger, than the one they'd faced at the castle. If believed, it would place the count of those tainted beyond salvation near a thousand. And that in the Borders alone.

She tried to keep from clutching her reins too tight. The news unsettled her, even without adding the dread of what they might be forced to do if they encountered another of the mobs, a notion that seemed likely, since they rode with their auras unhidden. When Effie had asked whether obscuring themselves would be prudent, the warden had argued for a scheme involving snares and bait.

His plan offered little comfort. She knew full well what part he intended her and the other men to play. But for Caledon she would gladly take such risks.

A hooded crow fluttered in to perch on her shoulder. She barely twitched this time. She'd tried to send the thing and its mate away earlier, but they'd clung on, taking turns circling Effie's mounted party on silent wing or nuzzling against her cloak's hood. At least they remained quiet, with only the occasional croak between them.

The rider who'd lent her the cloak stared at her. "Sorry, miss, only it's you, isn't it?" he'd asked when he'd first laid eyes on her by the burn. "The one they say can make trees sprout from the cobbles and giants bend the knee?"

"Yes," she'd replied simply and without embarrassment. His jaw had gaped and eyes gone wide. He had a scruff of ginger hair atop his head and wore a tweed riding coat patterned with greens and yellows. She'd come to find out he was called Alan Thornwood. He hailed from the village of Denholm originally and had worked with his father on the grounds of Sir Walter Scott's Abbotsford home for a time. Though he'd never met the late writer, he spoke of that employment with great pride.

Effie glanced askance at him. He blushed and turned away. They all had stared at one time or another, the riders from Hawick. But the three with her and Gaelyph had leaped to join their hunt, despite its dangers. She wondered if that made them heroic or overly foolish. The remainder of the riders had stayed at Hermitage Castle, along with the injured soldiers and the men Sergeant McGrady had tasked to seeing to their wellbeing.

The sergeant huffed behind her. "Nonsense," he uttered in a harsh whisper. "The crown will never allow it to pass."

"The French have recalled their ambassador, it is said," came a deeper baritone. "Their ships load arms and soldiers at ports from Calais to Le Havre, and that is just for a sea crossing. Never mind what might come from the sky. They intend to invade. This Lord Granville only delays the inevitable. War will be declared before the week is through."

Effie caught the name and turned in her saddle. The man who spoke had a thick nose and dark hair. He clutched a spear in one hand and a torch in the other. His horse clomped along with its head bent against the rain.

"It is Lord Granville who begs for peace, you are certain?" she asked.

"Aye," said the man. "But peace with the French alone. For the Scots, he begs for more regiments to repel this plague of barrow wights."

"Plague of barrow wights." Brandon snickered. "Perhaps Grigg's nan had it right."

Effie chewed her lip. Lord Granville no doubt saw only his own interests in his actions, but she would need to thank him all the same. If he could hold back war with France a few days more, it might make all the difference. Yet none of it would matter if the Barrow Witch were not stopped. The riders of Hawick had not stumbled on the mob at Hermitage by accident. They had tracked it from a local village that now stood abandoned, its inhabitants fled, slain, or cruelly enslaved to the will of the Sidhe Bhreige.

The riders had spoken of other villages equally ravaged. The town of Kelso had seen a devastating fire, and a pack of wulvers had been spotted near Jedburgh, the largest gathered since the Horned Host had descended on Caldwell House.

"Whatever they are called," she said, "their threat will not end, nor their numbers truly dwindle until their master is put down."

"You mean the Hag o' Maiden Paps?" Alan Thornwood asked.

Effie started. The Maiden Paps were conical hills rising close to Hawick, but she had never heard of a hag, or any creature, related to them. The crow squawked a protest at the sudden movement and fluttered its wings.

Alan read the confusion on her face. "The Hag o' Maiden Paps is an old tale," he said. "Some say it was she that whispered in the ears of the de Souleses of Hermitage Castle and drove them to the black arts. Boiled alive by his tenants, one of them was, wrapped in lead. Another tried to steal the crown after dancing in the moonlight with the hag's barrow wights."

He leaned closer. "Thomas the Rhymer said the barrow wights protected her, striking down any who seek her earthen tomb. That's why none has ever laid eyes on her and lived. The Rhymer ken all

kinds of uncanny things, it is known, learnt from the fey queen
herself."

"None lived until recent days," said the man riding behind Effie. His
tone sounded more worried than boastful.

"Och, aye," Alan agreed. "Ask Donald Langthumb. Seen her, he has."
He hooked a thumb at their companion, a dour looking man with sunken
eyes and loose jowls that wobbled as he turned his head.

A jolt of energy washed through Effie. "You've confronted this hag?"

"Confronted? Nay, I wouldn't say that." The man shifted in the saddle
with a bit of discomfort. "I was standing atop the Mote the night the
thing came for poor Maggie Stewart. I saw it lurking about in the trees
below, all spindly armed and pale faced. Thought I mustn't be seeing
right. But when Maggie's husband came after her, the hag made this
unholy noise and called down lightning from the heavens."

Alan shook his head. "Burnt the poor fellow with blue hellfire."

"We tried to give chase," said Donald Langthumb. "But by the time I
climbed down from the Mote—it's an auld hillfort mound, you see—the
lads and I couldn't find a whiff of the hag. Or of Maggie. That's the last
we've seen of either of them."

"Ack," said Brandon. He slapped his thigh. "It were probably just a
play of the moonlight."

Donald Langthumb's jowls quivered as he glared.

"I seen the scorch marks with mine own eyes," said Alan. "George
Gresham did too." He indicated the man riding behind Effie. "Unnatural,
they were."

"I believe you," said Effie. Her heart had quickened as the tale
unfolded. It pulsed with a steady ire. She held a picture in her mind of a
creature who wielded blue fire in such a manner, but it was not the
Barrow Witch, nor a hag. It was a grindylow. Tallia lurked somewhere in
the darkness.

"This Hag o' Maiden Paps is the same who captured our steward,"
she said. "She is the very creature we hunt."

The hooded crow cawed madly and took wing. It quickly disappeared
into the night.

Sergeant McGrady cleared his throat but abandoned whatever he'd
meant to say as a lone howl rang out. The chorus of a pack followed it,

high-pitched and frenzied. The howls sounded close, yipping and crying out all around them.

Barnaby panicked. Whinnying, he pulled against his reins. Effie fought to calm him. She whispered soothing words and nudged with a bit of Fey Craft. The men around her struggled with their mounts, and she widened the sense of calm she cast out. She didn't know quite how she'd learned to do the trick, but quelling animals, especially those familiar to her, had always come easily to her.

"Wulvers," said Gaelyph. The warden drew his sword.

Suddenly, feeling eyes watching their group, Effie scanned the fields and trees around them. Goose pimples rose on her flesh. Though she had faced the creatures before, the fact that she had escaped those encounters did nothing to quell her fear. Wulvers might well be a smaller cousin of the wolf, if a wolf could walk upright and have fangs longer than her fingers, but they moved at great speeds and bore fangs and claws to rival a lion.

"There!" said Sweet Tom Reedling. He'd unslung his rifle and waved it toward a cluster of ash and alder trees barely lit by their torchlight. Brandon followed the lad's aim with his own rifle. Sergeant McGrady cocked his pistol, holding it pointed skyward and peering at the trees.

Effie squinted and caught movement. Dark shapes slinked toward them, moving through the grass like beads of water dripping down a window pane. She reached for the wulvers with her senses but could not feel their auras.

The hairs on the back of her neck stiffened. These were not a random pack. Someone masked them with Fey Craft. Effie cast her senses wider. Hunters by nature, wulvers would attack animals they considered prey, even humans. But their predatory nature also allowed them to be easily manipulated by the Sidhe Bhreige and Unseily.

Sweet Tom Reedling's rifle cracked. The weapon jumped in his arms, and his horse danced to the side. The bullet thunked into the distant trees, but still the dark shapes slinked toward them. Brandon sucked in a breath, held it, and fired.

One of the wulvers jerked with a yelp. Brandon fired again, and it lay still. Howls sounded from the trees and from the fields lost in darkness around them. The wulvers that had been brave enough to approach snarled and yapped before turning and fleeing.

Brandon and Sweet Tom Reedling levelled their rifles. Sergeant McGrady urged his horse forward a few steps. "Save your bullets, lads, and keep an eye to our flanks," he said. He waved his pistol from side to side.

The riders of Hawick wheeled their mounts, scouring all around. Effie saw the worry etched on Alan Thornwood's face. Donald Langthumb had pulled a small woodsman's axe from his belt. She wondered how he managed to grip the thing as she saw now the meaning of his name. His right thumb ended in a short stump, the top missing above the knuckle.

"Where are they?" asked George Gresham. He yanked at his reins, spinning his head about, wide-eyed. His torch and spear flailed as he moved.

The question was met only by the patter of rain and the sound of their breathing. Some came labored and quick from a few of the men. It drowned out any noise coming from the fields.

"They flee," Gaelyph finally said. He held his chin high as he studied the tree line. "Their duty is done."

Effie frowned. She force her breathing to slow and find steady rhythm. As her racing heart calmed, she tried to deduce his meaning. "They only meant to scare and delay us. Their master seeks more time, a chance to gain distance..." She let the words trail off. She met the warden's gaze.

"No." She corrected herself. "They had two days at the least to slink into whatever dank hole they chose. She lures us into a trap." *She*. Tallia, Effie knew it had to be.

"We should return to the castle and fetch the rest of the lads," said George Gresham. "We can come back on the morrow in force and flush the things from their warren."

"If we tuck our tails, they'd only ride us down," said Brandon.

"Wait over the next rise until I return," said Gaelyph. Effie studied the warden and shook her head, but he hurried off into the darkness before she could stammer a word. Her mind whirled over what game Tallia might be playing at.

"Should we let him go out there alone?" Alan asked.

"Better him than us," replied George Gresham.

"Aye," said Brandon, twisting the man's meaning. "He is better than the lot of us with that sword of his."

"Come," said Effie. "We will trust in the warden." She made her voice sound steadier than she felt. In truth, she wanted nothing more than to chase after him. Patting Barnaby's neck, she flicked his reins. The horse plodded forward. Hooves clomped behind her as the other men followed.

The rain lessened to a gentle mist as they crossed over the rise and settled into a shallow dell full of bramble. Effie pulled down the hood of her cloak and felt Alan Thornwood's eyes on her again. She turned to him, resting her cane across her lap.

"What caused you men of Hawick to abandon your town and fight?" she asked.

"Honor," said Donald Langthumb. He pulled back his shoulders.

"Abandon?" asked George Gresham. "Nay, lass. These hills and waters are our homes."

"I wanted to ask the same of you, miss," said Sweet Tom Reedling. "Was it the adventure tales of your Mr. Robert Louis Stevenson?"

"His aren't as fanciful," Brandon answered for her. Torchlight flickered across his face. "Fiendish fey hounds prowling the night. Men and women wandering about like the dead come to life."

The presumption of his response rankled Effie. She was about to come to her employer's son's defense, but stopped and sucked in a breath. *The dead hunt the hills.* Conall's translation of Jean-Nicolas Durand returned to her. Had the man been in the Borders before his flight to Aberdeen? It would make sense, given their deduction of the Barrow Witch's location. In an odd way, the state of his mind, too, resembled that of the men and women they'd faced at the castle.

She pictured Scotland in her mind and wondered over the caches of Aerfenium. Certainly for Durand to have obtained a measure from Edward Waite, he need not be anywhere near the Borders, but it made a kind of sense that one would be hidden here. The area was rife with tales of fey lore. Squeezing her eyes shut, she drew a mental line from the

Storr to Edinburgh. The same line, if stretched farther, would run past the city and shoot like a dart for the Eildon Hills near Melrose.

"Are you all right, miss?" asked Sweet Tom Reedling. "I meant no offense."

"Thomas the Rhymer," she said. She tried to recall the auld tales. "The tree where he met with the Fey Queen is near to the Eildon Hills, is it not?"

"Aye, on the way from Melrose to Dryburgh," the lad answered. "I've seen it myself."

She had no time for another thought. The howls of the wulvers started once again. But this time, as the cries tore through the night, the auras of the pack flooded into her awareness. More than a score of the creatures spread in an arc behind them. At their center, a pair of bogills stood like huntsmen eager to flush their prey into a frightened flight.

Effie searched for Gaelyph. But of the warden, she could find no trace.

"Too many," said George Gresham. His mount wheeled in circles, bucking in panic. Effie urged their mounts to calm, but the same thought flashed in her mind. They would not be able to stand against so many, and they could not run. Their only hope lay in her Fey Craft. She had to wrestle the attention of the wulvers away from their Unseily masters and drive them off.

Steeling herself, she let her senses meld with the pack. She felt the hunger that drove them into a frenzy. She tasted the slaver on their tongues. She knew better than to try and quell that desire. Instead, she pulled at it, bringing forth the image of a drove of hares fleeing in panic through the grass-covered fields.

She had done something similar years before, when she had only begun to learn of Fey Craft.

The wulvers howled. Their chorus sang through the night until Effie couldn't hear the men around her. She saw only the quiver of their mouths as they gestured and peered into the darkness, waving with their spears and rifles.

Effie began to shape her next image of Fey Craft, but as she did she felt the familiar touch of a fetid weed. It snaked around her waist in a damp strand, slimy and oozing, yet firm. She ripped at it, severing the link from its owner, and a dozen new strands took its place.

The bogills sought to entangle her, she recognized, as she tore at the phantom weeds. If they succeeded, they would block her from her fey senses, removing her ability to work Fey Craft. Effie dropped the image of the hares. She couldn't hope to win the wulvers to her will, not as she struggled to defend against the bogills. The concentration needed was too great. But the wulvers were not the only creatures roaming the night. With a small sliver of thought, she scoured the area around her companions.

Sweet Tom Reedling's rifle popped in rapid succession. Yet the soldiers were not trained cavalry, nor the horses battle-tested mounts. The lad struggled with his seating, yanking hard at the reins to keep his balance. Effie couldn't see what he had fired at, but she sensed the wulvers stalking forward as a pack, tightening their arc.

A howl went up, and the creatures broke into a four-legged gallop. George Gresham saw them first. "Ride!" he hollered. Ducking low, he urged his horse to flee.

"No!" Sergeant McGrady swiped at the man's reins but missed. "Stand and fight!" he cried. He waved his pistol feebly at the man's back.

Gresham's horse gave a terrified squeal and dashed away from the charging wulvers. Alan Thornwood let out a noise—half battle cry and half wail—and followed. Their horses thundered across the field. The halo of their torchlight dimmed as they fled.

Donald Langthumb watched them go, a dumbstruck expression etched on his face. A few wulvers raced after the fleeing men. Their sleek bodies and iron muscles flitted through the fading torchlight in flashes of dark fur and gleaming fangs.

Sergeant McGrady fired at one. The bullet whistled harmlessly into the night. The rifles of Brandon and Sweet Tom Reedling cracked and popped until they were spent. A scattered chorus of yelps followed the shots, but they were drowned out by a symphony of growling and snapping jaws.

Exhaustion weighed on Effie. It clouded her thoughts as she ripped and tore at the endless onslaught from the bogills. She'd let Barnaby roam free and found herself apart from the soldiers. They'd separated no more than a dozen paces, but as the wulvers entered the ring of torchlight, the gap might as well have spanned an ocean.

Effie readied her cane, for the little good it would do her. She had never swung the thing from astride a horse, and it was too heavy for her to wield with a single hand. The wulvers approaching her rose to their hind legs. The movement revealed the thick, curved shape of their claws. Their dark eyes held a tinge of red that seemed to burn with a cruel mocking. Their jaws hung agape, with their lips pulled back to display jagged teeth.

Barnaby reared, battering with his forelegs. Effie desperately clung to the saddle. Her concentration slipped, and she felt the phantom weeds of the bogills' Fey Craft lash across her flesh. Their piercing barbs made her gasp. Her blood ran cold. She could not let go of the reins. She could not swing her cane. The weeds squeezed at her throat and chest. The world shrank around her in a pool of darkness.

Stalking forward, the wulvers appeared to grin. A relishing gleam reflected in their lupine gazes. One dropped to all fours and scrambled forward. Each breath came in a grunting snort, slaver dripping from its maw.

Grey and black streaked across Effie's vision in a flurry of feathered wings. She jerked back as a hoarse caw broke through the night, piercing her ears. The hooded crow raked with its claws as it swooped past the wulver. The creature saw the bird late. Its jaws snapped as it jerked its head. The effort unbalanced the creature, and it toppled over.

Its companions howled. One rushed for Effie. Barnaby lurched, and her cane slapped against her face, rattling her teeth. A second crow, the other that had followed her from the castle, swooped past to attack the wulver. Beak and tooth met in a sickening crunch.

Effie managed to slide from her saddle and keep her feet. The side of her face throbbed, the pulse of it keeping time with her racing heart. Taking her cane in both hands, she hurled herself at one of the wulvers. She took the creature by surprise and cracked it across the skull. As she drew back to hammer again, she saw a flash of silver in the distance, as if moonlight had caught on a rushing burn.

She hesitated and stepped back. The night sky remained dark under a canopy of thick clouds. The flash came again, flaring to life like a beacon. She couldn't make sense of its meaning, but she guessed at its source.

Gaelyph had returned.

Turning, she could no longer sense the auras of her companions. They struggled, swiping with their rifles and spears as their mounts bucked and bit. Curses rang from their lips, mixing with the growls and snapping maws of the wulvers, and the heavy pounding of horses' hooves.

The phantom weeds slithered around Effie, pulling tighter, layer over layer. Before her next breath, she would sense nothing at all, the power of her fey blood stolen by the bogills. She had to lay her trust in the warden. She had to believe he would not let them all die.

Clutching the last desperate trickle of her Fey Craft, she felt her impression of calm wither away and be replaced by fear. Her companions' mounts shrieked in terror and bolted. She whirled, watching Barnaby join them. The men clung roughly to their saddles. A few dark shapes hounded at their heels, snarling and yipping away.

The last of her fey senses snuffed into nothingness. The sound of her companions' flight faded. Above the growls and soft pad of the wulvers around her, she heard the grass crunch. A pair of dark shapes moved before her. They stank of rot and dried sweat.

Effie's heart beat hard and high against her throat. But she was not alone. The knowledge lent her strength.

❧ 26 ❧

Feathers brushed Effie's cheeks as the pair of hooded crows swooped to perch on her shoulders. They dug in with their claws and screeched a harsh challenge at the bogills. Effie breathed in their sharp scent. They smelled of the fields and the sky above. Her heart slowed and panic lessened. She had been shielded from Fey Craft before and understood the trick. It involved a linking of sorts between her and the bogills, a sharing of their fey power. Or perhaps a lack of sharing would be a more fitting description. The bogills consumed the strength of her fey blood, pulling it into themselves. But that did not mean she could not seize it back. She needed only subtlety and to wait on the right moment.

"This is the one she wants." The deep timbre cut through the night, thick with a continental accent. Effie tensed but forced herself to remain still. She planted her cane before her and used its sturdiness for support.

"Where is the steward?" She made her voice as firm as she could muster. "Where is Caledon?"

"*Oui*," the other bogill said. The response dripped with disdain. "But we have played her game long enough. We should kill this one and do as Mother bade us. She waits to begin."

The first bogill grunted and muttered something in a language Effie didn't recognize. That the bogills came from different nations alarmed her, but her thoughts had already caught onto another riddle.

"Tallia. You speak of a game Tallia plays," she said.

The first bogill leaned closer until she could feel his breath wash over her like a putrid mist. Her crows cawed and flapped their wings. In the near darkness, the wulvers returned a rumbling chorus of growls.

Effie raised her chin in defiance. "You must take me to the steward. If he is with Tallia, I demand to see them both."

The backhanded clout took her at the temple. Its force made the world spin, as if she tumbled within crashing waves. The crows fluttered away, screeching in fury. She struck the ground and gasped for breath. Her hearing dimmed. Her mouth felt wet, her tongue heavy. She tried to touch her lips, but her arm didn't respond.

Strength and courage, she reminded herself, fighting the urge to close her eyes and rest. Gaelyph hadn't abandoned her. She wasn't alone.

The makings of a smile tugged at her lips. She wasn't alone, but nor would the warden expose himself to aid her. Not yet. Her safety wasn't his concern. She understood that. He tracked the bogills, not her, and he would wait until they led him to Caledon. What abuse she suffered, or whether she still lived, was moot.

An iron fist gripped her and yanked her upright. Her gut lurched. She swatted at the hand, but her thoughts lost focus. The world flipped over once more. Her eyes closed, and darkness dragged her away.

She blinked sometime later. Awareness returned. The ground swayed beneath her, or rather she over it, and she realized from the pressure against her torso that she jostled over the shoulder of one of the bogills. She felt the muscles of the thing's back working beneath her dangling arms—her loose arms. That was something, at least. She had been stripped of her cane, but at least her hands were not bound.

The touch made her recoil. Shifting her weight, she shoved against the bogill's neck with an elbow and kicked. The sudden movement threw the larger man off-balance. He stumbled, and she slid free. A meaty hand swiped at her, scraping at her arm.

"Stop!" she commanded, holding up a feeble hand. "I will march where you please, but I will not be carried like a sack of grain."

She crouched, expecting another swipe. But none came. The bogills studied her, and in the silence she realized the night had changed. They had left the rolling fields below and clambered up a steeper hillside coated in short, billowy grass. The cloudy sky had broken as well. Dim starlight shone down, illuminating everything in a silvery hue. She considered the change and tried to judge how long she might've been asleep. But she might as well try to count the number of midges in a swarm.

The trickling of the Hermitage Water no longer sounded nearby. That told her they had abandoned their previous path. She could not see clearly over the rise of the hilltop, but it looked as if a ring of miniature trees topped its crest. Of the wulvers, she could no longer see nor hear them, but she had to imagine they had not strayed far afield.

The bogills regarded one another. Something unspoken passed between them. "March. Do not run," said the one who had carried her. He prodded and Effie lurched forward. The victory was small and perhaps meaningless, but she carried on with her shoulders held back and her lips closed.

The ground felt slick as she ascended the hilltop, as if the recent rains had fallen more heavily on the higher ground. *Raindrops will find a route over any leaf.* One of her mother's sayings came to her. It meant one should be open to unexpected paths in life, but now it made Effie think of the fetid weeds binding her Fey Craft.

Like the raindrop, she would need to find the right crevice. Ever so slowly she felt along the barbs and strands of the phantom weeds. With her fey senses dimmed to almost nothing, the sensation of their touch was like that of a spider's web—one she could not see but only feel the irritation of across her flesh. She tried to pull at one of the strands, softly, but she was not subtle enough. The strand tightened at her lightest touch. A giant hand clapped her back, and she stumbled forward, flailing to keep her balance.

"No." The bogill's warning sounded like a growl.

Effie tensed. To avoid any further reproach, she asked the first question that popped into her head. "What game does Tallia play at? Why do you follow her commands?"

"No," came the stern reply.

The way steepened as they crested the last part of the hill. Atop the rise, she realized the trees were not trees at all. Nine stanes rose in a circle, each like a stone finger in a pair of cupped hands. Effie gasped. Caledon lay in the middle of the stanes. His form was limp and lifeless. Only the shallowest of breaths let her know he still lived. Blood streaked his forehead. His clothes were torn.

She rushed for the steward but stopped short as cackling echoed from behind one of the taller stanes. Tallia stepped into view. The glow of her stardust device illuminated her grey flesh and scarred face. Her shoulders hunched forward. Her lips pulled back in a sneer.

"I have observed your feeble attempt to save the steward," she said. "It amused me greatly. I would keep you as a pet, but it is Mother's will that I put an end to your intrusions. It is her will that all shall be as it once was, and you have not the stomach for that."

"If any harm befalls Caledon, you will feel the wrath of Elphame," said Effie. Anger flared inside her. She edged a few steps farther away from the bogills. She didn't know how the Fey Queen would react to an attack on her steward, but she tried to sound threatening.

Tallia's laughter came like a wheezing cough. "We have no fear of the usurper. She and those of her court will soon suffer a just fate for abandoning their masters."

"Kill her and be done with it," said one of the bogills. He strode forward. Starlight painted his hardened gaze.

Effie scampered away from the large brute. "Elphame is warned of your plans," she said, hoping the surprise would keep them talking. "The Seily Court is prepared for your coming. Your invasion will not succeed."

The bogill hissed. He muttered a curse in French. "We should not have delayed."

"Fool." Tallia spat the word at him. "Her taunts have no consequence. Let them prepare. They are ever weak. We will have our victory."

"What of Caledon?" asked Effie. "Let me trade my life for his."

Tallia's cackling came once more. Her head tilted as she watched Effie. "You are in no position to trade anything. I have you both. The steward will lead Mother's armies into Elphame as you lay decaying in the dirt of this hilltop."

Effie's flesh prickled. She felt the blood drain from her face. It made her head swim. She reached out her arms to steady herself. "No!" she yelped. Her gaze whipped to Caledon, to the pallor of his cheeks. Her chest clenched in pain.

"Yes, you see it now," said Tallia. "You are too late. He has joined our host, whether he willed it or not." She turned to the steward. "It is unfortunate he fights the change. I would have cherished to see him strike you down. It would have been a fitting end to your meddling—the blood of the steward having its revenge on your grandfather's progeny."

Swallowing, Effie fought the urge to charge at Tallia. Her only hope lay in Gaelyph springing whatever trap he laid. But the words stung, the reminder that all fey seemed to know her grandfather's legacy—that he had let the old steward die in order to save a human child.

Effie ran her senses along the fetid weeds of Fey Craft that bound her fey powers, prodding for a weak point, anywhere she might rip and tear her way free. The weeds constricted at her caress, offering no purchase. The bogill moving toward her grunted.

"Seize her!" Tallia shouted. She flicked the slender stick toward Effie, and the stardust burned brighter, flooding the night with a blinding azure glow. The dark shadows of wulvers raced along the hilltop, ringing the stanes and allowing no path for Effie to flee into the darkness of the fields beyond.

But she had no intention of abandoning Caledon. She had caught a sound on the wind that met her ears like a clarion cry of fellowship. It told her what she must do.

"You will not see your Mother, the Barrow Witch, claim victory," she hollered as she ducked behind one of the stanes. The cold of its stone bled through her damp coat and into her bones. The bogills lumbered after her, giant boots stomping the grass. Their snarling faces were lit by the glow of Tallia's wand.

One stopped and cocked his ear. His eyes widened. He raised an arm to shield his face as hooded crows swarmed the nine stanes on near silent wings. In a heartbeat, the area flooded with the darting and swooping birds. Their feathers whipped the air. Their squawking deafened the hilltop.

A burst of stardust screamed through the night. The crows in its wake screeched and fell. But the murder remained. Their number, illuminated by the burst, had grown since the swarm at Hermitage Castle.

Effie couldn't fathom how. She hadn't called to them, nor had she bade them come to the hilltop. She had not felt their approach, either. They had simply appeared. Yet somehow she knew their allegiance was born of the same kinships she had always known with animals, an innate bond that sprang from her Grundbairn nature.

A gift from her mother, her grandfather, and her unknown ancestors for millennia before that.

Ducking her head around the stane, Effie spied Tallia. The grindylow slashed with the wand, sending another burst streaking into the night. But the crows' fervor didn't lessen. They pecked and scratched, squawked and flapped. Tallia and the bogills swatted with arms too slow and clumsy for the crows. Blood welled in gashes on their faces. Fiery red welts rose on their exposed flesh.

The wulvers leapt and snapped their jaws at the birds. Quicker than their masters, they pulled down crows by the maw-full. Effie cringed at the sight but knew she could do nothing to stop the beasts. She had only her bare hands and not even Fey Craft to aid her.

Her feet moved all the same. She stumbled across the hilltop in a scamper. The crows parted for her, darting for the wulvers who dared rush forward, and creating a wall against the bogills.

Tallia saw her come. She swiped at a crow with her free hand and brought the other up, leveling the glowing device toward Effie. Its stardust tip flared, turning white with heat. The grindylow's face scrunched. Her brow pulled low and lips quivered in a sneer.

Effie's legs churned, but her stride was not long enough. She wouldn't reach the grindylow in time, not before the stardust burst tore through her. Grunting, she pumped her arms harder. She willed herself to fly as fast as the crows.

Drawing back the wand, Tallia snapped her wrist. As she did, a crow swooped past in a streak of long black feathers and short brown tufts. Its claws snatched at the wand, knocking it aside.

Effie shivered as the burst of stardust streaked past her. Its heat felt like that of a roaring fire thrust against her flesh. But unlike the last time she faced Tallia, she did not raise her arm or dive aside. Instead, she kept on and lowered her shoulder.

She caught the grindylow in the gut. The pair tumbled over and landed hard against the beaten earth of the hilltop. The impact drove the breath from Effie. Tallia's sharp nails raked across her back. They gouged painful lines, but her coat stood against them, keeping her flesh from ripping apart. She kicked and rolled aside. Her eyes scoured the ground searching for the stardust device. She found it just as Tallia plucked it from the grass.

The grindylow loomed over her. Effie tensed, heart thumping. The azure glow of the device's tip wavered a few feet from her head.

One of the bogills cried out, his bellow raised above the din of the crows. Effie didn't dare take her eyes from Tallia, but she felt what had happened. She knew Gaelyph had come. Her fey senses flooded into her as half the fetid weeds restraining them dissolved into nothing. She ripped away the rest with a giant surge of Fey Craft.

She didn't wait for Tallia to react. She formed a simple glamour, producing a shimmering green orb that hung between her hands. To it, she added heat. When it began to singe her flesh, she let it float higher before her and conjured a wave of mist to seep from the ground. The cool vapors billowed upward and kissed the orb, letting off a blanket of steam.

Tallia's gaze narrowed. "What's this? Do you think simple tricks can fool me?"

Effie felt pressure against her glamour. She enlarged the orb and flattened it. Raising it before her like a shield, she caused the mist billowing about the hilltop to rain sparks like emeralds falling in a hailstorm. She let the whim of her senses take over while she listened. She could feel Gaelyph and the other bogill circling in a dance nearby. The swooshing of a sword cut through the night. Across the hilltop, wulvers snapped at the crows, while the birds screeched their challenge in return. In the distance, thunder began to build.

Tallia cackled at the display.

"Is that what you have learned?" Her tongue clucked. She swatted aside a hooded crow that darted for her nose. "It displeases me that Mother gives you such credence. In Edinburgh, you stole away my playthings and left no greater challenge than what a sheep faces to produce a dropping."

Her head cocked to the side. A shiver passed through her. "Yes." She hissed the word, and Effie realized it was not for her own ears. Tallia spoke to another, someone who watched from afar. The grindylow waved her open hand and yanked it back. Effie's glamour was ripped from her control. The weight of the flattened green shield shoved against her and flung her to the ground. It pressed against her chest like a slab of stone.

"Mother begs of me," Tallia snarled. She thrust the stardust device at Effie. "Tell me where it is, and perhaps I won't make you suffer...too much."

Effie blinked. She tried to deduce what the fey woman might mean, that which the Barrow Witch coveted, but she could not think of a thing that would cause Tallia to delay the killing stroke. The Unseily had the steward. They had allies from the continent and those they needed to invade Elphame. The armies of London could not stop them. They knew not where the host gathered, and even if they did, the banshee's touch would rip through their ranks.

"Your flesh is failing you, as are your wits, Tallia." Effie spat the words. She knew not what else to do. Even knowing the glamour for a trick, she could not free herself from its weight. Its heat scalded her flesh. Her breath came in shallow gasps. "Are you now a leashed pet made to heel?"

She risked a glance for Gaelyph. The mist she had conjured had dissipated, but she could not spy the warden, nor the remaining bogill. She knew only that they fought near the stanes on the far side of the circle.

The once-distant thunder rumbled louder, coming closer. The wulvers began to howl a cry of warning.

Tallia didn't notice. She bared decaying teeth that had broken and turned yellow. "Tell me!" she screamed. "You must have it. It is your nature to seize control. You do not trust your pathetic allies!" She marched forward and shoved the stardust device into Effie's face.

Effie blinked away the sudden brilliance. When her vision cleared, she saw clearly for the first time the object lashed to the device's tip. It was a stone covered in runes. A thunderstone meant to channel stardust rather than divine Aerfenium.

The riddle fell into place. The Aerfenium thunderstone—that was what the Barrow Witch coveted, the reason why Tallia had not yet killed her. Effie tipped her head back and laughed. Tallia and her Mother believed Effie foolish enough to have brought the stone with her, that her lack of faith in the Seily Court, in those from Elphame, and in London would drive her to be selfish and act in solitude.

But she did trust. She trusted in the duke and the soldiers who'd fought at Caldwell House. She trusted in Caledon and Jaelyn and Rose. She trusted in Stuart Graham and Thomas Stevenson, and so many others. She'd even trusted in Jack Canonbie after he'd betrayed her. And if she once doubted Gaelyph, she trusted in him now.

She was a part of them all and they a part of her. She didn't need Fey Craft to know that for the truth. Her family, her community, needed no such tricks.

"Tell me!" Tallia shrieked. She flung her wrist forward.

A blast of stardust burst from the wand. It exploded into the ground next to Effie's head. Chips of rock and mud showered her. Effie grinned. The thunder had reached the hilltop. Rifles cracked in a volley. The wulvers' howls turned to yelps.

Tallia whipped her head at the charging riders, the men from Hawick. Red coats dotted among their number, the sergeant and his soldiers. They carved a path through the wulvers and claimed the hilltop. The crows swooped among them. They perched on the stanes and fluttered to the grass. They could rest. They had stalled long enough. Their work was done.

Effie felt a frigid flare of power rush into her. Gaelyph linked with her, not with fetid weeds but with the sturdiness of oak. She surged her Fey Craft outward, spreading calm and a sense of hope to her companions. Her hand shot up and grasped the wand. With a deft twist, she snapped it.

The thunderstone fell to the ground. As it did, the glow of stardust winked out.

Tallia recoiled. She stumbled back and stared blankly at the broken wand. A rifle cracked. She jerked and spun around, stumbling to her knees. Hacking, blood dripped from her lips. Her gaze found Effie. Her eyes shone with a malice that would scorch the sun. They lingered on Effie for only a moment before sliding toward the center of the ring of nine stanes, toward where Caledon lay motionless.

The grindylow snatched the thunderstone. Effie lunged to wrestle it away, but Tallia battered her back. Effie raised her arms to protect herself. She rolled aside and came to her feet, balanced on her toes. Something slithered across the ground before her. Dark shapes twisted and hissed through the grass. The riders hollered, struggling to control their mounts as hundreds of snakes emerged from the dark shadows of the stanes.

Effie countered Tallia's Fey Craft. She pulled on the strength Gaelyph lent her, redoubling the sense of calm she sent to the riders and horses, and reshaping the snakes into flowery vines that swayed as if taken by a morning breeze.

The thunderstone flared to life in Tallia's clutched fingers. Where the azure glow of stardust touched her hand, it seared the flesh away. The grindylow shrieked in agony. Her arm blackened. Turning to Effie, her shrieks became a gurgling cackle.

A burst of stardust shot from the thunderstone. Effie had no chance to leap aside. She managed to tuck her shoulder, and the burst ripped across her back, scorching her to the bone and setting her coat alight. She was flung back. The cold kiss of grass scratched along the wound. It made her cry out in pain, but at least it snuffed the flames.

Cringing, she expected another burst. She heard the ragged clomp of footfalls stumbling away from her instead. Tallia staggered toward the center of the stanes. She passed the thunderstone to her other hand as she went. The first was spent. The arm dangled, coal black, rent, and dead.

"Mother, save me!" Her desperate cry came as a choking rasp.

Scrambling to her feet, Effie lurched after the grindylow. She spied a loose stone but knew if she stooped to pick it up she may not rise again. At least, not until it was too late to save Caledon. Her feet had turned to lead. Fire rippled across her back. She felt a wetness there soaking her shirt.

The steward must have sensed the coming doom. His head rolled toward Tallia. His eyes fluttered, the first movement Effie had seen from him since her arrival on the hilltop. Her heart seized. The steward had believed in her when no other fey had. He had rallied the Seily Court around her intentions and seen she was treated with respect.

And he had done all of this while others ostracized her. They blamed her family for the death of his kin. They blamed her for conspiring against their kind and her mother for shunning their traditions. But he only saw her for who she truly was—not as a fey, or an orphan, or the blood of a betrayer—but for the merits of her own worth.

She would not let him die, no matter the cost.

Tallia raised the thunderstone. Its glow cast a halo around her that fell onto the prone steward. As she plunged her arm downward, the halo narrowed and strengthened in intensity. The azure glow turned into blue flame that licked and hissed like the gas lamps of a city street. She shrieked as she dropped to her knees and shoved her fist toward Caledon's chest.

Effie smashed into her. As they toppled over, blue flames burst into the air between them. The heat seared Effie. It scalded her neck and singed her arms. She ripped at her coat, tearing it free. Gasping against the shock of agony, she rolled along the grass.

Shrieks rang out behind her. She whirled around to see Tallia rise. The grindylow's tattered clothes had also caught alight. Flames billowed from head to foot. Her arms flailed. But they were too charred and dead to dampen the burning stardust.

Sergeant McGrady stepped into Effie's line of sight. Mud caked his boots and coat. His cheeks were flushed, and his breath came in panting huffs. Raising his pistol, he fired.

Tallia twitched and collapsed. Her shrieks ended. Effie sensed her aura fade away. Across the hilltop, none of the grindylow's companions remained. The bogills were dead, the wulvers likewise or fled. A few of the crows squawked. They flapped their wings and resettled. The horses snorted and stomped their feet against the cold night air.

"No." Effie whimpered. No joy rose in her at Tallia's death. She crawled on her hands and knees toward Caledon. Each movement stung. Her flesh ached. It throbbed to the pulse of her heart.

The grass near the steward's head smoldered. Whiffs of smoke rose from it, smelling oddly sweet. Caledon lay still, but his gaze studied her. He breathed. His chest rose and fell in a shallow rhythm. Bruises ran along his neck. The sickly pallor of his face and the way sweat trickled from his brow gave indications that he fought a fever.

Effie took one of his hands in her own. The effort made her wince. Casting forth her senses, she scoured his aura. It had changed. The beacon of light it had once been was now a cruel and twisted thing, as if a cheery hearth, warm and offering protection, had become a frigid and boggy mire full of menace.

The grass crunched as Gaelyph came to stand over them both. His sword was slick, his face a stone mask. But she read the doubt in his eyes. It troubled him what he thought he must do.

"There has to be a way," she said. "It must be possible to remove this taint of the Unseily."

"Effie." He squatted and reached out with the back of his hand. His fingers stopped short of caressing her cheek. He didn't disagree with her, but nor did he show concern for the steward. His attention didn't waver from her. His gaze flickered across her arms and chest.

It took a moment for her to understand. Death hung in the air. She closed her eyes. A shudder passed through her. Her heart started to race.

"We are not too late," she said, gritting her teeth.

"You would make a grand steward. I see it in you, as surely as I read it in the stars." Caledon's voice sounded weak, barely above a whisper. "But I have long known you would never accept such a mantle."

Effie blinked, confused. She felt the night slow around her, as if she had been cast underwater. Slowly, the starlight was dimming.

"You have much of your mother, and of her father, Arnwyrd, in you," the steward continued.

"Betrayer's blood." The words tasted fuzzy on her lips.

"Fey blood," Caledon replied. "We are one. Our history is shared. You must have faith in that." His gaze found the warden's unsheathed sword. "I fight her, Gaelyph. I am strong, but I cannot resist forever. You must do what must be done."

"No." Effie barely managed the word. She refused to believe that the Caledon they knew would never return. They were not one, despite what he said. He was the stronger, the better. He was the heart of their people.

Someone sucked in a sharp breath. Dark figures loomed over her, she realized. She couldn't make them out. Her vision had become a haze of shadows. But she knew them by their auras—Sergeant McGrady, Sweet Tom Reedling, and Brandon. The men from Hawick stood around her too, all save George Gresham.

What would they do without the steward? She ignored the deeper part of her that wondered whether the question had become moot for her. Her wounds were grievous. She had seen that in Gaelyph's expression. She knew the fading pain, the numbness, was not a good sign. Yet she still drew breath, and she refused to abandon her friends without hope.

She delved into the steward's aura, probing for the traces of light she had known for these years since their first encounter on the shores of Skye. She remembered its immense strength, like that of a stag who stood with antlers reaching the heavens. But a coldness had come to its normal cheer. It no longer felt as of a hearth. The vast, boggy mire it had become stretched larger than a sea. Dead things floated there, stuck within its filmy grasp. She brought the image to mind, to help her make sense of what she felt.

But the image warped. It spun, making her dizzy, and she found herself curled on the ground beneath the boughs of a giant oak. She had seen it before and knew its limbs. Mistletoe draped along its bark. A familiar fey woman in a shimmering silver tunic perched in the large hollow of its trunk. Lines of age gave a noble cast to her sharp features.

"You have lost," said the Barrow Witch.

"I am dying," Effie replied, though she felt no fear or sorrow in the statement. "If I was to be your prized possession, perhaps it is you who have failed."

The Barrow Witch's face lit up in amusement. She chortled and rubbed her hands together. "Oh, that is good, my child, and bittersweet."

Effie stood and raised her chin, glaring at the fey woman. "Have you come for your thunderstones? The one Tallia wielded is where she dropped it when she died, as you must already know. But the other—you will not have its location from me."

The Barrow Witch's expression remained amused. But her silence made Effie wonder. She had assumed the Sidhe Bhreige had first come to her out of anger years before, threatening with vengeance after the defeat of her brethren. Her second attempt, after the capture of Cyrus Reed, had likewise been meant to instill fear. But their encounters afterward had changed. While meddling with *Les Revinirs* and again in Aberdeen, the Sidhe Bhreige had sought her as a willing ally, or at least as a captured pet.

It made no sense that she would present herself to Effie now, unless it was to gloat. Yet Effie couldn't fathom her demise mattered so greatly. The fey woman had much larger concerns to consider—unless.

Effie's mind raced. "You fear some knowledge I possess," she said. "That is why you have come to threaten me, and me alone, these many months." She held no ability of Fey Craft that would warrant the attention. Almost all fey besides Clara Bowman knew more tricks of fey blood than herself.

"Tsk, child. Do not consider yourself special. I coveted your betrayer's blood, nothing more," said the Barrow Witch. She cast her gaze aside, indifferently. "The steward was a fool to trust it. In time, you would have seen him for the puppet he was and come begging to join me. But that matters not, presently."

Effie saw through the lie. It rang with a self-serving hollowness. The Laird of Aonghus had made such proclamations. He had demanded her allegiance as her would-be savior. But, in truth, he had only sought the strength of her fey blood to add to his host. She sucked in a quick breath. Grasping onto the strands of that thought, she took a step back and clutched at the hem of her dress.

A dress! The feel of the fabric made her start. She had not been wearing the green, woolen frock on the hilltop. *We are one. Our history is shared.* Caledon's words of comfort returned to her. They bolstered the idea germinating within her. She reached out her hand. A cane appeared in her grasp. Jack Canonbie's cane. She smiled. The weight of the cane gave an anchor to her thoughts, a sense of certainty. The Barrow Witch might hold more power than she, and have centuries' greater knowledge, but that did not alter the fact that they shared a common ancestry. Just as in Aberdeen, that meant she could manipulate whatever Fey Craft the Barrow Witch worked to trap them in this dream state.

Effie pulled at the giant oak, forcing it to unravel like a spool of yarn. A prism of colors whirled around them and in its place, a ring of stanes rose. Between the stanes, grass sprouted, thick and wild. The horizon filled with scattered forest and rolling field. An earthen scent filled the air along with a heavy dampness. The effort made her queasy, and she could not shake the notion that the place was not hers to control.

Removed from her perch in the hollow, the Barrow Witch floated to the trampled grass. Her eyebrow raised. "The hour is late for you to play at childish games."

As she spoke, hooded crows popped into existence. They flooded the fields and grass. They flocked through the sky, squawking and swooping in circles.

"I have no need for games," said Effie. "I have uncovered your secret, the reason for your fear. The knowledge I possess."

The fey woman cackled. The noise sounded similar to that of Tallia. "You have not the Fey Craft, nor the wits, to invoke fear."

Striding closer, Effie planted the cane before her. Crows fluttered to rest on her shoulders and atop the cane. "We are all of a shared blood, but I am a Grundbairn."

The Barrow Witch's eyes narrowed to tiny slits. "Do you think that matters now?"

The defiance gave Effie courage. "Even with the strength of the steward's blood, I could not have scoured the whole of the empire to find you. It would have taken years and been like uncovering an iron bit in a sea of steel. But I no longer need to scour such a large area, do I?" Her muscles pulled taut. She knew she gambled, yet she managed to keep her voice firm. "You are near the Eildon Hills, perhaps close to the tree of the usurper, as you called the Queen of Elphame." She had deduced as much when speaking with Sweet Tom Reedling.

The Sidhe Bhreige clucked her tongue. "Clever child, well done." Her gaze slid to the side once more. "A pity for your friends you will not survive long enough to divine the exact location before your steward leads my host into the fey realm."

Effie flinched. She could not imagine such a thing. She ran a hand along the cane. Missing chips and rough notches gouged its once smooth surface. Each reminded her of its previous owner, and of his sacrifice. Jack Canonbie had plunged himself into danger so she remained unharmed. Her head tilted. Her smile broadened, mouth parting in wonder. What she must do shone before her like a beacon that blotted out the sun. The answer had been within her all along. She did not question it. She knew in her heart it was right.

"No," she said. "I don't believe he will do any such thing. I was wrong. You do not fear I will uncover your dank lair. The knowledge I possess is something older, something from the time of Righm and Bhreige."

A fitting end—the blood of the steward having its revenge. Tallia's proclamation would prove more right than she would ever know. But it was the grindylow's final act that now fixed in Effie's thoughts. Tallia had not unleashed her fury on Effie. She had used the last of her breath to assault Caledon. The act made no sense unless she had cause to believe the steward was not fully tied to the Unseily Court.

Or unless such a thing could be reversed.

"We are one." Effie spoke aloud the steward's words. "It is a simple truth not much thought on these days. Our blood and history are shared. And so are our auras. It is the basis of all Fey Craft."

The Barrow Witch's eyes widened. Effie saw a hint of doubt creep into them as the world around her burst into flame. The hooded crows took wing, a whirlwind of black and brown feathering against the flicker of purple and blue fire. Their flapping beat back the crackling blaze and buffeted Effie with a cool breeze.

Shoots of gnarled bramble sprang up around the stanes. Their barbs were sharp as steel. They dripped with a sickly yellow ichor. The bramble wove together, forming a thick web overhead. The crows squawked and fluttered in its wake. Where the shoots closed in a tangled mesh, scores of the birds disappeared.

The light of the sun followed. The web of bramble became an oppressive weight that hung down like the ceiling of a cave. Dripping yellow ichor kissed the ground. The grass sizzled and died.

Effie barely noticed. She had lost sight of the Barrow Witch, but whatever Fey Craft the Sidhe Bhreige used to present herself in this dream state mattered little. Effie had to focus on the pain of her wounds, the real wounds she had suffered from the burst of stardust. She had to wake herself, as the sharp scent of Salt of Hartshorn had in Aberdeen.

The ground at her feet turned to water. She plunged into its depths. The shock of it made her gasp, and she gulped in a mouthful and choked. Her arms flailed. Her legs kicked. The water tasted putrid. It was thick with peat and decaying root and weed.

She scolded herself. *The pain, focus on it*. She stopped struggling and let herself sink. She had no need to breathe. Not anymore.

A dull ache spread along her back. Its throbbing seemed a distant figment of her imagination. She pulled at the sensation, and it started to burn.

Vines lashed onto her arms and legs. They slid around her like eels. She let them yank her limbs and slice through her flesh. That pain meant nothing. It wasn't real, only the effects of the Barrow Witch's dream-like glamour.

Underwater, the world turned pitch black. The darkness helped her concentrate. She pulled at the burning that ran along her arms and across her chest, stoking it like she would a hearth fire. Its bite grew sharper, but still she did not wake.

She knew the young orphaned lass she had once been, cold and frail and lost in the world, would have panicked. The woman she had grown to be these past years yearned to rail against the Barrow Witch's tricks, to rage alone even as friends surrounded her. But she was no longer either of those past selves. They had been born of mistrust, and she had finally learned a simple truth. Better yet, she had come to believe in it. She was not alone and never had been.

Her blood had given her that gift since the moment of her birth.

A new thought came to her. Straining, she listened. The sound came from a great distance at first. But as she focused on its rhythm, it neared. An inhale. An exhale. Other sounds joined the breathing—the creak of leather harnesses, the stomp of boots trying to warm cold feet, and the quiet murmur of concerned voices.

Effie focused on them all. Her bodily pain returned with a fierce intensity. It made her cringe and cry out. A gentle hand found her leg, the pressure meant to keep her still. The touch, warm and caring, yanked her from the dream. Her eyes snapped open.

"Effie." Gaelyph's voice drifted to her as her vision focused.

She wheezed through a raw throat. The hand belonged to the warden. He pulled it back and studied her with a concerned gaze. She ignored him. She didn't have time to be thankful. She hadn't time to debate her intentions. Caledon lay next to her, and if she had any chance to save him, she dared not focus on anything else.

Delving into the steward, she sought through the mire of his aura, peeling back the sense of him layer by layer until she found a spark of life. The steward himself had taught her how to accomplish such a feat. He had guided her to do the same with Jack Canonbie. Her grandfather had also done the same, all those years ago. Blood Craft, she had assumed the trick to be—something foul and wicked. But she understood now what it meant to be of a people, one with shared blood and gifts of great power born of community.

What power that could lend.

"Wh...what are you doing?" The warden stammered the question. His eyes widened. "You cannot!"

Effie barely heard the words. She had been right. She had surmised the Barrow Witch's fears correctly. The steward's life force glowed like an ember, but something shrouded it, dampening its vigor. The taint of the Unseily Court.

She plucked at the shroud. But it was like plucking threads from a scrap of cloth—pluck too many strands, and nothing would remain. The steward's life force dimmed as she worked, coming ever closer to winking out.

She had been right about that as well. Clara Bowman had said the Fey Craft of creating Unseily involved consuming the blood of innocent fey. It made a perverse sense that its reversal would likewise require as great a cost. Oddly, the knowledge did not upset her. She no longer mistrusted. She would place faith in her friends and welcome the faith they placed in her. She was ready. All it would take was her life.

Reaching within, she delved to the core of her own being. An ember flickered there, similar to the steward's. Its pulse was not as great as it had once been; its heat would barely rival that of a candle. It had shrunk to nothing more than a speck and seemed as if the slightest puff of wind would snuff it out.

She hoped it would be enough. Jack Canonbie's ember had been as faint, and it had proven sufficient. Her body trembled at the memory. It came to her in a sadness of what might have been.

Bracing herself, she ripped at the steward's shrouded ember, snuffing out all that was tainted, pulling loose the final threads. At the same time, she plucked free her own ember and shoved it into the steward.

❧ 28 ❧

Effie did not expect to ever wake again. She had nothing left to sustain her. She had given up her life force, her ember, to save Caledon. The choice had been easily made, and her certainty unflinching. She had not allowed herself any hope of rescue or revival. There was no need. She was content. She had done, in a sense, the same that her grandfather, Arnwyrd, had done so many years before. She had made a choice to save one life over another. That he had chosen to take a steward's life, and she to save one, brought on her a small amount of irony.

She would never learn how the Seily Court would judge her, nor the empire. She only hoped both survived long enough for there to be such a judgement.

Water babbled over stone. She cocked her ear to it, noticing for the first time that the earth felt damp and soft beneath her. Thin muck sluiced through her fingers as she clutched her hands into fists. Her head pounded. Her throat was parched. She wondered at both and blinked, startled, as if the memory of such sensations were a foreign thing.

A stone wall lay near her feet. Its height was slight and ran in a broken line before ending in a jagged gap. The breach allowed her sight of the river where the water lapped along a reedy bank.

Leather and wool rustled. A figure dropped to a knee beside her. The man's face was shadowed, but she would recognize its shape anywhere. He no longer wore his arm in a sling but kept the limb loosely pressed against his side.

"Conall!" She sprang up and buried her face into his dark curls. She ignored the pounding in her head and ache of her shoulders, though neither felt as sharp as she thought they should. Running her arms around his coat, she clung to his warmth. Tears blossomed in her eyes. A part of her refused to believe him real, but no dream or memory could ever replace him so fully.

Guilt followed her elation. It balled in her gut, and she realized the regret that ate at her from their last parting. She shifted, and he must've read her expression.

"For a later time," he whispered.

Pulling back, he rose and helped her to her feet. From her higher vantage, she saw the stone wall was part of a castle that sprawled in ruin atop the riverbank. Tufts of grass sprang amid the tumbled stone. Where it sometimes sprouted higher, it buried any evidence of the once-mighty fortress.

Her wounds felt newly healed, the flesh numb and joints stiff, but they brought her only a slight discomfort. The marvel of it rushed through her, followed by a jolt. She remembered what had transpired at the nine stanes. "Caledon?" she asked, bracing herself for despair.

"With the duke in Hawick," said Conall.

The response made her dizzy, and he grabbed her arms to keep her from stumbling. She shook her head. "But how? I...I don't understand."

"You showed us the way," came a new voice. Gaelyph leaned heavily on Jack Canonbie's cane. His face appeared sallow. His eyes ringed with dark lines. "I was wrong, as wrong as I've never been before."

Effie broke from Conall's grip and strode with a wobbling step to the warden. She saw behind the fey the ginger tresses of Ana and Rose, and the plump cheeks and high collar of Freiherr Jörg. Her friends approached, beaming in delight.

"The steward is no longer Unseily?" she asked. "The taint is removed?"

"Aye," the warden answered, "but that is not of which I speak." He ducked his head in deference. "I should never have doubted the steward's wisdom. You are no outcast of our Seily Court, Effie of Glen Coe."

Effie relaxed at the proclamation, as if some hidden part of her could finally release a tension that had built up since the moment of her first breath. Her hands found her hips. Her foot began to tap. Another riddle came to mind.

"You hid the crows from Tallia," she said. She recalled her surprise at their sudden appearance. At the time, she hadn't considered the warden would do such a thing for her benefit.

His lips tugged into a grin. "I did, but it was for you they came. I had no part in their calling."

A pair of throats cleared. Effie laughed, but her mirth waned as she turned her attention to the ginger-tressed women. Their complexion was as sallow as Gaelyph's. Ana's posture, normally stiff and militant, sagged, as if with age. Rose merely hugged herself to the autumn-colored shawl she'd wrapped about her shoulders.

"The warden has finally discovered what the rest of us have known for truth, though it be scrawled on his head the entire time," said Ana. "Men, eh?"

Gaelyph ducked his head in acknowledgement and gave no reply. It was Conall who blustered. "I have...from the start. I..." But his voice trailed off at Ana's raised eyebrow. Freiherr Jörg shuffled his feet and studied his clasped hands.

"It matters not," said Effie. "You saved me at a cost greater than I could ever ask." The words tumbled out as understanding dawned. She had solved the riddle of the Unseily. Their taint needed the consumption of another's blood. In reverse, the Fey Craft of restoration involved the willingness of others to give. She took in her friends and had to strain to keep her knees from crumbling once again. "All of you." She shook her head. "But without Caledon..."

"You saved him," answered Rose. "With his steward's strength we were able to save you." She strode forward and embraced Effie. She smelled of her namesake and a hint of honey. "You have a part of us in you now, each as much as we could give."

Effie's throat tightened. She clung to the woman who had become like a mother to her. Her friends had risked themselves for her before, but this was something more. They had given a part of themselves, their very essence, to rescue her from death. She had no words to express her gratitude. She doubted she would ever find any, so simply embraced each in turn. Their blood had always joined them, and now the life force of their auras did as well.

"What of Clara Bowman?" She felt guilty to ask.

"We will save those others we can in a similar fashion," said Gaelyph. "When we can." He rested a hand on his sword's pommel. "But presently we are to answer the steward's call to arms. We are the vanguard—we here at Roxburgh and the regiment of queen's soldiers mustered in Kelso."

"Eildon Hills, Caledon heard you whisper, and it is to there he has bade the duke to march his army," said Conall.

"The army will take time," said Ana. "We are closer."

"Yes," Effie agreed. She swung her gaze between her friends. "We must hurry. The Barrow Witch waited on Tallia to return with Caledon before beginning her invasion of Elphame. It was only Tallia's hatred of me that has delayed the Sidhe Bhreige. She will act swiftly now that Caledon is hers no longer."

"Effie," said Rose. Her tone held a hint of warning. "The Eildon Hills are not such large slopes, and none too distant from Melrose, as to hide an army of Unseily from plain sight."

A flitter of doubt crept into Effie. Had the Barrow Witch played yet another trick? She tried to recall the fey woman's exact words, but it was another's who came to her unbidden. *Find the darkest crypt beneath a shadowed hill.* Jonas, the fey of *Les Revinirs* that had remained true to Cecily McCray, had spoken the words upon her death. Her foot began to tap.

"We seek a barrow," she said. "A fey hill infested by Unseily and those twisted to their will. The Barrow Witch may be full of tricks, but I saw her hesitation. If she is not at Eildon, she is close." She met Rose's gaze. "Close enough for a Grundbairn to uncover, now that the area is not so large to roam."

Reaching out her hands, she closed her eyes. Ana took her right palm and Rose her left. They need not touch for the Fey Craft to work, but Effie cherished the warmth of the contact. She sensed Conall join the circle by his aura, and Freiherr Jörg and Gaelyph. Those of fey blood offered themselves to her, and she pulled at their strength, linking with them and binding their auras to her own.

The sensation felt like being doused in icy water. It made her giggle to know her aura was merely a collection of theirs to begin with. She hoped for time later to wonder whether that had changed her in any tangible way. She trusted Jaelyn would let her know, when she saw the brownie again. Her friend was never one to hold her tongue.

The strength of fey blood pulsing within her, Effie quested once more for those that took wing in the neighboring hills. To lapwings and rooks, hooded crows and woodland grouse, she called. She beckoned them to scour the hillsides and cry warning of any creatures they found.

Birds rustled in the reeds near the riverbank. They chirped from the trees lining the higher ground and squawked as they looped on updrafts high above. Effie roamed with her senses, picking out those who sent impressions of alarm.

A mile distant, a crossbill, slight and swift, panicked over the presence of a red fox. Along the river, a grouse had lost track of its young. Here and there, the crows told of roving packs of men and women—those who'd fallen prey to the banshee's touch, Effie had no doubt. But it was to the south and east of the Eildon Hills that seized her attention. There, the crows and sparrows alerted her to the presence of giant birds larger than a cottage, and of a teeming mass of horned pigs, hairy men, and oversized goats that strode on their haunches.

Effie opened her eyes. She had finally found the Barrow Witch.

❧ 29 ❧

Effie blew out a breath to steady her nerve. She ran a hand along Jack Canonbie's cane, gazing as she did across an open field at an ancient hillfort made of three concentric rings. The largest and lowest sprawled as wide as Edinburgh Castle and ran as long as three New Town city blocks. Each ring had been hewn from an existing hill by men and women long forgotten, perhaps even from the days of the Sidhe Bhreige. They were overgrown and undulating, yet their form remained visible to the naked eye.

The hillfort bustled with Unseily. Bogills stood sentry in camps along the host's flanks. They were dressed for war. Leather jerkins covered their hairy chests. A few sported wooden bucklers, and some even heavier rounded shields. They carried a mismatched assortment of rough-hewn clubs, fine broadswords, and short spears.

Trows and wulvers roamed here and there, the former in their way of almost dancing, and the latter prowling as if ready for the hunt. Spriggans, the troll-like imps Effie had encountered at Caldwell House, rode their tusked pigs as goblins scurried through the shadowed grass. Other creatures unknown to her filled out the host in a mass of sharp ears, fangs, and tusks.

The grunting snorts and clang of metal made Effie wonder why the host still kept their auras hidden. The clamor would be heard for near a mile distant. But she did not have to wonder for long. She realized the obscuring was not to hide where the host gathered, as much as what gathered within it.

Atop the hillfort, a pack of beasts emerged into sight. "Oversized goats," she said, remembering the impression the crows and sparrows had sent. Blinking, she strained her eyes. She had faced down giants, but never had she witnessed such an intimidating foe. The beasts stood twice the height of a man and half again as broad. Large, clawed feet supported legs as thick as trees. Like the bogills, coarse hair coated their limbs in a pelt. Only theirs was white, more suited for blending against a snowy field than a Scottish bog. Their faces were scrunched and rounded, their arms long and dangly, capped by paws that would smother her face.

"Thurs, they are called," said Rose. She stood next to Effie with her arms folded beneath her chest. "I have heard tale of them from the huldrefolk in Norway." She nodded to another creature a few spans away from the beasts. "Och, and there I spy an ogress from the Bordeaux region, if the cut of her tunic be any indication."

"France and Norway," said Effie. She took in the ogress, who stood almost as tall and stout as the thurs, only with considerably less hair. Wisps sprouted from her broad pate. The flesh beneath held a greenish tint. "The continent has come to join the Barrow Witch."

"Nay," replied Freiherr Jörg. The gnome tugged at his high collar and smoothed his beard. He stood on the other side of Effie. "The barrow witch has no such strength to bespell them all. Not yet. These be fiends of foul blood, too few to stand against their own courts in their own lands."

The Unseily host did not look few to Effie. She could count a hundred of them for each finger and still need another hand—perhaps a pair—to tally them all. But she held her tongue. Her friends did not need to be told the disposition of their foe. They could see it for themselves. They stood around her at the edge of a crofter's field. Where the crofter or his family had gone, none could say. But by the disrepair of the squat stone cottage, Effie guessed the place long abandoned.

Gaelyph hissed. "They have a pair of redcaps among them. I can

sense their foul blood even with their auras obscured." The warden's
hands flexed and curled into fists.

Clomping boots drew Effie's attention. Sergeant McGrady had
returned. At the mention of redcaps, his face soured, mustache drooping
as his cheeks puckered.

"Lieutenant Walford sends his regards," he said. He gave a curt nod
to Effie before turning his attention back to the hillfort. "The men are in
position, but the advantage is not in our favor. Word has been sent that
several airships are landed on the far side of the encampment. We are
outnumbered, outgunned, and will be assaulting from the lower ground."
He clapped his hands together and rubbed them against the cold. "This
is not to mention what the barrow witch might do to spread her madness
among the men."

"You are right," said Effie. She turned to him and leaned on her cane.
"If we could wait for the duke to arrive, we would."

"The Unseily can sense us, each and every one," said Rose. "That they
do not come tells us they are preparing to invade Elphame."

"Or that they do not consider us a threat," said the sergeant.

"We will break through and delay them," said Gaelyph. The warden's
sword scraped free of its scabbard. He judged the light. The sun was
hidden behind a bank of dark clouds, but a few rays painted a golden hue
to the sky. Still, the day had turned cold and promised a freezing night.

Freiherr Jörg drew himself rigid. "Allow the Order of Freiwald to lead
the charge. It would give us great honor."

It was not the first time the wizened gnome had made the request,
but the Order's talents in Fey Craft were needed far more than the
accuracy of the bell-shaped blunderbusses they carried. Effie was about
to remind the elder fey as much when the echo of rifle reports rattled
across the fields. The assault had begun.

Effie thought first of Conall. The man, lacking a place among
professional soldiers and fey, had volunteered to act as a runner for the
lieutenant. She couldn't deny him his willingness to fight, but her chest
pulled tight all the same. She would rather he had fled to Hawick, or
even to Edinburgh, than to be far from her sight on a field of battle.

She couldn't spy the lieutenant's position from where she stood, but
she could hear it. He had taken his some fifty men and spread them in a

copse of pine and birch opposite a part of the hillfort he judged the soldiers could easily scale. The crackle and pop of their opening volley waned. It was replaced by shouts of command and a chorus of bellowed war cries.

The rifle fire had ripped through a group of bogills, felling perhaps a dozen. The Unseily nearest the assault frenzied. Sharp, high-pitched cries came from the trows. The wulvers howled and raced as a pack down the slopes of the hillfort. The remaining bogills lumbered after them, barking at one another and screaming curses in a hodgepodge of continental languages.

"There! They are linking," said Rose. She pointed atop the hillfort. Three grindylows had appeared. They stood studying the lieutenant's woodland cover.

Effie marveled at her friend. It reminded her once again how much skill in Fey Craft she had yet to master. Opening her senses, she allowed Rose to join with her. She ignored the frigid sensation and weaved what she imagined was a tangle of vines. Yet no sooner had Rose pushed the vines toward the grindylows than Effie felt the familiar weeds and thorns of the Unseily. Effie ripped and tore at them, starting to pant from the effort.

Rose was smarter. She burned. Tiny flames flickered around her in a defensive swarm, setting to light the Barrow Witch's attack. Effie cursed herself a fool and mimicked the flames. Born of Fey Craft, the flames and burning weeds produced no smoke and left no smoldering remains. Both simply vanished from thought, as if they'd never been.

Sergeant McGrady hollered. He gave no reaction to the struggle of Fey Craft. He could neither see nor sense it. But he had spied the trows and wulvers who surged across the field toward them. A few bogills joined them, their bucklers and basket-hilted broadswords waving wildly as they charged.

The sergeant drew his pistol but did not fire. Their foe was still too far distant for the accuracy of the weapon. Instead, the man put a whistle to his lips and shrilled a single, long blast. From near the crofter's cottage came the reply. A dozen riflemen stood at the ready, flanked by a pair of gnomes from the Order of Freiwald.

Effie watched the blur of red coats hustle past. Metal clinked and boots thumped as the men formed ranks. She spotted Brandon's familiar face among them, but of Sweet Tom Reedling, she saw no sign.

Sergeant McGrady barked an order. Rifles snapped into firing positions. Barely had the sergeant grunted the command than did the air near Effie explode. The tang of gun smoke filled her nostrils. She flinched at the fury of the volley. Bullets hissed. They whistled across the field and thunked into flesh.

The charge of Unseily slowed, but it did not turn back. Effie glanced toward Lieutenant Walford's position. Red coats spotted the tree line, but none had crossed the ground to the hillfort.

"What is keeping them? They must advance!" she cried above the din. Her gaze swung back to where the thurs gathered near the grindylows. The giant beasts roared and thumped their chests but made no move to join in the fight. The collection of spriggans and bogills and wulvers around them remained equally as motionless.

Waving at the sergeant, she stepped forward. "If we do not engage those atop the hill, they will be in Elphame before the duke arrives!"

"We have no field guns to reach them," shouted the sergeant. He met her gaze with uncertainty but pulled straighter as he realized her intentions. His eyes hardened as he took her in. His mouth clamped shut, and he nodded.

Effie did not wait for his command. She hefted her cane and started forward. Gaelyph and Freiherr Jörg strode at her sides. Rose, she knew, would remain near the cottage. But she felt the fey woman still linked with her. Together, they pushed back the onslaught from the grindylows in a silent struggle.

A thought came to Effie. "Call down your glamours on the hilltop," she said to Freiherr Jörg.

The gnome looked at her askance. "The Unseily will know them for a trick."

"Yes," she agreed. Peering over her shoulder at the soldiers fanning out behind her, she grinned. She almost felt her eyes twinkle. "But they will not. Give them something to encourage victory."

Freiherr Jörg's eyes did twinkle with mischief, though he didn't break stride. A rumble built overhead. The clouds began to swirl. Effie's flesh prickled at the power of the glamour. The winds gusted. Static built in the air.

The sky crackled with energy, splitting apart in a slash of brilliant white. The lightning forked as it struck along the hilltop, its thunderous boom deafening. Those above barely moved, but that did not lessen the effect among the soldiers. They cheered in wonder and broke into a trot, rifles leveled.

Effie let them pass before speeding her own pace. Rifles cracked before her as lightning slashed and thunder boomed. Wulvers yelped as bullets tore through them, flinging them aside. But still they came.

The bogills outpaced their trow cohorts. One reached the soldiers and swung a thick blade. His target scrambled aside and only barely managed to bring his rifle up in defense. Steel clunked into wood. Before the bogill could swing again, another of the queen's men shot him in the back.

It pained Effie to know the bogill might be an unwilling fey. Whether each Unseily they encountered was like Tallia or Clara Bowman, they had no means to uncover. But Effie could not let the guilt distract her. She knew well enough it was a price they would have to pay, and hers the lesser.

She wished they'd time to decipher Tallia's thunderstone. What she would give to be able to hurl stardust at the grindylows above! As she drew closer to the base of the hillfort, she spied more of them. They had crawled out from some dank hole, no doubt, the same as where their master hid.

Gaelyph's sword whirled before her. The blade slashed through a wulver who'd tried to backpedal on its hind legs. Its snarl vanished as it toppled over. The warden's blade kept its arc and glanced off the leather jack of a bogill.

A pistol popped. The bogill grunted and dropped to its knees. Effie barely had time to take in the sergeant before a trow leapt before her. She swung her cane with both hands. The trow darted aside. Its narrow eyes pulled wide, ears flopping like a rabbit's as it bounded around her.

Swinging again, her arms rattled as she connected. The trow swayed in a daze. Effie spun the cane and drove the tip of it into the thing's chest. As she did, the trow's aura popped into her awareness. A flood of the Unseily followed. She flinched at the suddenness of the host's presence. Her footing slipped, but she caught herself.

A cold bead of dread ran down her spine. She could think of only one reason the Unseily would unmask themselves. They prepared the invasion.

Her legs churned. She blurred past a bogill. A pair of wulvers chased at her heels. She was only vaguely aware of Gaelyph hounding after, sword slashing out, keeping the beasts at bay.

As fast as she rushed, she knew she would not reach the grindylows in time. If they had begun the invasion, the hilltop would be empty by the time she reached the second ring. The battle would rage in Elphame, and the Barrow Witch would no doubt slink into whatever hole she desired and vanish until victory was hers.

Something flitted past her vision. Effie didn't make sense of it until a second spear landed at her feet. Its haft was thin and short, and tipped by crude stone. She skipped aside to avoid impaling herself. Gaelyph knocked into her. Grunting, she sprawled, landing hard.

Spears rained down from above. She heard the spriggans cackling in delight as they set about their work. The warden grabbed her shoulders and yanked her back onto her feet.

"We must reach the protection of the slope!" he shouted. He breathed heavily. His face was pale. He had not yet recovered from saving her.

She muttered no reply but scurried forward, an arm futilely raised to protect herself. The dread she felt pounded within her. With every glance above, she thought she saw less of the Unseily host gathered. But the angles had changed. The host moved, warping and flexing in her line of sight. She could not tell for certain they had gone, and she convinced herself not to abandon hope.

Lightning flashed, blinding her. Spears fell like raindrops. The clap of thunder and rattle of distant rifle fire mixed with bellows and cries of alarm. Effie no longer smelled gunpowder and wondered if that meant Sergeant McGrady's soldiers had fallen. If she tried to glance back, she knew she would tumble, so she kept going forward.

It wasn't until she reached the embankment of the hillfort that she realized her hands were empty. She had left Jack Canonbie's cane where she had sprawled. There was nothing for it but to carry on. She could not go back for it.

Pressing herself against the grassy slope, she craned her neck upward. Something struck her in the forehead. She flinched, trembling, until she recognized its icy kiss. It was a snowflake.

30

Freiherr Jörg's glamours had masked the approaching storm. Snowflakes swirled in the wind, melting where they kissed the ground. With her back turned against the embankment of the hillfort, Effie saw Sergeant McGrady and his men. Less than a handful remained upright. Those formed a line just out of reach from the falling spears. Bullets whistled past as they fired at the spriggans and other Unseily above her head.

Far across the field, she heard the roar of a charge. Lieutenant Walford's soldiers broke free of the tree line and surged across the grassy span to the base of the hillfort. They were met with spears and hurled rocks, but their numbers kept the advance. Smoke burst in puffs from the gnomes' blunderbusses. Whistles shrilled. Red coats clumped and spread out like ants falling on biscuit crumbs.

Effie strained to spy Conall, but as well spot a midge from the far bank of a loch. She scoured for his aura, her concern welling. But the effort left her open. She had to abandon it.

Weeds born of Fey Craft snatched at her. She flicked fire at them deftly and without thought. They hissed as they singed and shriveled away. She allowed Rose to consume the bulk of her strength of blood.

The elder fey woman worked what tricks she could, but Effie could spare no attention for them.

Soon! The sending from Rose startled Effie with its ferocity. It stole what little warmth she had left. Soon the Unseily host would invade Elphame and join in battle there. She imagined the lords of London would consider the fate just—a fey end to a fey problem. But the Barrow Witch would not stop there. With Elphame conquered, her host would stand large enough to sweep through the empire and spread across the continent. To allow her Elphame was to allow her all of Europe and more.

A trickle of blood ran along Effie's arm. She hadn't felt the cut and knew not whether it came from spear or scrape. She fixated on the bead's progress and let it form her thoughts. Pressing both palms against the embankment, Effie closed her eyes and delved. She caressed the thin yet hardy roots of the grassy slope, felt the moist soil beneath, and deeper still the tiny channels of water that fed life into the flora.

If she could pull more water into the roots, perhaps she could bend the grass to her will. She had done such a thing before, in Glasgow. But she had now neither the strength of Caledon's blood, nor the sacrifice of Jack Canonbie.

The water seeped meekly toward her. Her arms shook from the effort. Her heart thumped against her breast. The world spun, and she gasped, collapsing against the embankment.

It would not work. The hillfort was too large, her need too great.

But she had sensed something buried beneath the roots and rock and earth. It was something she hadn't fathomed would exist there, but something she could use to her advantage, if given the chance.

"Along here," said Gaelyph. He didn't wait for her reply. He set off along the embankment, hugged against its grassy protection.

Effie followed. Exhausted from her delving, she stumbled the first few steps, fighting the urge to slump to the ground. She found one of the spriggans' spears and grabbed onto it. It had not the sturdiness of the cane, but it returned a steadiness to her.

The warden led them to a place where the slope of the embankment lessened. They scaled quickly and mounted the level area atop the first ring of the hillfort. The path there was wide enough for perhaps three abreast before the slope resumed its climb toward the height of the second ring.

Wulvers streaked toward them. Effie took in the slit of yellow eyes and slathered fangs as the things barreled past spriggans and goblins. Their legs churned low and fast to the ground.

Soon. They could not scale any higher. The wulvers would tear them down from behind if they tried. *We are too late.*

Effie braced herself. She levelled the flimsy spear. The lead wulver leapt. She ducked under it and thrust the spear beneath its ribs. Its claws raked her shoulder. Fire burned where it touched.

The impact knocked her down. The spear snapped from her grip. She kicked and punched, her hands meeting coarse fur and her feet hard bone. One of the creatures rose to its hind legs and leered over her. Delving into its mind, she ripped at the binds of its Unseily masters. She flooded it with images of greater prey—of thick deer and fat hares. Those, it wanted, not her, she tried to convince the wulver.

It faltered, turning its head aside and sniffing the air.

The weeds of Fey Craft slithering from the grindylows surged. The strands doubled, growing thicker, their thorns sharper. Effie cried out from the phantom pain. Her bursts of fire could not keep the weeds at bay.

Soon! Effie gritted her teeth. Her cries became a growling challenge. Anger flared from an inner part of her. How could the Unseily enter Elphame when even she knew not the way? *No,* she corrected herself. She had not been allowed the way. She had been barred, the secret kept from her because she had not been trusted.

Not as the grindylows, once Sithlings of the Seily Court, had been.

Her breath caught. "Fool lass." She spat the words. The fire of her wounds dulled as the chill of the falling snow numbed her flesh.

Lashing onto one of the thorny weeds, Effie spun strands of her own phantom grass and wove it tight against the shoot. She sensed the grindylow attempt to dissolve the weed, but she would not let go. Snaking her grass strands up the slope, Effie entangled them with the weeds until they had locked into an impenetrable knot.

She had been a fool earlier. She had no need to bend anything to her will other than the grindylows. The Fey Craft of linking and blocking were intertwined. Tallia had unwittingly passed her that knowledge in the bowels of Edinburgh.

Rose understood her gambit, and Effie felt her full blood strength return, bolstered by her friend's own. The rush of sensations surprised her. Within the span of a breath, she could feel each and every living thing atop the hillfort—and beneath it.

The grindylows recoiled. Their snares of weed and thorn shrank back as Effie's grassy tethers surged. But she would not let them go so easily. She had started to sense another Fey Craft at work. With a flicker of thought, her tethers became a sticky web that entangled a dozen of the grindylows. She could feel them ripping and tearing as she had done to counter their assault. Her webs spread and thickened.

The Fey Craft she sensed flexed as if it were a kaleidoscope. Images flashed through her link to the Unseily. A blanket of stars rotated around a silvery moon. Beneath, steep crags gave way to the bowl of a long and narrow glen. The image burst, replaced by that of a rough sea, white caps spraying foam in violent gusts.

An anchor, Effie recalled from what Rose had said at Skye. They sought an anchor into Elphame, the aura of a fey known to at least one of them. That was how the traveling worked.

A rough hand grabbed her by the waist and pulled. She stumbled back a step, only vaguely aware of a sword flashing before her and of the squeal of some creature. Labored breathing reached her ears. Sergeant McGrady had come. The man had lost his helmet and half his mustache. His men fired up the slope to the second ring.

Effie shaped an image, that of an ancient oak. She thought it a fitting device to counter the Barrow Witch's host. Tendrils of moss dripped from its limbs. A deep hollow shadowed its upper trunk. Its leaves had turned a bevy of reds, yellows, and oranges. The tips of its branches swayed under a breeze.

If the Unseily needed to fix on an aura, she would divert them with one of her own.

The oak pulsed through her web, through the link she held tethering the Unseily. The grindylows shoved against her, yanking and ripping at the web strands. Rose worked with her, she could tell, but Effie did not have the elder fey's subtlety. She stood her ground as stubbornly as the tree she conjured. Her body trembled. She panted. Her throat ran dry.

The grindylows fought for their anchor into Elphame. They scraped at the oak, turning it to ash. The glen returned, sprouting in its place. Effie devoured it and regrew the oak. The sea, she drained when it came again. The images the Unseily spun began to imprint in her mind, yet with each cycle her strength waned.

She could not stand against them forever. They were too many. She reached for Freiherr Jörg, but as she did her concentration slipped. Some of her web flared and dissolved into a horde of midges that swarmed about her. They bit her mercilessly. They crawled down her throat as she gasped for air.

The grindylows wove a ward against her. She smashed through it and clutched desperately to the image of the oak. Her limbs felt like stone. She couldn't tell whether hands clutched her, or whether she had tumbled down the embankment. Her ears had numbed to the popping rifle fire, the howls of the wulvers, and the chittering of trows and spriggans.

Soon! Rose's cry of warning pulsed through her. Her heart raced to it. But she focused only on delaying the Unseily. Her friends would come, she trusted.

She had faith in them.

31

E ffie drifted in a haze. She could not tell whether she dreamed. She knew only the pain—the burning in her lungs from gasping, the fire that throbbed along her shoulder where the wulver had rent her flesh, and trickling doubt that weighed heavier with each passing moment, as if she stood at the bottom of an hour glass with specks of sand cascading off her head.

Soon she would suffocate. Soon she would be buried. Her webs of Fey Craft were all but spent. She sensed Rose's strength had dwindled, and every time the gnomes of the Order of Freiwald tried to reach her, they were blasted back until Effie could barely sense they lived at all.

A cry echoed across the hillfort. Effie shuddered in its wake. The cry meant hope. It meant her faith was just. The Scots had come—fey and man alike.

"*Teribus ye teri odin! Teribus ye teri odin!*"

Horns blared. Drums rumbled. The thunder of hooves rattled the ground. A soothing caress washed over Effie as Caledon's blood strength joined with hers. His hand was deft yet made of steel. *Rest.* He sent her the impression of a doe drinking by a hidden pool, having defended its warren. His assault on the grindylows came in a flurry, faster and stronger than Freiherr Jörg's lightning. It was a storm that drove them reeling into submission.

Effie released her grasp on the oak. Clutching at the grass to keep herself from tumbling over, she sank back onto her heels. She expected night to have fallen. She expected for days to have passed. But the sky still held light, and the snow drifted lazily in a thin dusting. She remained atop the first ring of the hillfort.

"They have come," said Gaelyph. The warden stood next to her. Wonder painted his expression.

Effie followed his gaze and took in the duke's army. Ranks of red coats marched in a line that stretched to the horizon. Riders flanked them. On one side rode the queen's cavalry. On the other trotted the men of Hawick with their pendants flapping in the breeze.

Airships slid across the sky, bobbing as gusts knocked against their great balloons. She counted four of them and gasped in bewilderment at their colors. Not all were the queen's. The French airship she had seen in Aberdeen floated among a trio of sleek British gunships. The former was painted blue, with a deck shaped like a long canoe. The gunships bristled with the muzzles of rifles. A pair of crank-guns were mounted on either side of their steel-banded hulls.

Trows and goblins squealed above Effie's head. The clamor along the second ring and hilltop gave evidence to the scurrying of clawed feet and stomping hooves. Spears no longer fell. A roar came, something vicious and untamed.

The gunships made a pass overhead. Their crank-guns burst into action, spitting a hail of fiery lead. Where the bullets landed, Effie could not see, only that the flashing streaks ended atop the hillfort. The gunships banked. Gouts of white smoke billowed from the portholes where their guns were mounted.

Effie turned to Sergeant McGrady and flinched in shock. The man looked to her in question. She saw Brandon and a few of the others doing likewise. Even Gaelyph seemed to hesitate, taking a step neither forward nor back.

They waited on her to instruct them.

She nodded to each in turn. Blood marred their faces from cuts and gouges. Bruises welled. Their uniforms were torn and soiled. Sweat and spent powder hung about them in a cloud of perfume. She stood no different, and yet she would no sooner abandon the hillfort as host a tea for the lords of London. Besides, she had seen what she must do. She had felt it as she delved.

"We use the distraction," she said. "The steward may have the strength to hold back the invasion of Elphame, but we will need to deal with the Barrow Witch herself."

The sergeant nodded. He barked a command, and his men went about their rifles, checking their load and inspecting the weapons. Gaelyph squatted and reached out a hand as the grunting and huffing of Freiherr Jörg reached their small band.

The gnome had abandoned his glamour. He'd slung his blunderbuss over a shoulder and struggled his way to reach the height of the first ring. His cheeks puffed red from the effort, but once mounted, he tugged his coat straight and motioned that he was ready.

Effie eyed the pouch of powder strapped to his belt and grinned. It must've looked devilish, she thought, as a chuckle trickled across the sergeant's men.

"For the fey of Elphame," hollered Brandon.

"For queen and country," Effie replied, to a chorus of cheers.

They followed Gaelyph up the slope of the hillfort's second ring. The way was steeper, the grass slicker from the wet snow. Effie hauled herself with both hands, marveling as she did how the soldiers managed the feat with rifles clutched in their arms.

Above, the gunships had restarted their hammering barrage. But they no longer fired on the hilltop. They engaged a foe some distance from where the Unseily host swarmed, and Effie recalled Sergeant McGrady's report of airships landed on the far side of the hillfort.

Taking a moment to catch her breath, Effie eyed the gunships' line of fire. The enemy airships were no longer landed, she judged. But there was nothing she could do to aid or hinder their involvement. She returned to climbing, clawing her way up and digging in with her boots.

They had almost reached the lip of the ring when the head of a trow popped into view. Its ears flopped and eyes went wide as it screeched. A dozen of its cohorts joined the first. Their squat snouts twitched as they hopped back and forth flinging rocks down the slope.

Effie gasped. Her mouth ran dry. She ducked her head. The rocks thunked into the grass and sailed far below. A few struck the soldiers, and one man lost his purchase on the slope. He flailed as he slipped. Effie reached out, but his weight was too great. He smacked into her arm and tumbled past, landing hard against the flat surface of the first ring top.

Yelping, Effie snatched the arm in close and waited for the numbness to pass. A rock clapped off her back and sent a jolt down her spine. She gritted her teeth. A snarl escaped her lips, and she surged upward.

Rifles cracked next to her. The closeness of their fury brought a whine to her ears that drowned out all other noise. One of the trows bounced snout over heels past her. Another simply slumped to the grass and slid.

The assault of rocks lessened. Effie shook the ringing from her ears, clearing them just as a deep thump boomed from the direction of the approaching army. She whipped her head in time to see the rings of smoke billowing from the cannon. The device itself she could not see for the distance. Its shot screamed overhead. Chunks of the embankment exploded where it struck, raining down clumps of dirt. The cannon adjusted. Its second shot flew farther, blasting away at the hilltop.

Two more joined the first, but their thumping booms disappeared under a cacophony. Crank-guns rattled high above as the airships swooped and banked. The enemy craft had risen aloft. Their designs reminded Effie of giant bugs with their jaggedly ridged keels, outrigger sails like wings, and pointed battering rams.

Below her position, rifles popped like a crackling fire. The soldiers of the main army had reached the field and begun their advance on the hillfort. Their charge was more orderly than hers had been. They scurried in ragged ranks. Bayonets gleamed at the tips of their rifles.

Effie ducked her head and clambered over the lip of the second ring. She flinched as a wulver barreled down the slope from the hilltop. Brandon shot it before swiveling his rifle down the flat area atop the ring. There, the Unseily scurried in chaos. Some of the trows fled, rocks still in hand. Spriggans waved their spears, crying out some unfathomable taunt. Their porcine mounts squealed and pressed against the shelter of the embankment.

Slipping past the smaller creatures, a group of bogills bounded toward Effie. They didn't make a dozen paces before bullets zipped from below and peppered them to a halt. One shied, raising its buckler, only to be knocked aside by a larger brute. The impact sent it reeling down the slope Effie had just climbed.

Freiherr Jörg's blunderbuss blasted fire from its bell-shaped muzzle. Effie spun in time to see the ogress she'd spied earlier rumbling down from the hilltop. She carried a wicked blade, like a butcher's knife grown ten times too large. Her head was shaped like a melon, with a squat nose and close, beady eyes. Barely a wisp of hair remained to cover her scalp. The greenish tint she bore reminded Effie more of a fungus than moss or leaf. Her stench echoed the impression.

The ogress roared a challenge. A cloud of tumbling rocks and clods of dirt flew in her wake. The swipe of her blade cleaved into a trow and sliced through one of Sergeant McGrady's men. Brandon yanked the poor man back. He raised his rifle barely in time to catch the ogress' next stroke. It clacked off the wood and rattled the weapon from his arms.

"*Verdammt!*" Freiherr Jörg cursed next to Effie. The gnome labored to reload his blunderbuss. Cold dread washed over Effie. She reached a trembling hand toward her friend, ready to shove them both over the embankment and out of the ogress's path.

Gaelyph's sword whirled. But the warden struggled to reach the ogress on the narrow ring top. He could only approach straight on, and the ogress drove him onto his heels.

Fear for the warden constricted Effie's muscles. Her thoughts sprang to Rose, lost in the fighting below, and to Conall—*what had befallen him?* She clamped her hands into fists. Such fear would serve none of them.

Flashes of green and gold and pink swirled past Effie, blinding against the cold grey of the clouded sky. The wee forms of pixies swarmed the ogress, darting in and stabbing with tiny blades like needles. Their squeals sounded like the clamor of tiny bells chiming in fury.

The ogress bellowed, swatting at the wee assailants.

Effie jolted in shock. Her tight muscles melted. She had never seen so many pixies together, not even during the moots at Skye. Watching in awe, she couldn't fathom from whence they came. But come, they had.

She allowed her senses to roam and found that Caledon had brought with him a host of fey she did not recognize.

"The Erbgraf," said Freiherr Jörg. "He has sent allies from the continent to throw back the Unseily." The gnome brought his blunderbuss to bear on the ogress.

"Ana, as well," said Effie. She understood some of the pixies' squeals. The words were French.

The cannons boomed once more. They were closer. Their shot whooshed overhead, thumping into the hilltop. Effie's teeth rattled, and she snapped alert. She could worry over giving thanks later, if she managed to survive.

Gaelyph lunged with his sword. His boot skidded, scraping over ice-encrusted dirt. He caught his balance, but the ogress saw the hesitation. Her meaty fist drew back, blade raised high. As it did, Sergeant McGrady let out a hoarse cry. He stomped into a lumbering charge. His pistol clicked empty in his hand, but he didn't slow.

The pixies renewed their flurry. A pair poked at the ogress' nose and ears. The creature's raised hand came crashing down at them, smashing into the side of her own head. It staggered woozily.

Sergeant McGrady barreled into ogress. The impact flung him aside. He grunted and landed hard.

The ogress toppled. Her arms reached out for purchase but found only empty air and the soft kiss of snowflakes. She made an awful noise, like that of a starved sow, before her weight sent her plummeting down the slope of the hillfort.

Cries rang out from the soldiers below. Rifle fire erupted, but Effie barely registered it. Her attention had been drawn across the fields.

"There!" The soldier next to her pointed. At first Effie saw only the flurry of red coats beneath the light drift of snow. In the distance, along the edge of the horizon, it was difficult to distinguish one man from another. Their shapes blurred and blended, five men becoming one, and then ten. But she saw the struggling, the way their arms flailed at one another, the stomping and thrashing. Her heart sank as she peered. Her dread returned.

The banshee's touch consumed the duke's army.

The madness crawled toward the hillfort in a steady wave. The surge from behind caught those before them unaware. The soldiers pummeled with fists and fired randomly with their rifles. Shouts began to reach her and her companions, some in anger and others in panic.

"More come," said Gaelyph. The warden nodded to Sergeant McGrady before turning his attention to the rise of a hill behind the crofter's cottage. The slight gesture spoke a volume of gratitude and respect.

Brandon helped the sergeant to his feet. "All of Melrose has come." He whistled. "And Selkirk too, by the look of it."

Men and women, young and old, finely dressed and bedraggled, roamed over the hill in an endless mass. They moved like a horde of locusts, having neither direction nor aim. Their minds held no faculty. The banshee's touch had consumed them as fully as those at Hermitage Castle.

Effie's heart had sunk before, but now it seized. She eyed the soldiers of the duke's army. Already, a pitched skirmish consumed half its strength. Its officers had dissipated, enthralled by the same Fey Craft as their riflemen. Those who remained untouched shouted impotently, their cries drowned out by the angry murmur of the Barrow Witch's growing mob.

Feeling for her link with Rose, Effie scoured the mass. The elder fey woman flared a response of desperation. Relief flooded Effie, knowing her friend was unharmed. But panic blossomed with it at the danger Rose now faced. Exhaustion pulled at Effie from the mix of emotions. She ignored it. There was no time. Nor was there time for delicacy. She ripped randomly at the invisible bonds of the banshee's touch, and hoped that none of its victims had been so fully corrupted that they would never recover.

Others joined her. She felt Freiherr Jörg's deft Fey Craft, and the pixies. Some fey she did not know, but a few from Skye she did. Together, they strained and ripped, but those they freed did not run for safety. They merely milled about in a daze until the Barrow Witch's touch found them again.

Panic rose within Effie. It took no military mind to see what the Sidhe Bhreige intended. "They will trap those who escape her touch against the embankment," she said. "They will be caught between the Unseily above and the mob before them."

"Trapped," said Sergeant McGrady. "Nay, they won't hold fire." He ran an unsteady hand through his moustache. "It'll be a massacre."

Gaelyph spoke, but the rattling pop of crank-guns drowned out his words. Bullets zipped past them, kicking up puffs of dirt and thunking into the grass of the embankment. One of the sergeant's men cried out. So did Brandon. The man clutched at a bloody leg.

Effie dove into the grassy slope as one of the duke's gunships drifted lazily overhead. It was low enough she could count the rivets on the steel that banded its wooden hull. Its great balloon sagged. Scorch marks ran along its belly.

"Bollocks!" Sergeant McGrady cursed. The crank-guns continued to spit fire, hammering at the hilltop. The line of destruction raced down the embankment and scattered across the crowded field. Soldiers and townsfolk alike fell before the onslaught.

A smaller airship chased the gunship. Oval-shaped sails hung beneath it like swept-back fins. At its prow was a spiked ram carved like an open maw. Angled above, the smaller craft rained globs of fire down on the duke's gunship. The incendiaries popped as they struck, sending out sheets of flame.

The gunship made no maneuver to evade its pursuer. Effie didn't need to guess the reason why. It was clear the Barrow Witch had the crew within her thrall. Delving into the craft, she found those who manned the gunship and strained to free them.

"Leave them, Effie." Gaelyph had to step before her to get her attention. He spoke above the din but did not shout. His words were hard and meant for her alone.

Her ire rose. She made to shove the warden aside but stopped herself. She met his gaze and understood. He wasn't speaking out of cruelty or indifference. He was right, as the grindylows and Barrow Witch had proclaimed. She could not save them all. Perhaps she would not be able to even save her friends—or herself.

Her gaze swung from the burnt and failing gunship to the bloody field below. The duke's army had fallen off the attack. Bodies piled like bales of hay across the ground. Horns blared a retreat. The cannons had fallen silent.

No amount of Fey Craft could save the army. She had to let them go. She had to get to the Barrow Witch before Caledon's strength failed. Before the battle was lost.

※ 32 ※

E ffie sensed the steward's struggle. The weight of it fell over the hilltop like a blanket of iron. He kept the Unseily host from Elphame through strength of will. Gone was subtle craft and skill. Even with the immense power of the steward's mantle, he tired.

"Let us end this," she said to Gaelyph.

"Aye," said the Warden of the Hunt.

She had sensed earlier the pockets of Unseily fey who roamed within the hillfort. Deep passages ran beneath the earthen embankments, a warren of tunnels and caverns. She eyed the slope above. The shadows cast by stone and crevice reminded her of where they had found young Clara Bowman.

But which hid an entrance into the warren beneath? She bit her lip, considering.

Gaelyph answered her unspoken question with one of his own. "Would you hide behind a scrawny pine bough when a palisade stood next to it?"

Effie grinned. "You've watched the thurs."

"And the bogills." He nodded and pointed at a shadowed area halfway up the slope to the hilltop. "They emerge from the cleft there."

She could've hugged the warden. While she fought the Unseily directly with her Fey Craft, he used his hunter's guile.

Grabbing Sergeant McGrady by the coat, she yanked the man forward. She had no more time for words. His attention snapped from the chaos below. He turned to shout an order at his men, but his jaw slackened in shock. He had none left to command.

Brandon sat in the dirt with his back against the embankment. He held his rifle at the ready and waved it for the rest of the group to leave him. The other soldier the gunship had felled lay on his side. Shallow and weak breaths gave the only sign he clung to life.

With effort, Effie pried her gaze away and forced the wounded from her thoughts. She had to remain firm in her resolve, no matter how much it panged her. They had all come to save the empire. To a man, she knew they would rather she carry on than risk defeat.

She ignored the distant rattle of crank-guns, the grunts of bogills and chittering of trows. Men screamed. Wulvers howled in misery and hunger. The wafting stench of spent gunpowder, churned earth, burnt wood, and smoldering canvas met her nose. Snowflakes fluttered before her face as she raced along behind the warden. Ice crunched beneath her boots.

Freiherr Jörg struggled to keep pace behind her. The gnome huffed with each stride. Sergeant McGrady came at an easier gait. He had holstered his pistol and snatched up a rifle from one of the fallen. His hands clutched it hard enough to turn them white. His face was a stone mask.

They encountered few Unseily. Those who'd gathered on the second ring earlier had either run off or been slain by arriving riflemen of the duke's army. A pair of wulvers, one with a bloodied maw and the other with a lame forepaw, growled at them as they passed. But neither moved from their huddled position.

A goblin fled before them. Its flopping ears wriggled as it loped. It made a chittering squeal as it went, until it flung itself onto a boulder that protruded from the upward slope.

Only a bogill dared to stand against them. Tall and lean, the hairy creature howled a challenge at Gaelyph. Its muscles pulled taut, hands curled like claws. Sergeant McGrady shot it twice before the warden's sword brought a final silence.

As the slope grew steeper, Effie scrambled upward on her hands and feet. The drifting snow did not pile high, but where it landed the earth had frozen and become slick. Her fingers quickly numbed. Her grip became less certain, and she was forced to slow.

Her head whipped about at the boom of an explosion. The smaller airship of the Unseily had downed the duke's gunship, she saw. It sprawled in a flaming mass across the field, sending up a black plume of smoke. But the explosion had come from the smaller airship. One of the gunship's sisters had swung around and launched a broadside. Its crank-guns had torn through the smaller craft's wooden hull. Gouts of flame streaked from the breach.

The airship wobbled under its balloon. Pieces of its outrigger sails caught fire and came loose. The crank-guns opened up again, raking across the craft's rigging.

Effie wrenched herself away from the spectacle. It would do her no good to know its outcome. Shambling up through a ridge of stone, she peered into the cleft where Gaelyph had led them. Her vantage revealed a deep shadow nestled into the embankment. It was the mouth of a cave.

Her neck stiffened. She lurched in shock. Her vantage had revealed more than the cave. Red coats dotted the far side of the cleft— Lieutenant Walford's men. She could spy the man clustered with a few of his soldiers.

Their rifles cracked, taking aim at a band of Unseily who guarded the cave's entrance. The size of the thurs made Effie's throat run dry. From a distance, they had appeared like undersized giants, but that gave not enough credence to their sheer mass. The hulking creatures had arms like smokestacks and legs that could drive back a steam carriage.

They smelled, too—not like the decay of the bogills and grindylows, but of a powerful musk, like that of eggs left too long in boiling water. Effie gaged and covered her mouth.

Gaelyph flung himself into the cleft. Sword darting and slashing, he cut down a bogill before the creature could raise an arm to shield itself. The thurs roared. Tusks the size of iron spikes hung from their upper jaws.

Freiherr Jörg's blunderbuss thundered. Smoke blasted into the cleft. One of the thurs howled. Sergeant McGrady took aim on the creature. The thur jerked as the rifle hammered. Its white fur streaked with blood, but still it lumbered forth.

As the warden readied himself, Effie heard the crunch of leather on stone above her position. Red cloth flashed. But it wasn't that of the queen's soldiers.

"Gaelyph! Redcap!" She shouted the warning as a tumble of stone rained down.

"Ack!" Freiherr Jörg cried out as a stone whacked into him. He skidded down the slope, groping for purchase with his hands. His boot caught Effie across the jaw. Her teeth rattled. Her vision blurred.

Sliding to rest a few feet down the slope, she blinked and worked her jaw. Gaelyph had flung himself toward the redcap, but a pair of thurs stalked the warden. Lieutenant Walford's men let loose volley after volley from their position on the far side of the cleft. A few bogills tried to reach them but were repelled by the onslaught.

She had no weapon, no means to aid her friends save Fey Craft. She eyed Freiherr Jörg. The gnome sprawled next to her. Blood and a wicked gash marred his brow. He held a hand to it, in a daze, but made no move to rise.

Her eyes narrowed, fixing on a pouch at his belt. She had Fey Craft, but a different plan formed in her thoughts. It was one she hoped the Barrow Witch could not counter, one that would take the creature by surprise.

"No!" Sergeant McGrady screamed. Effie's gaze didn't budge. She could feel the banshee's touch crawl through the cleft. She knew it sought the lieutenant's men.

They had run out of time.

Her hands lurched. Snatching Freiherr Jörg's pouch, she ripped it free and tucked it into her belt. His blunderbuss lay near his feet, but the thing was too heavy for her to wield. She stooped and yanked out its slow match, hoping the gnome wouldn't have dire need of it.

"Effie," he whispered. His gaze trained to her.

"Tell Rose," she said. She didn't wait for a response.

Clambering over the ridge, she dropped into the cleft. A thur roared at her. She ignored it. Her feet churned as fast as she could lift her heavy boots. Shadows passed overhead. A sudden heat billowed against her, roasting her flesh. Wood and ash rained down from the sky. One of the airships had broken apart, but she knew not which.

She had eyes only for the cave's entrance.

❧ 33 ☙

Arthur stomped after Effie. Smoldering ash fell into her hair. Her breath came in panting huffs. Shouts echoed around her as rifles cracked and bullets whizzed.

She took no note of the warnings. She hoped that only the single thur had spotted her. She hoped Gaelyph could stand against the rest of the Unseily, or at least have sense enough to fall back. But she hoped most of all that Caledon's strength would hold out for a little while longer.

The cave entrance opened before her. She could see now it was not natural. It had been dug out with tools. Scrape marks scored the stone. A thick timber formed the entrance's lintel. The passageway leading beyond was regular and uniform.

A blast of cold air enveloped her as she passed into the Barrow Witch's warren. The ash and snow stopped abruptly. The crunch of ice beneath her boots turned into the clop of slippery muck.

She had no need to stoop. She cursed the luck and tried to gauge whether the thur pursuing her would even need to slow.

Something tickled in her senses from a few spans away. A familiarity she hadn't expected popped into her awareness. It had been there since she reached the cleft, she realized. She had only been distracted.

Skidding in the muck, she grabbed for the cave's earthen wall and smacked into it.

The click and boom of a blunderbuss rattled through the cave. Wood creaked and splintered. A crash of rock and dirt followed. Effie ducked and raised an arm to shield herself. By the time the cloud of dust settled, the cave had plunged into near darkness.

Only a single torch flared. It illuminated the form of Conall Murray. He held the light in one hand, a blunderbuss in the other. Her eyes squinted to make him out. He didn't grin, but his expression held a mix of wonder and smugness.

Smugness! She fought the urge to clout him up the back of the head, even as a flood of relief overcame her. He was safe. She had not lost him.

Glancing sheepishly away, he turned his attention upward. "I saw a trap rigged over the entrance." He shrugged. "It seemed as good a way to stop the thur as any."

Effie felt her eyebrow rise. But she could not deny the results. A furred paw large enough to span a swaddling cloth protruded from the pile of collapsed rock. It wriggled in spasms.

When she didn't respond, Conall stepped closer. "We saw the cave and fought our way toward it. I thought you would... I knew the danger..." He shrugged again and stared into her eyes. "It seemed the place you would be."

She tried to feign irritation at the jest, but a stronger desire to feel his touch won out. Grabbing his coat with both hands, she tugged him down until her lips found his. She didn't fully understand the impulse, but nor did she care. She wouldn't question it. It was a day for foolish actions. Heat rose from her toes to the tips of her ears.

Conall let out a yelp of surprise. But he softened and fell deeper into the embrace. Wrapping the arm with the blunderbuss around the small of her back, he pulled their bodies together. The hand with the torch he held aloft and at arm's length.

Effie remembered Freiherr Jörg's slow match and started. She had it clutched against Conall's chest along with the lapel of his coat. The tip dangled perilously close to the pouch she'd stuffed into her belt. Pulling back, she gave him a final peck.

"The redcaps must've set the trap," she said, finding her voice.

"There may be more of them." She glanced down the passageway. The torchlight made the earthen walls glow an amber hue.

"Redcaps?" asked Conall. As he spoke, an explosion from outside echoed through the tumbled rocks blocking the cave's entrance. A few stones trickled down the pile.

She shook her head. "There's no time."

"She's here, isn't she? The Barrow Witch?" He peered into the darkness before studying her. "You mean to confront her alone?"

A smile broke her lips. "No, not alone. Not anymore."

He grinned. His posture relaxed. "Never again."

Effie felt the weight of his declaration wash over her. The truth of the statement had sunk home on the riverbank near Roxburgh Castle, but it seemed now as if the final blinders she'd worn since a child had fallen away.

She had known friendship. She had known family. She had even known notoriety. But never had she experienced the certainty of living not as an outsider, but as part of the heart of a community, a people. Her chest pulled tight, and she marched down the passageway, lest she be overwhelmed. Her legs had turned to lead from the climb up the embankments. Her shoulder burned from the rake of the wulver. She had no need to add to her encumbrances.

Conall's mirth waned as she led them down the passageway. It sloped from the cave's entrance. In the steeper places, she heard the snowmelt trickling. The sound made her wonder how many entrances the warren might have, and by the same measure, how many escapes.

She sensed a handful of fey nearby. They were separated by mere spans of what she hoped was solid rock and earth. The Barrow Witch was among them.

"She leads us into a trap," she whispered over her shoulder. She had no other explanation for why the Sidhe Bhreige allowed her position to be known—and why she did not assault Effie as she had done so frequently with ease.

Effie patted Freiherr Jörg's pouch. "But I have a surprise of my own."

Conall nodded. He held up the torch and studied the wall. Running a hand along one of the exposed stones, he said, "These here are cut and formed on purpose." Those he indicated formed a vertical pillar. "And here." He pointed at similar stones on the opposite wall. "The warren might've been carved by the owners of the hillfort some millennia ago. Perhaps they used it for storage, or as a crypt."

Effie took note and examined the ceiling. Such places provided opportunity for the redcaps to work their fiendish tricks. She saw no sign of a trap, but still her heart thumped harder as they carried onward.

Placing each boot with care slowed their pace. It felt like an age had passed since they left sight of the cave's entrance, though she doubted they had travelled the length of an airship.

As the way turned, it widened into a chamber. The torchlight painted the ceiling above their heads, yet in front of them it drifted off into an open space. The walls gave way as well. Shallow pools of water collected in the depressions of the floor before them. The air grew colder and danker.

"It is good you have come to me, child." The Barrow Witch's voice echoed throughout the chamber. It seemed to come from all directions and none.

Scratching, like that of claws across rock, followed the greeting. Effie guessed the source to be trows, by the impressions of their auras. Perhaps a dozen of them lurked in the darkness. The spacing of their auras gave an impression of the chamber's scope, nearly a quarter the breadth of the hillfort above it.

Effie strode forward into the chamber. It was time to set her trap, but she would need to be subtle about it. She opened Freiherr Jörg's pouch. Her fear of the redcaps had lent her an idea, and she gestured for Conall to step beside her.

"You are wrong about me," she declared. "I hold no betrayer's blood. Mine flows strong and loyal." As she spoke, she delved with her senses as she had before. She searched the warren and the ground beneath for the substance that would form her ruse.

"Loyal?" The Barrow Witch cackled. "That is an odd word for one who basks in enslavement. A flea-ridden hound is loyal. Is that all to which you aspire? It is a pity. I have watched you for many long years. I had higher expectations of your fate."

"The Laird of Aonghus sought to twist me to his will," said Effie. She reached into the pouch and clasped some of its contents. The black powder felt like sand. "He failed, as will you. You are the same."

The Barrow Witch's tone sharpened. "You have seen my power and know that I am greater than that blustering fool." A shadow moved at the edge of the torchlight. Effie recognized the form of the elderly fey woman.

"Do you not realize I can grant you the treaty you have so long desired?" the Barrow Witch continued. "Join me, and I will give you this feeble empire and all within it. You will witness fey and man living together in peace, as you've so yearned. The Seily Court will bow to your authority, no longer abandoning its own to the winds. And as for these so-called lords of man, they will cow to your pleasure. They are too weak to offer you anything more. You must see they hold against you the very compassion you grant them."

"And you?" Effie swallowed. A part of her wondered how much truth was in the Barrow Witch's words. She let some of the black powder trickle through her fingers. In the darkened chamber, it was easy to conceal the movement—or so she hoped. "Where will you dwell once this empire is mine?"

"Why I will rule in Elphame, my child," the Barrow Witch replied. "That is a certainty you cannot alter. Your decision to accept my terms matters not."

Effie sputtered into laughter. She couldn't hold it back. "You cannot enter Elphame. Your corruption is too vile." She reached for another fistful of powder and felt the pouch was almost empty.

"I will find a means, in time. But my offer to you will not wait any longer. Would you rule as the steward of my Unseily Court? All I ask is a pledge of your...loyalty."

"As you took from Tallia?" Effie inhaled a deep breath. Pulling with her fey senses, she envisioned the swirl of prismatic colors she had witnessed at Caldwell House. The vapors of Aerfenium they'd conjured then had been cast into a circle of urns. She had no vessel, but she had no need of one. The tendrils that began billowing from the ground she swirled into a giant ball before her.

They had errored in their assumptions while using the thunderstone at the Storr. The Aerfenium cache had not been in Edinburgh. She had deduced as much earlier, yet even having expected the cache near the Eildon Hills, when she first sensed it in her delving, it had surprised her. Surprised, and terrified.

Its presence meant the Barrow Witch could summon allies. The Sidhe Bhreige could release her brethren with a simple act of destruction. And yet, it had taken Effie only a fleeting moment to determine the Barrow Witch would not. All of her ilk held a single-heartedness that blinded them to such a possibility. Like the Laird of Aonghus and Piper of Ceann Rois, the Barrow Witch would rather face defeat than allow an equal to stand at her side. She had proven as much these past months. She'd had ample opportunity to destroy the caches she'd uncovered and had not.

Effie meant to use the knowledge to her advantage.

The Aerfenium felt like liquid silver. It hissed like steam as she pulled it from root and soil, from its ancient nest where it had lain for millennia. She imagined her ancestors standing in this same place, casting out the Sidhe Bhreige to imprisonment in the Downward Fields. The thought gave her strength.

"What is this?" demanded the Barrow Witch. She eyed the gathering vapors with uncertainty.

"You have lost," Effie replied. She was emboldened by the shock in the Sidhe Bhreige's voice. Her nerve remained steady. She raised the slow match for the Barrow Witch to see. "I mean to bring the hillfort down on top of us. You may have escaped the Downward Fields, but you will not escape death."

The swirling colors of Aerfenium caught on the Barrow Witch. Her flesh flashed in violets and greens and blues. Her red eyes pointed like daggers. Her brow scrunched in fury. Effie sensed the Sidhe Bhreige's assault and flared a golden shield before her.

A mountain slammed into it. Barbs shot through the shield, expanding and ripping it apart. Effie threw up another, but as she did a bramble of decaying vines wrapped about her legs. The shoots snaked from all around. They filled the darkness at the edge of the torchlight, from the floor to the ceiling high above.

Conall cried out. He dropped the torch and clutched his head. Effie reached for the vines that carried the banshee's touch, but the effort left her exposed. Barbs pierced her flesh. They drove deep and stole her breath.

"Do you think I am to be toyed with?" asked the Barrow Witch. She strode forward. "Your bluff is ill considered. You would no sooner destroy this Aegirsigath than would I." The Sidhe Bhreige used the ancient fey term for Aerfenium.

Effie forced herself to shamble backward. Pain lanced through her. Conall's screams tore at her heart. "I have no need to bluff," she said. "Your brethren won't escape their imprisonment with the loss of the cache here. We have made enough Aerfenium to seal them away forever. It is only we who shall perish."

The effort to speak shot fire down her throat, but she spoke with a conviction that belied her fear. The words rumbled from her like a growl. Raising her arm, she launched the slow match across the chamber.

Effie's aim was true. The slow match landed in the pile of Freiherr Jörg's black powder. As the smoldering wick hissed and caught alight, she gave herself over to the thorns and vines that ensnared her. Using all the strength of her fey blood, she sucked the Aerfenium from the chamber, driving it back into the depths beneath the warren.

The Barrow Witch wailed. She flinched backward, raising an arm before her face. Effie's shrieks echoed the Sidhe Bhreige. But hers were born from the pain of the thorns that lanced through her, piercing from head to foot.

The pile of black powder ignited in a whoosh of flame. The heat of its harsh smoke washed over her. Her eyes stung. A racking cough collapsed her to a knee. She tensed as darkness claimed the chamber. Without the colorful spray of Aerfenium, only Conall's torch remained to shed any illumination, and that had almost snuffed out. It lay smoldering near the man, its halo dwindled to a few paces.

The Barrow Witch's cackling began as an uncertain trickle, as if she disbelieved what her eyes and fey senses told her. Yet it became raucous as the air of the chamber stilled. She had every reason to gloat. She had guessed correctly. Effie had bluffed.

"Pathetic," said the Sidhe Bhreige. "I should not have wasted my efforts on you, but now that charity is at an end." The Barrow Witch's shadowed form stalked through the halo of torchlight. "Your friends have abandoned you. Your army is defeated. Open your senses and know that I speak the truth. I have won."

Effie felt the vines and thorns relent. She gasped as the pain fled. Like other glamours born of Fey Craft, it vanished as if it hadn't been there at all. She rubbed at her arms anyway. The smooth flesh pimpled as she shivered.

She had no need to reach out with her senses. She knew already that the Barrow Witch spoke the truth. Rose Brewer and Gaelyph, Warden of the Hunt, were gone. They had fled the battle along with dozens of other fey. Those of Scottish blood. Those of the Seily Court.

All save Caledon had winked from her awareness only moments before she'd thrown the slow match.

But they had not abandoned her.

She did not know how the duke's army stood. She could sense only a mass of men and a scattering of women outside. She hoped desperately that those who remained to fight would hang on for a short while longer, until the madness of the banshee's touch could be eradicated.

Conall cradled his head in his hands. He'd fallen and sat whimpering.

Hold on! Effie willed herself to keep from reaching out to him. It was almost time. She could not miss her chance no matter how much it tormented her to watch him suffer. But her will must be for the greater good.

"Yes, child," said the Barrow Witch. "You realize your foolishness now. I see it on your face. But it is too late. I have tricks of my own to reveal."

The trows began to chitter, yet as they did their timbre deepened to hoarse rasping. Their auras warped. A veil dropped, and Effie jolted in shock. Similar to obscuring auras, the Barrow Witch had tricked her into believing only trows skulked within the chamber. She sensed now a dozen grindylows.

They edged closer at a shuffling pace. Their rasping laughter echoed the cackling of their master. Effie crouched as the circle tightened. The shield of Fey Craft she'd formed before she readied once again. Waiting, she rose to the balls of her feet. Her breathing came quick and shallow.

But the assault of thorn and vine did not come. They meant not to subdue her, she realized, but to slay her.

Scouring the ground for a weapon, she caught movement in the reflection of one of the shallow pools. She dove forward. Nails like talons raked her back. A hiss of fury followed. Her momentum sent her rolling. She tucked her shoulder and felt lines of fire race across her flesh.

She smacked into the legs of a grindylow. Lashing out with a boot, she kicked herself free. Her hands found only dirt, but she grabbed handfuls and flung it, choking as a cloud ballooned over her.

She needed to find something sturdy, something strong. She cursed herself for dropping Jack Canonbie's cane. Her gaze caught on the smoldering torch, and she scrambled for it. Anything was better than her empty hands.

Her knees scraped. Her palms bled, scratched by sharp stones. Water splashed as she clambered through the shallow pools of snowmelt.

A foot, pale and deathly, slapped the water next to her head. Her head snapped back. The grindylow held her hair in its grip. Her neck strained, throat exposed. The face staring down at her was shriveled and sickly. Its breath stunk of rot. Its eyes were filmed and weeping.

Effie sucked in a panicked breath. With balled fists, she pummeled the grindylow. The creature growled, flinching against the onslaught. It raised its free hand to strike, fingers curled to reveal thick, yellow-tinged nails.

As it did, the chamber blossomed with the auras of the Seily Court.

All the breath rushed out of Effie. Her fear vanished. It was the moment to which she had attached all her hope. Her friends had finally come.

"You were wrong," she hollered at the Barrow Witch. "No one abandoned me." She giggled, overcome by joy. Their gamble, her final trick conceived in the shadows of the Storr, had worked. "They did what your foul host could not. They invaded Elphame. And now, they have returned."

Gaelyph stepped into the halo of torchlight as if summoned from mist. His sword flashed, and the grindylow holding Effie jerked. Its head splashed into the shallow pool.

Jaelyn howled with glee. Her dirk already dripped with blood. Rose Brewer and Abigail Salisbury stood shoulder to shoulder. Bursts of white light popped throughout the chamber, each explosion banging like a drum. Hogboons and pixies flooded the area, and a few Sithlings, too. They had used her as an anchor, returning to the very spot where she needed them most.

"You were meant to wait for me, Effie of Glen Coe," said Gaelyph. "You were not meant to stall the Barrow Witch alone." His sword did not slow, nor his feet.

"I managed," she said, panting in relief. "And I wasn't alone." Pulling herself to her feet, she lumbered over to the prone form of Conall. She ran a hand along his brow and through his curls. His face was pinched. He murmured something inaudible.

"Effie!" Rose shouted in alarm. It carried over the din of the fighting. Effie whirled and saw Jaelyn and the brownies of Clan Kae surge against a pair of grindylows. Pixies, including wee Alison of Tarves, zipped about one another as hogboons swung their wild and meaty fists at it.

But it was for the Barrow Witch that Rose had shouted. The Sidhe Bhreige stalked toward Effie in a crouch. Her eyes narrowed to slits as Effie regarded her. The dead grey flesh of her brow tightened. Her lips pulled back in fury. The silver of a dagger flashed.

Effie jerked aside and fell over Conall. Kicking with her legs, she scrambled to distance herself from the blade. But the next attack did not come. The Barrow Witch darted away from her.

Cursing, Effie realized the ancient fey sought not vengeance, but only to escape the chamber. She sprang to her feet and lunged. She couldn't let the creature flee. She didn't know how many other exits there might be from the warren.

Her arms thwacked into flesh and bone. The impact rattled though her body and sent her back into spasms. The Barrow Witch crumpled. Swiping back with the dagger, she thrashed through one of the shallow pools.

Her wail pierced Effie's mind as if a butcher's pick had been driven into her eyes and ears. But Effie did not let go. She clawed her way up the Barrow Witch's legs, feeling the cold steel of the dagger bite at her arms.

Conall's torch winked out. Effie reached back for him just as the chamber floor dissipated, and she dropped into an empty void. Darts whipped past her. Some snagged in her hair. Others pricked her flesh. She felt her blood run free, dripping upward as she plummeted.

It was all a trick from the Barrow Witch, she knew. She had come to recognize the Sidhe Bhreige's manipulations. Vines, healthy and verdant, shot from her hands. She formed a sphere of pulsing light, like that of a star, and snared it with the vines from one hand. The vines of the other, she hurled as far as she could.

Her descent jerked to a halt. The darts changed course, whirling through her vines and shredding them. They were black shadows against her starlight, she saw, nothing more than a clouded thought from the Barrow Witch.

Effie ignored the glamour. She reached through her vines, stretching them out of the darkness like extensions of her own fingers. She found purchase on a clump of dried and forgotten weeds. Their thorns withered to dust as she gripped tight and yanked.

She felt the banshee's touch crumple away from Conall. As it did, her sphere exploded and flung her hard enough to crush the wind from her lungs. Searing heat melted through her clothes and rent her to the bone.

As she bent her head to scream, the glamour disappeared.

She blinked. The white heat vanished along with its blistering agony. No cuts marred her flesh. The void had not taken her. She lay on her side, with a hand trembling in a puddle of snow melt.

Conall swayed unsteadily next to her. An amber light from somewhere nearby painted his silhouette. He held the blunderbuss by its barrel, gripped in both hands. The limp form of the Barrow Witch sprawled in front of him. Effie had freed him from madness, and he had brought an end to her torment.

A snarl curled his lip. Raising the blunderbuss, he hacked down using his full weight. The crunch echoed through the chamber. The silence afterward brought with it an onrush of elation and relief. And, Effie had to admit, hidden beneath was a small measure of sadness—for the lost, and for the senselessness of it all.

Jaelyn clomped to halt before Effie. She had relit Conall's torch. The flame highlighted the brownie's face, which wore an expression as jubilant as Effie knew her own must be. Muck and blood stuck to Jaelyn's cheeks and coat. Her ginger hair was wild. Behind her, Rose and Gaelyph, and all the others of the Seily Court stood and regarded Effie with grins of disbelief. Seeing their faces unleashed a torrent of relief that shook loose a joyous sob.

"Aye," said the brownie. "It's done."

❈ 35 ❈

The steam carriage rattled. Its engine puffed thick black smoke, but Effie was grateful for the warmth the burning coal emitted. The afternoon wind cut through her woolen coat and dusted her with the morning's snow. At least the sun hung above the hills, free of clouds. Its presence brought a cheeriness to the day, fitting for Clara Bowman's departure.

The lass clambered into the steam carriage and sat on its worn bench. The wood creaked despite her slight frame. As the driver banged the door shut, the carriage rocked on its spoked wheels. The man doffed his hat to Effie and eyed the road to Balclune with a pinched face. Ruts and sloshed snowmelt gave evidence of the many steam carriages that had already come and gone throughout the day.

Clara put her head to the open window in the carriage's door. Her gloved hands gripped its sill. "If I might beg of you, Green Lady..." She broke off and ducked her gaze. "What I said in Syke...about what I asked of you..."

"It is forgotten," said Effie. She placed her hands on top of Clara's. "We have all of us suffered, for good and ill. My hope is that we will now claim the former and learn from the latter."

Clara nodded but kept her gaze ducked. "I would've been lost were it not for the belief you inspired." She smiled and finally met Effie's eyes. Her face brightened. "I am not alone in that regard."

Effie's throat tightened. Moisture came to her eyes. It had been a day of leave-takings, but Clara's words bit deeper into her than those of earlier departures. Perhaps it was the time she'd spent searching for the lass, or perhaps it was the reminder of how close they had all come to losing everything.

After the demise of the Barrow Witch, she and the rest of the Seily Court had captured those Unseily they could, and the old distillery near Balclune where they'd once stored Aerfenium had turned into a house of healing. Many of the bogills and grindylows at the hillfort, those not slain outright, had succumbed to their wounds. A few had fled the fray as defeat closed in. But of those taken alive, almost all were now restored to their true and former selves.

Of the wulvers and trows, thurs and spriggans, not many survived. Effie feared she could do little for those who had, but she had at least convinced the duke to forestall execution until the matter was discussed more fully. They lived now in a giant pit dug like a quarry, with sheer sides and an armed guard.

The driver worked a lever, and the steam carriage squealed into motion. Effie stepped back, patting Clara's hand one last time. "Fare thee well," she said. "Until the next time we meet." She made a note to check in on the lass in a few months' time. Clara's smile didn't wane as she pulled back into the shadows of the carriage's compartment.

Effie had many such notes—friends to thank, debts to repay, and promises to keep. She would start in Aberdeen with a rat who was owed a bit of cheese and see to the rest over time. That the effort might take many months did not lessen the joy that sprang from thinking about such a leisurely adventure.

A wave of fatigue passed through her, all the same. She folded her arms and closed her eyes. The effort to restore the Unseily had taken a great deal, both physically and mentally. She still recovered from her cuts and bruises suffered during the battle. Her shoulder ached. Her back spasmed if she slept too long. But she refused to sit idle while others of the Seily Court, many of whom tended their own wounds, took turns giving a part of themselves to save their brethren.

"My lady." Jane Porter's soft call carried to her as the pop and shudder of the steam carriage drifted away. "I am sorry to disturb you, but Mr. Alpin is making his demands again."

Effie's eyelids squeezed harder as her expression tightened. The old Fey Finder had brought his usual bluster and intolerance to their restoration efforts, but he had been ordered by the crown to oversee the work, and there was nothing she could do to send the man away.

A door banged open. Boots stomped through the snow. Raised voices and a familiar hacking cough carried to her. She took a deep breath before turning to greet them. Fergus Alpin's wrinkled face and frail frame charged her direction. Samuel Harper followed, flanked by a pair of brownies. The trio wore similar coats of a russet wool, though the soldier stood twice as high as his companions and did not have so sharp of features.

Alison of Tarves buzzed about the Fey Finder's ears in her azure gown. How her wee body did not freeze to death, Effie could not fathom. She could see Fergus Alpin straining not to swat the pixie away. She giggled to herself, remembering. Jaelyn and Ana had seen to this newfound composure. They had threatened to remove the man's hands. Effie wished her friends had remained, but they had left with Freiherr Jörg and the gnomes of the Order of Freiwald to track down a thur spotted near Goswick.

The last of the group storming from the old distillery was Gareth. The hound wore a happy winter belly that wobbled as he trotted through the snow. He kept his head cocked, watching Alison flit about with his tongue lolling merrily.

"See here, Effie of Glen Coe," started Fergus Alpin, but his words trailed off into a fit of wheezing. He put a handkerchief to his mouth and stooped from the effort.

"He says she's evil," squeaked Alison. "He says she don't want to repent." The pixie fluttered to land on Harper's shoulder, waved her arms as if to prove her point, and zipped off again.

Effie raised an eyebrow. She idly reached to scratch at Gareth's neck as the hound pressed against her shin. "We have been through this before, Mr. Alpin." *Several times, in fact*, she did not add. "What is it about this woman that convinces you of her wickedness?"

"Something in her eyes, he said." Samuel Harper planted himself next to Effie and shook his head. The young man had been granted leave by the duke himself to lend what aid he could to Effie.

"Her pale complexion," said one of the brownies.

"Her long nails," said the other.

"But of course she has those things. She hasn't been healed yet." Jane started, as if surprised by the bite in her tone. She swept a loose strand of hair from her face. The white of her dress shone through the open part of her heavy coat. She had become bolder over the past few weeks, taking charge of organizing many of the gathered fey's daily needs.

The change wore well on her, as did her acceptance of Edgar Talmadge's proposal. The pair would marry in the summer. Jaelyn had teased the young woman would need to find a dress of a different color come autumn. The jest had made Edgar blush deeper than Jane.

Fergus Alpin raised a finger to thrust at Effie but thought better of it. Dropping the hand, he said, "You cannot be sure this healing will make the creature good again. You cannot be sure of it!"

"No," Effie agreed. "We most certainly cannot. But we must try anyway." It was true not all of the Unseily they had healed had been grateful. After all, not all had been forced against their will. Some had been like Tallia, bent on delusions of the Barrow Witch's grandeur.

"It would be better for the empire to put the thing down," said Alpin. "One does not let a rabid dog play with the sheep."

Gareth whined and thumped his tail. Effie felt the gazes of those gathered. They looked to her to guide them. Even Fergus Alpin did, in his own grumpy manner. Perhaps they had for quite some time, in some regards. She had only needed to learn how to trust and accept her place among them.

"Nor does one cast out an unfortunate soul whose poor circumstance was no cause of their own, Mr. Alpin." She raised a hand to quiet the Fey Finder. She leaned toward the man. "I will not stand for abandoning a single victim of the Barrow Witch. Their bent, whether good or ill, will not be decided for them by a presumption of tainted blood. The days of that absurdity have ended."

Effie's hands started to stray to her hips but she pulled them back. It was too cold for such a stance. She hugged her coat closed. "The matter is settled," she said, striding for the warmth of the old distillery. "Let us get out of this chill air."

Fergus Alpin grumbled behind her but made no further objections. She warmed at the small victory and realized, not for the first time, that her authority no longer felt so odd a mantle to bear.

EPILOGUE

Conall Murray slapped a hand against his knee. "It is madness and an insult," he said as he and Effie settled within the compartment of the steam carriage. He wore a formal coat trimmed with the green, blue, and red striping of his family's tartan. "I am restored to Fey Finder General, to the dismay of John Billingsley, and bestowed a knighthood. Caledon is made Keeper of the Wards. Lieutenant Walford is given a commendation." He thumped his cane on the carriage's floor. "Even those men of Hawick received a royal declaration of gratitude."

The steam carriage creaked as it sputtered forward. Effie swayed with the gently rocking compartment. She held her gloved hands in her lap, feeling stiff and awkward. She was ready to be rid of the embroidered gown of emerald and silver she had donned for the evening. It felt too much like wearing a mask, like the animalistic ones of *Les Revinirs*.

"I have all I desire," she admitted. "The treaty is signed by the royal hand. The Sidhe Bhreige are defeated. I have no need of a title or compensation." She meant the sentiment, but it had not been lost on her that none of her gender had ascended in rank as the queen bestowed her blessings. She grinned at the irony of trading one prejudice for another.

"The treaty." Conall shook his head and thumped the cane anew. "It could not be written more vaguely if it contained no words at all."

Effie put a hand over his to still the cane. "It is an agreement of peace, something we fey have never had in our lifetimes. It is something to us." Her hand slid to his knee. "I think I liked you better melancholy. This cheerless passion does not suit you."

"Och, I am sorry. It is only that I want you to have all you deserve, and you deserve more." He cocked his head and eyed her with a smile. "It was satisfying to see Lord Granville humbled. I've never seen the man sweat so much and say so little."

Effie had to agree. "He has fallen from a great height and may never recover." Word had spread that the lord used crown funds to hire thugs bent on repressing worker unions through violence. The mob justice had caused the deaths of dozens in Manchester, and the scandal had led to many further admissions by his associates. All were nefarious. No one yet knew when or where the allegations might stop. She only hoped Catherine Granville's name would be spared. The man's daughter did not deserve such disgrace.

Regardless, her debt to the vile man had been fully paid.

As the steam carriage trundled along, the lights of Edinburgh flashed through the compartment's window. Conall studied one of the tall, stone buildings before returning to his musings. "His legislation for the crown to formally seize control of Aerfenium will pass," he said.

Nodding, Effie said, "It must. But not with his name as its architect. There is a very large and intimidating microscope pointed at the empire from across the channel. If London did nothing, it wouldn't take more than a match to inflame tensions to the point of war."

"Aye," Conall agreed. "The continent watches, ready to pounce. They will hold the empire to the coals to ensure another Sidhe Bhreige does not escape the Downward Fields. They will do even more to ensure the empire cannot use the substance while they have none. It would tip the balance too far in our favor."

"The Sidhe Bhreige will not escape," replied Effie. "We will see to it, though men like Sir Walter Conrad will play both sides while Caledon is caught in between." A new home to store the substance would be found, and caches great enough to withstand even a major loss would be created. Plans for both had already commenced.

Conall chuckled. "Keeper of the Wards. I thought my new position a hen in the fox house. Some lords already call for an invasion of the Downward Fields. Others want to use Aerfenium to reclaim our lands abroad. But none of that bluster is as dangerous, or as devious, as a mind like Sir Walter's. The man will not be appeased until his name waggles on the tongue of the most backward sots from Boston to Sydney."

"It will be to you to aid Caledon," said Effie. Her hand pressed farther up his leg. "Conall Murray, Fey Finder General."

His eyebrow raised. "That is Sir Conall, if you please."

She traced his leg with a finger. Where she passed, a tiny blue flame ignited. She put no heat into the glamour, but Conall yelped all the same and brushed frantically at his trousers.

"Sir Conall," she said, giggling. She removed her hand. The flames disappeared.

He leaned into her, pressing himself against her. One hand closed about her waist. The other cupped her cheek. "I am due that respect."

Effie muttered her agreement as their lips found one another. A flutter stirred within, a lightheadedness came on that numbed the world and left only the two of them in focus. She could feel her body wanting more. Now it was his touch that drew fire.

"Her Majesty has bestowed upon me the honor of the realm." His hands moved through the silk of her dress.

She gasped. "Please don't mention the queen just now."

"It is because of the time I saved the empire, you see." Pulling back, he slid the window curtains closed. He turned the single oil lamp of the compartment down so that its orange glow barely painted their flesh.

She didn't need the light, nor her fey senses, to know his yearning. It thrummed within her equally, as if they had already joined. Gripping him tight, she had no cause to resist. "Oh, well that is a tale best saved for our children." She breathed the words into his ear.

* * *

Gwendoline screeched into the night from her favorite perch by the garden well. The noise made Gareth thump his tail, though the hound didn't move from his position by the hearth. Effie peered out the windows of Bonny Law, her cottage near the village of Westley. Night was about to fall, and the dim haze of dusk blurred her view.

But she could sense Caledon and Rose approaching. "They've come," she said, taking in the dormant tulips and wild flowers of the garden. An earthy moss peeked through a blanket of white frost. Wood smoke and honeyed tea filled her nose, the scents of winter.

A chair creaked behind her. Stuart Graham crossed the small room to stand next to her. He held his pipe in one hand but smelled more of whisky. His eyes had glazed, and he had a soft choke to his voice.

"It is too bad Conall's nae here," he said. "He should be giving you the sending, not we old buggers." He nodded behind them to where Thomas Stevenson rested in an oaken chair, blanket pulled across his knees.

She saw the father's pride in his expression and felt her throat clench. For a week she had kept her emotions in check, tricking herself into believing Elphame had never been her desire. But the place meant more than a physical realm. It was the tangible notion that she belonged to the Seily Court, that she was trusted finally and fully.

As stoic as she'd tried to be, her defenses had failed her at the last. Understanding both sentiments to be already true could not remove the trembling from her legs or flittering swirl of butterflies from her gut.

"He will be distraught," she agreed. "But I would not have either of you miss this. It is you who have taught and guided me into the person I've become." Wrapping her arms around Graham, she hugged his thick frame. There was no holding back the tears, though they gathered heavier on the old man's cheeks.

Her thoughts turned to Conall as Gwendoline screeched again. She missed him dearly. They had rarely separated during the previous weeks. Yet his duties had taken him away a few days earlier, and she could not fault a second of his commitment. Together they would change the Fey Finders to work in harmony with the Seily Court. Their order would take charge of settling disputes amicably, and their sniffing would remain only for the Unseily.

It was a far cry from the days when the Sniffers imprisoned and hanged any they suspected of fey blood, days when she had lived in constant fear of any stranger.

"My Robert should write a story of you someday," said Thomas Stevenson. His tone had lost some of its firmness through the years, but not its kindness when it came to her.

She snorted but smiled at him all the same. "I hope my life is not so adventurous as to warrant that," she said.

Breaking from Graham, she strode to the door and opened it just as Caledon and Rose stepped to the threshold. The fey were locked arm in arm. They had traveled to Elphame for a time at Gaelyph's request and returned to gather her. She greeted Caledon with a toothy grin and Rose with an embrace. The pair traded pleasantries with the gentlemen, but the steward declined a warm cup of tea or glass of the stronger.

"It is time for you to see Elphame, Effie of Glen Coe," he said. "Effie of the Shadows, Effie the Hidden." His eyes twinkled with mischief. She laughed. She had been those things once but could never be again.

Cold washed over her as their auras linked. She caught Rose's hand. Her toes wiggled in anticipation. She thought of her mother, and of her grandfather, and knew as the room began to swirl in a blur of colors that their blood was carried with her, reunited at last with the fey of the Seily Court.

THE END

Thank you for reading! Did you enjoy?

Please Add Your Review! And don't miss more fantasy novels like, MUD, by City Owl Author, E. J. Wenstrom. Turn the page for a sneak peek!

SNEAK PEEK OF MUD

A stair creaks.

With the rain pounding down on the temple's rattling roof, the human may not have even heard the sound. But I do. It is too close, just outside the door of my tower. I look up from the Texts and listen.

There it is again.

A cold darkness tosses in my stomach.

Another stair creaks, and I know I'm about to kill again. The boiling thrill for blood rises within me and I know better than to bother suppressing it. It will happen anyway, no matter how much I try to bury the monster I really am.

Over the centuries, I've at least learned how to make it quick. My hand has already dug the box from the breast pocket of my cloak. I stride across my small room, my bare feet collecting dust. My back to the door, I lean on the mantle to lure the Hunter in. Then, I stare at the blank dusty wall and wait. The rustle of his cloak breaks the quiet with each step.

I want this over.

I hold the box high in my hand for him to see, as if I am inspecting it. So small, so delicate. It nestles easily against my palm, comfortable and sure. It knows I must serve it.

Padded steps lift from the wood and onto the worn rug. My spine prickles with anticipation. Dread, heavy and thick like a storm cloud, wells up inside me. Have they learned nothing from their many losses? So many I cannot count them anymore.

I lay the box on the mantle for him to reach. My fingers itch for the fight, but I will not destroy the human of my own will. He must bring it on himself. I step away from it, leave it there for the Hunter to set his fate.

A rustle of rushed steps, a grunt, and a blade slices through my back, cool and slick. They keep trying to hurt me as if I were human, as if I felt the pain as they do. I reach around and remove the blade from my back. The skin knits itself back together.

I turn to him. Rain beats at the window. Wild dilated eyes peer up at me from under a deep red hood. Young. The cloak slips at his neck, too large for his growing body. It is the same deep red cloak all the others wore. Rich, dark, velvety, with the same gold braided trim. My own cloak, worn and ripped, seems even worse next to it.

The boy is trembling inside it. Waiting.

Has he even experienced a true fight before? Why did they send someone so young? Guilt twists through me.

"It's not too late. Leave." My voice is rough with disuse.

I shift the knife in my hand, holding it away to show him I don't mean him any harm, not if I can help it.

Like their cloaks, the Hunters' blades are fine, an elaborate pattern carved into its handle. It seems out of place in my hand, even after so many times. I run my fingers over its familiar ridges and wait. My ears are hot with anticipation, with dread of what I know comes next.

He gapes up at me, my monstrosity. I fight the urge to drop my gaze to the ground and instead keep my eyes locked on his. I try to will him to turn away, to go back to wherever he came from.

But I already know he won't. They never do.

Instead, he gives himself a quick shake and recovers his warrior's front. "The Sworn will not rest until it is destroyed. Give me the box."

Courage glows in his eyes. Strong. Fresh. What a waste of a life.

The Sworn? What is the Sworn?

"I cannot."

If only I could. It would save both of us.

He reaches for the box on the mantle.

"*Don't—*"

His fingers wrap around it.

The box's force takes over and my arms reach for him. I wince as my hand slips the Hunter's own blade through his soft middle. In the back of my mind, years and years of all the others who came before him flash through my memory. My hands buzz with mad hunger for the fight.

But it's already over.

He gasps, clasps his hands to his open belly, trying to hold it in. Then he slumps to the floor, spilling his life across the wooden panels. He opens his mouth to gasp, but it comes out as more of a gurgle, blood rising in his throat.

Not much time left. I try to push down the throbbing anger, the monster in me that hungers for the fight. I kneel beside him, gripping his head urgently so he is looking at me.

I hold the box to his face. "What is in it? Why do you come for it? Who are the Sworn?"

A red line dribbles down his chin. He looks up at me, trembling, shakes his head side to side.

"You don't know?"

His words come out in a hoarse whisper. He is shaking all over now in a struggle for his life. He opens his mouth again, tries to push out more. But the dark puddle grows fast below him, and it is over before it begins. Again, I am alone in the heavy dark of the temple tower.

* * *

The Hunter's eyes are cold and dead and open wide.

Watching, judging, condemning.

And they should. They have seen what I am.

I used to tell myself I would get used to it. I got used to snapping bones, last cries, pools of blood. But the eyes. The eyes freeze in an echo of their final panic and pain. When they realize these are their last breaths. Paled. Filmed. Hollow.

The Hunter's eyes stare up at me and I can't bear it.

I step out onto the balcony to escape them. Try to clear my head, still buzzing and grainy from the kill. Rain squeezes out of the sky like teardrops over the cobblestone streets in the marketplace below, over the thin rotted roofs of the laborers' quarters beyond it, over the wall that traps them within the city's borders. Even over the city center, where Epoh's elite rest, safe and dry. It pounds down on me, drop, by drop, by drop.

So close, yet again.

I set the box next to me on the railing, finger the curves of the delicate patterns painted over it. Such beauty. But it's what's inside that the Hunters come for, die for. That much I know. If only it would open. If only I knew what my body betrayed me for, why my hands are covered in blood yet again.

They will send another. They always do. I will be waiting. It goes without end, back further than I can remember. Centuries. Years trudge by, bodies pile up, the weight grows heavier.

I cling to my new clue. *The Sworn.* The phrase is meaningless to me, but it's a little more than I had before. Next time, maybe I can learn even more, if they keep sending their young and untested.

Already the dark sky is lightening toward a troubled gray. Another weary day is here in the city of Epoh.

Which means I'll be stuck with the Hunter's cold stare all day. There's no time to move the body now. Soon Epoh's Silencers will be out, the city's guards who keep the order with fear and clubs. Ever since they burned down the Holy District and all the Texts so many years ago, anything related to the Three Gods makes them jump. Any sign of movement from a temple like this would trigger a full search of the grounds. Then where would I go? There's nothing else left beyond Epoh's walls. Nowhere else to go.

It wasn't always like this. The realm was happy once. There were tons of other cities like Epoh, and they were thriving. But something shifted in the Second Realm War.

Some say the Three saw the destruction and anger and hate that spread throughout the realm of Terath in the Second Realm War and abandoned it. Others say the Three themselves were on the battlefield, and They came with Their soldiers to beat at Epoh's wall, begging to be let in and shown a little of kindness—care for wounds, a drink of water—but the people would not let them in for fear of the rebels, and They gave up on us. Others say the Gods simply saw how few men dared fight for Them and turned away.

Whatever it was, the Gods are gone, and the people won't dare invoke Them for anything, afraid of Their wrath. The realm is in ruins. Only the Gods know what lies beyond Epoh's high walls. If They care enough to look.

That's why I hide here, in the temple. I keep to where the humans don't dare wander. The Gods don't worry me. They forgot this realm long ago.

I force myself back inside and quickly step toward the body. I drag my fingers over the grayed lids, closing them. I untie his cloak and pull it from under him to mop up the congealing blood from the floor. With his eyes off of me, my entire body finally begins to relax again.

It must be such great relief, knowing you can end. I envy them that, the humans. But not like this. Not before your time. Not alone, with no chance.

When I'm done with the floor, I lay the cloak over the body. His legs jut out at the end, the hand still pushing against the sliced organs. A grotesque empty shell.

The eyes still haunt me through the cloth. But there's no time to do anything more.

I pick up the Texts from the mantle and move quickly past the body to the window, trying to push the Hunter out of my thoughts. Below my feet the ornate rug, once rich and brilliant, is worn so deep I can feel the wood's grain under my toes. Decades of standing in the same place day after day after day. Here, I am in the shadows. A human peering in from the streets would not see me. But I can see out.

I watch them. Completely alone, silent, still, there is nothing else to do.

My temple tower rears up against what's left of the holy district, tall and tired, leering over the market. I watch each day play out on its wide streets and small carts. Behind it, the expired grandeur of the aged towers rises, a rotted reminder of a lost past.

There was a time when Epoh was Terath's shining jewel. Its streets bustled with life at all hours. But the Second Realm War changed everything. The First Creatures tore through the realm like it was paper, their battles destroying men's cities, homes, the land itself. And the men, they took part. Some stood up and fought for their Gods. But others turned away from them in anger. Others' loyalty was easily bought with magic, jewels, or promises of safety after it all ended. Still others ran, cowered, and just waited for it to end.

I'd never, in all my years, seen such destruction.

This is when Zevach arrived at Epoh, with his flock trailing behind him, desperate to believe his promises of protection and hope. Then Zevach told his followers if they wanted the city, they must take it for themselves. Desperate and scared, they fought their way in and destroyed most of its people.

They should have known then what he would become, that this is the city's fate. I should have.

The sky turns from pitch black to a troubled gray. The rays of light touch over the battered city. Silencers' boots tap against the pavement. Another weary day in Epoh is here.

* * *

Don't stop now. Keep reading with your copy of <u>MUD</u> available now.

And visit www.craigcomer.com to keep up with the latest news where you can subscribe to the newsletter for contests, giveaways, new releases, and more.

Don't miss more fantasy novels from Craig Comer coming soon and find him at www.craigcomer.com

Until then, get your fantasy fix with MUD from City Owl Author, E. J. Wenstrom.

* * *

Torn apart by war and abandoned by the gods, only one hope remains to save humanity. But the savior isn't human at all.

Trapped by his Maker's command to protect a mysterious box, Adem is forced to kill anyone who tries to steal it. When a young boy chances upon Adem's temple, he resists temptation, intriguing the golem. As the boy and his sister convince Adem to leave the refuge of his temple, the group lands in a web of trouble.

Now Adem will do whatever necessary to keep his new young charges safe, even if it means risking all to get rid of the box. Their saving grace comes in the form of an angel who offers to set Adem free of the box's magic by granting his greatest desire—making him human.

But first, Adem must bring back the angel's long-dead human love from the Underworld. In doing so, he will risk breaking the barrier between the realms, a cataclysm that could launch the Third Realm War. To set things right, he may be forced to give up the only thing he's ever truly wanted...a chance at a soul of his own.

* * *

Please sign up for the City Owl Press newsletter for chances to win special subscriber-only contests and giveaways as well as receiving information on upcoming releases and special excerpts.

All reviews are **welcome** and **appreciated**. Please consider leaving one on your favorite social media and book buying sites.

For books in the world of romance and speculative fiction that embody Innovation, Creativity, and Affordability, check out City Owl Press at www.cityowlpress.com.

ACKNOWLEDGMENTS

Thank you to everyone at City Owl Press! Tina Moss and Yelena Casale, your passion, support, and knowledge know no bounds. An author could not hope for a better champion of their books. Heather McCorkle, thank you for your patience and enthusiasm. Your editing insights have once again made Effie's tale more polished and vivid. I hope vast, powdery slopes be forever in your future!

Ahimsa Kerp, thank you for always being blunt and honest, and for always taking the time to read through what is often still a bit of a mess. To you, I owe a softball-sized samosa. You know where to find them!

Thank you to my family for asking after me and my writing, for helping peddle books at fairs, and for being my most loyal fans.

In preparation for this book, my wife, Martina, and I went for a little walk around the Borders region of Scotland, and I want to thank her immensely for humoring my little diversions—day after day, for a fortnight—to climb ancient mounds, seek out ruined abbeys, and stroll through Victorian prisons. I don't want to travel with anyone else, for more reasons than I can count, and I can't wait until our next adventure together. I am also ever thankful to her for putting up with my constant questions and musings over the book's direction, its characters and plot, and for reading early drafts and making invaluable suggestions. Without her support, there never would have been an Effie, and without her unwavering encouragement Effie would still be dawdling around Ben Nevis, lost on page one of the first book. This book, and the entire series, is as much hers as mine.

ABOUT THE AUTHOR

CRAIG COMER is the author of the gaslamp fantasy novel THE LAIRD OF DUNCAIRN and co-author of the mosaic fantasy novel THE ROADS TO BALDAIRN MOTTE. His shorter works have appeared in several anthologies, including BARDIC TALES AND SAGE ADVICE and PULP EMPIRE VOLUME IV. Craig earned a Master's Degree in Writing from the University of Southern  California. He enjoys tramping across countries in his spare time, preferably those strewn with pubs and castles.

www.craigcomer.com

 facebook.com/craigscomer

twitter.com/CraigComer

ABOUT THE PUBLISHER

City Owl Press is a cutting edge indie publishing company, bringing the world of romance and speculative fiction to discerning readers.

www.cityowlpress.com

www.ingramcontent.com/pod-product-compliance
Lightning Source LLC
Chambersburg PA
CBHW030401020726
47493CB00003B/903